What reviewers are saying about the stories in
Bonds of the Maleri'

Bonds of the Maleri': Mate Hunt

"It was a delight to read about two such wonderful men finding each other and pursuing a loving relationship. I highly recommend Bonds of the Maleri': Mate Hunt to anyone who enjoys erotic love stories with a twist."
 -- *Regina, Coffeetime Romance Reviews*

Bonds of the Maleri' 2: Double or Nothing

"What a unique and intriguing story! The sex scenes are hotter than a bushel of jalapeno peppers and left me wanting more."
 -- *Susan White, Coffeetime Romance Reviews*

Bonds of the Maleri' 3: Between Love and Law

"5 Stars! Ms. Steele takes her superb talent for writing science fiction romance and puts it on full display in this offering."
 -- *Keely Skillman, eCataRomance Sensual Reviews*

Bonds of the Maleri' 4: Ride 'Em Cowboy

"5 Stars! This story had beautifully descriptive scenery and a mystery to solve. I was enthralled throughout the entire book and was sorry that it had to end."
 -- *Marcy Arbitman, Just Erotic Romance Reviews*

Bonds of the Maleri' 5: Redemption

"The love scenes are delicious in Redemption. There is such emotion in the coming together of the men."
 -- *Tara Renee, Two Lips Reviews*

www.ChangelingPress.com

Bonds of the Maleri'

Kate Steele

All rights reserved.
Copyright ©2008 Changeling Press LLC

ISBN: 978-1-59596-481-6

Publisher:
Changeling Press LLC
PO Box 1046
Martinsburg, WV 25402-1046
www.ChangelingPress.com

Printed in the U.S.A.
Lightning Source, Inc.
1246 Heil Quaker Blvd
La Vergne TN 37086
www.lightningsource.com

Anthology Editor: Connie Alberts
Cover Artist: Bryan Keller
Cover Layout: Bryan Keller

The individual stories in this anthology have been previously released in E-Book format.

No part of this publication may be reproduced or shared by any electronic or mechanical means, including but not limited to reprinting, photocopying, or digital reproduction, without prior written permission from Changeling Press LLC.

This book contains sexually explicit scenes and adult language which some may find offensive and which is not appropriate for a young audience. Changeling Press books are for sale to adults, only, as defined by the laws of the country in which you made your purchase.

Bonds of the Maleri': Mate Hunt

Kate Steele

Prologue

"Col, can you hear me?"

Coltas Oldarie stirred at the sound of his name and opened his eyes. He lay still for a moment, then commented in a resigned voice, "It happened again."

"Yes."

His gaze wandered the room, a utilitarian yet pleasant place, equipped with a bed and a small table with two chairs. It was a typical room in the Contaral Healing Complex, the kind he was well familiar with as this was where he worked.

Col let his gaze connect with his friend's. His green eyes flared for a brief moment and Geral's gray eyes echoed that fleeting flash. Geral smiled. "It's past time, Col. You have to seek your mate before you can continue your work. Your mind has absorbed all it can. Unless you want to end up a permanent patient instead of blacking out a time or two, you need the relief only your true mate can provide."

"I know, it's just that..." Col swallowed, unable to finish his thought.

Geral caressed Col's face, brushing a lock of sable hair from his forehead while his eyes filled with understanding. "You know Sam and I would keep you as our third forever if we could. We both love you, but we all know that's not possible. You must seek your mate, and Sam and I will bring another of our brothers into our home until such time as he, too, is ready to leave." Geral grinned and winked. "Besides, it would be selfish to deny you the opportunity to discover for yourself the joys of being mated."

Col grinned in return. "You mean the nagging, chiding and scolding?"

"Hey! I resent that," said the man entering the room. He frowned, his brown eyes filled with ire at the two already present, which brought a laugh from them both.

"I'm only teasing, Sam. We felt your approach and it's just too much fun watching you rise to the bait," Col confessed.

"Hmm, I suppose for someone with so little imagination you have to get your jollies somewhere," Sam replied with a satisfied smile.

"Is that any way to talk to an invalid?"

"Invalid my ass," Sam snorted and approached the bed. His hand cupped Col's cheek and he leaned down, kissing him gently on the lips. Col responded by sliding a hand to the back of Sam's head and holding him while his tongue slid between Sam's parted lips for a leisurely exploration of his mouth.

When released, Sam drew back and gave him a skeptical look. "Yeah right, *you're* sick," he responded sarcastically. "If you were any healthier, I'd find myself riding that," he accused, pointing to the growing bulge in Col's pants.

"That's actually not a bad idea," Geral said, giving his mate a look filled with heated intent. "I think Col deserves an appropriate send-off." He turned his gaze to his friend. "Col, go lock the door."

Sam's chest rose and fell at a more rapid pace as the rate of his breathing increased. "I should have kept my mouth shut," he quipped, even as he returned the growing look of arousal in his mate's eyes.

"Oh no, lover, I want your mouth open," Geral replied, shaking his head.

Col watched their exchange with an anticipatory smile before sitting up and swinging his legs over the side of the bed. He stood, crossed the room and locked the door. By the time he returned to them, Geral had Sam in his arms, his mouth engaged in a passionate kiss.

Col waited a few moments before joining them. To watch them kiss always stirred him, not only his desire but his heart as well. Their kisses were sensual, warm and loving, no matter how passionate they became. Their mouths pressed and moved, sliding against each other as their tongues danced and caressed, leaving moisture, slick and gleaming, on their lips.

Col's heart beat faster as he moved in behind Sam, spooning the smaller man's body between his own and Geral's. His hands cupped Sam's nicely muscled shoulders, his mouth descending to the back of his neck where he started nibbling and licking the sensitive skin. Sam shivered and moaned making Col smile against his skin. The back of Sam's neck was one of his more sensitive areas and caresses there never failed to elicit a response.

In front of him, Geral had moved back slightly to work open the buttons on Sam's collarless shirt. He spread the fabric open, his hands sliding in over Sam's smooth chest, his palms brushing the tiny nubs of his nipples. Sam's gasp was audible when Col pulled his shirt back and off, one of his hands finding Sam's nipple and lightly pinching while Geral bent to tongue the other.

Col and Geral set a deliberately slow and sensual pace, their hands gliding over Sam's smooth, warm skin, their bodies touching and undulating, a basic primitive movement that made their passions rise higher. Col's mouth followed the center line of Sam's back, first downward then back up. His tongue slid, leaving moisture in its wake, while his lips pressed into and skated over the wet flesh.

Returning to his neck, Col nibbled and kissed his way upward to Sam's ear, suckling the lobe and biting gently. Sam shuddered and pushed himself closer to Col with a murmured "mmmm" of pleasure at the tiny, stinging bites.

Geral was doing *his* share to ready Sam. His hands moved down until he clasped the rounded mounds of Sam's ass, kneading them, while digging the tips of his fingers as deeply as possible into the fabric of his pants and the center seam that ran between his cheeks. He pressed himself tightly against Sam, his erection and Sam's rubbing against each other through their clothing. Col pressed against the back of Geral's hands, enjoying the movement against his cock. It was trapped in his own pants and Geral obligingly turned one hand, finding the stiff bulge, massaging it with his fingers and drawing a groan from Col.

Col eagerly thrust against Geral's searching hand and, growing impatient, he slid his arms around Sam's waist. His hands went to the top fastener of Sam's pants, popping it open before carefully sliding the zipper down. Together, he and Geral pushed the pants down and off, exposing Sam to their now unfettered touch. Geral went to his knees, his hands sliding down the length of Sam's torso until he reached his already swollen cock.

Once there, he slid his tongue over the reddish, throbbing head, giving it teasing licks that drew husky groans from Sam. Holding Sam tightly, Col was able to look over his shoulder and down the length of his body, his own cock jumping in reaction to the sight of Geral sucking on the plump cap of Sam's cock. He released Sam and stepped back slightly, quickly undressing. Naked, he pressed himself tightly to Sam's back. His own fully erect cock dug into the crease of Sam's ass while his arms encircled him, his hands playing with Sam's nipples.

Lightly aromatic moisture formed, drawn by the heat of their bodies where they pressed together. Col rubbed his face over the skin of Sam's shoulders and back, drawing in his scent, feeding on the heady tang while allowing it to flow through him until it engaged every needy impulse within.

When Geral engulfed the full length of his cock, Sam's head slammed back against Col's shoulder. Col reached up, captured his face and held him for a scorching kiss. His tongue ravaged Sam's mouth as the scent of ripe, raw testosterone rose with the increasing heat of their passion. Col released Sam's mouth and with his own, found the curve of Sam's shoulder and neck, nuzzling and licking him before baring his teeth and biting down. Sam bucked against him and Col undulated against Sam. All their movements were in concert with Geral's as he slid the thick, wet length of Sam's cock into his mouth, sucking him deep before letting him slide nearly free.

Col held the bite, but after the initial sting, reduced the pressure and merely held Sam's flesh in his mouth, his eyes closed as his hips thrust against the warm globes that cradled his aching cock. Pre-come, sweet and crystal clear, leaked from the tiny slit in the swollen head, anointing Sam's flesh until Col's cock was sliding easily between those fleshy, rounded cheeks.

Wanting more, Col went to his knees and Geral, knowing his intent, clasped his hands tighter on Sam's ass, spreading him wide, exposing his entrance to Col's fevered gaze. Col's tongue flicked out, finding the puckered pink opening, laving and swirling his tongue over the clenched velvet skin. He reached between Sam's thighs and pulled at his cock which Geral released with a sucking pop. Pulling Sam's cock down and back, Col slid his tongue the entire length of it from tip to balls and upward over the sensitive skin of his perineum until he again reached the wet pucker of his hole.

He repeated this action several times as Geral held Sam steady, then settled his mouth at Sam's entrance, softly drilling with his tongue while stroking Sam's cock, firmly milking him. Sam cried out, his hands desperately clasping Geral's shoulders as both men drove him mad with pleasure. Satisfied, Col released Sam's cock to Geral and was soon gently working first one then another finger into Sam's hole, easing him open, readying him to be fucked.

Geral had resumed sucking Sam's cock, but knowing his limits and feeling the increasing rigidity of his cock, released him and stood. Col followed his lead and while Geral undressed himself, he positioned Sam on the bed. Col went to the bathroom and returned with a small jar of lubricant. The bed was narrow enough that, positioned on his hands and knees across it, Sam would be able to suck Geral's cock while Col fucked him. It wasn't long before Sam was doing just that.

Geral groaned his approval as Sam's mouth engulfed him, his lips and tongue sliding up and down the thick rigid pole, nudging, teasing and sucking Geral's cock as though it were the best thing he'd ever tasted. Geral's hips moved in concert with Sam's strokes. Rasping words of encouragement, Geral was soon fucking Sam's face.

Moving into position, Col scooped a generous dollop of lubricant onto his fingers and liberally greased Sam's hole and his own throbbing rod. He pressed the plump head of his erection against the puckered pink entrance and pushed. The head slowly eased in then was suddenly engulfed. Col remained still, waiting for Sam's permission to proceed. It wasn't long in coming. Sam pushed back toward Col, encouraging him to move, and Col, more than eager to oblige, firmly grasped Sam's hips, slowly working himself deeper until he hilted, fully lodged in Sam's hot, clasping channel.

He carefully withdrew and again pushed deep until his cock was easily stroking in and out of Sam's tight body. Col's gaze met Geral's, their eyes sparking with heat and lust as each watched the other thrusting in and out of a hot, willing orifice. Sam, continually moaning his pleasure around Geral's rigid, glistening cock, easily took the thick rod down his throat all the while pushing back into Col's strokes which alternated between slow circling undulations and hard ramming thrusts.

The room was filled with grunts, groans, the rhythmic slap of flesh and the muffled jouncing of the mattress while the air was redolent with the smell of male rut. More dewy sweat formed on their naked skin, dripping from brows and sliding in tiny rivulets down backs and bellies. Geral reached his climax first, a muted, guttural roar tearing from his throat as he released spurt after spurt of tangy cream into Sam's eager mouth. Col followed, issuing deep, husky growls while his cock pulsed and drenched Sam's clasping channel with thick ropy streams of potent seed.

When Sam had taken all they had to give, Col and Geral easily rolled him to his back. Geral climbed on the bed, taking Sam's rigid cock in his mouth while Col, kneeling between his thighs, sucked and massaged Sam's plump balls with hands, tongue and mouth. It was the pleasurable work of only moments before Sam in turn reached orgasm, his body arching as his cock pulsed and gave its seed to his mate.

Geral swallowed the warm, white fluid Sam fed him then collapsed on the bed, pulling Sam into his arms while

Col sat back on his heels, his arms and forehead resting on the bed as Sam rode the receding waves of his climax. After resting a moment, Col stood and stretched out on the bed next to Sam so that he was sandwiched between himself and Geral. The three of them rested in silence, hands idly and softly caressing in random patterns over each other's damp and cooling skin until, with a sigh, Col pulled himself up and off the bed.

He went into the bathroom for a quick wash then returned to stand next to the bed while he redressed himself. His gaze fondly roved over Geral and Sam where they lay holding each other and he bent, first kissing one and then the other. "I'm going home to pack. I'll miss you both."

Geral sat up. "We'll miss you too, Col, but you know, no one's dying. You'll be back soon and with your mate, and Sam and I will be here waiting for the two of you. Now get going. Your skill is needed to fully heal Kiel if we're to prevent the war that's brewing between the Kasians and the Yalhandrans."

"As if I needed another incentive to hurry. When he's fully returned to us, I'm going to kick his ass for getting hurt. He takes too many unnecessary risks and for what? The thrill of it," Col replied with a grimace. "But I *will* hurry. I know where my duty lies."

"As do we all," Geral acknowledged, then smiled. "Safe journey, my friend."

"Safe journey, Col," Sam echoed, his eyes shiny with unshed tears.

Col winked and headed for the door. He unlocked it, checking to make sure the coast was clear when it opened, then took a step out into the hallway. Just before closing the door he looked back at them with a grin. "By the way, Head Nurse Arata is coming this way and she's looking a little grim."

As the two on the bed cursed and scrambled for their clothes, Col took off down the hall chased by the sound of Nurse Arata's voice. "Coltas Oldarie, what have you and your miscreant friends been up to in my room?"

Chapter One

His ship cloaked, Col set the controls to keep it in as close an orbit as possible around the planet Earth. He retired to his cabin and settled in his bunk, where after closing his eyes, he let his thoughts blank and drift free. Moving deep within, he opened a part of himself to snippets of thoughts and conversation that flowed in waves from the planet below.

Automatically his mind shields filtered anything that would jar his psyche, allowing only those mental frequencies that resonated with his own. Minutes, hours and days passed as his ship continued to circle over the planet. The computer made small adjustments to the orbit, constantly changing the latitudes and longitudes it followed while methodically sectioning the planet.

Col left his meditative state long enough for an occasional, sporadic meal, then returned to it until he found what he was seeking. Below, on the North American continent, in a state called Arizona, he found a thought pattern which drew him like a siren song. His body tightening with anticipation, he dressed in the clothes that had been prepared for him, typical everyday Earth garments that would draw no particular attention to him.

Though the clothes, jeans, T-shirt, leather jacket and boots, were everyday, the man was not. No matter how inconspicuous he tried to be, a man standing six feet nine inches tall with hard, heavy muscles that rippled with every movement would draw the eyes of many. He shrugged at his image in the mirror and, carelessly brushing back his gleaming sable hair, left the cabin, heading for the speeder dock.

Once there, he entered the sleek, powerful craft and quickly brought the systems on line, being especially careful to engage the cloaking shields. Setting the coordinates as close as possible to the person he sought, he launched the speeder and skillfully piloted it down, coming to rest in a slightly wooded area that was bisected by a narrow access road. Col synchronized his wrist tracker with the speeder's computer and was pleased to note that he was only a few miles from his goal.

Exiting the ship, he opened the storage hatch and wheeled a chrome and black Harley from inside. After securing the hatch, he reengaged the cloak and circled the Harley with a proprietary gleam in his eyes and a sudden grin. He loved riding this finely crafted machine and took every opportunity to do so. Mounting the bike, he started the engine, revving it, enjoying the rumbling purr while anticipation set his heart to beating faster. His mate hunt had begun.

* * *

"Matt! Go deep!"

Matthew Ashton took off down the field, checking back as he ran, preparing to catch the football his brother Eric was getting ready to throw his way. Eric let the ball fly and Matt could tell the throw was straight, true and headed right for him. He turned, his momentum taking him back a few more feet when he slammed into a brick wall.

With a whoosh, his breath deserted him as he bounced off the wall and hit the ground. He lay there, momentarily stunned, until his body reminded him of its need for oxygen. Matt took one deep breath and then another, his eyes closed as he concentrated on fulfilling his body's demand. He didn't look at the man who knelt beside him until the deep, sensual voice washed over him.

"Are you all right, little one?"

Who knew a wall could talk? Matt opened his eyes, blinking to focus. He stared into a pair of the deepest green eyes he'd ever seen. Images of evergreens and deep cool forests, lush meadows and stormy seas paraded before his eyes.

He felt a strange pull and was drawn into those eyes and the memories behind them. He saw a group of men. All of them were tall, muscular and handsome. Matt could see the aura of light that surrounded them, burning bright. There was something magical about them, some power that flowed between them and he felt drawn to that group. Especially to the one man who suddenly seemed to note his presence, turning his green-eyed gaze to Matt.

He blinked again and refocused on the mesmerizing eyes of the man in his vision. They stared back into his. A rim of silver glowed around the green of the man's irises, then receded. Matt shook his head. Had he really seen that ghostly glow or was it some trick of the light his dazed condition caused him to see? It was then the man's words struck him.

"Who are you calling little?" At six feet one, weighing in at two hundred ten pounds of muscular, well defined body mass, Matt hardly considered himself little.

"You," the man answered and rose, extending his hand. "Let me help you up."

Matt accepted the offer, clasped the man's sinewy hand with his own and was immediately, effortlessly drawn up. His stomach lurched. The trip up resembled an elevator ride, smooth and easy. He could feel the great strength in the hand that held his and something more, something that sent a current of tingling heat shooting straight to his groin, causing his cock to stir and plump.

The man's hand released his, an arm going around Matt's shoulders. "Steady, little one."

Despite the fact that this man's voice and touch were giving him an instant erection, Matt was getting irritated by his use of the term little. "My name is Matthew and I wish you'd stop calling me little." His gaze continued upward until he again made eye contact. "Jeez, what football team do you play for?" he muttered.

"None," the man answered with a teasing sparkle in his eyes. "I wish only to play with you."

Matt's eyes widened, his brows rising in disbelief while his cock lurched. He suddenly became aware of myriad details he'd failed to notice before. In addition to being extremely tall, the man who held him was sinfully handsome. He wore his thick, wavy sable hair pushed back from the sculpted planes of his face. His nose was straight, his jaw square and chiseled. His chin had a slight cleft, and his lips were firm, not thin, the bottom one slightly fuller, just perfect.

Matt appreciatively noted that his body was heavily muscled, his shoulders broad, waist trim, hips slim and thighs thick and well defined under the tight denim. One other detail stood out with crystal clarity. He was also aroused. A thick bulge strained against the zipper of his jeans and Matt felt his own cock thicken and throb in response to the sight and scent of the man whose arm steadied him.

The stranger took Matt's hand and drew it to his crotch, pressing it firmly against his erection. "You like what you see, as do I."

It was a confident statement of fact, not a question. He

released Matt's hand and placed his under Matt's chin, turning his face up. Matt watched paralyzed as the stranger's face descended to his, their lips meeting, clinging. In addition to the pleasure, Matt felt a building pressure, then an unexplainable connection forming between them. It felt as though the barriers between their minds abruptly dissolved and he was instantly plunged into a swirling morass of emotions, sights, sounds and smells that burst over his consciousness and sent him reeling.

Out of the blue, the name Col Oldarie was presented to him and he felt Col's arms wrap around him. "Hold on to me, Matthew. The first time is always the worst."

Stricken, Matt pushed at him, struggling to get away. "Not again," he gasped, shaking his head. "Please, not again. Let me go!"

"Matthew, it's all right, this sensation will not harm you," Col assured him.

Matt broke free, backing away, raw fear reflected in his eyes. "Won't harm me? What could you possibly know about it?"

By that time, Eric, who Matt could see was watching from across the field, covered the distance between them. He took up a protective stance at Matt's side. "What the fuck is going on?" he asked aggressively.

"Get me out of here," Matt pleaded, struggling to still the shudders that were shaking his body.

"What the hell did you do to my brother?"

"I meant him no harm. I've never heard of this happening before," Col tried to explain, concerned yet equally puzzled.

"Please, Eric," Matt murmured, placing his hand on his brother's arm. "Let's go. Let's just go."

"Wait, please," Col entreated. "Matthew, I must be

allowed to see you again."

"No! Just stay away from me!" Matt insisted and turned, striding away without a backward glance.

"You heard him. Stay away," Eric repeated, his voice menacing.

Catching up to Matt, Eric threw an arm around his shoulders. Matt leaned into his brother and the two of them made for the parking lot and their waiting car.

* * *

Dismayed and ineffably saddened, Col watched them go, his mind awhirl with confusion. It wasn't supposed to happen this way. The connection should have brought great pleasure when it was made, but instead of welcoming it, Matthew had withdrawn in horror.

Col cringed. Was the fault his? Was there something so wrong in him that Matthew couldn't bear being joined to him? Hurt and more than a little worried, Col decided to return to his ship and contact Geral. Something was terribly, terribly wrong.

* * *

"And that's where things now stand. Geral... what am I going to do?"

Col watched his friend on the vid screen as Geral considered his question. "Tell me again exactly what Matthew said after the connection was made."

Col carefully sifted his memory, wanting to be absolutely precise. "He said, not again, please, not again," Col repeated and the words brought a thickness to his throat as he remembered the tone Matt had used, the utter fear and helplessness that had filled his voice.

"Not again," Geral repeated. "That implies that something like this has happened to him before and it was not a pleasant experience. Col, you have to find out what happened. The only way you'll be able to take Matthew's fear away is to find out what has caused it."

"How am I going to do that when he's ordered me to stay away from him?" Col asked, raking his fingers through his hair in frustration.

"How soon they forget," Geral sighed. "Col, my friend, have you been gone so long that you've forgotten everything you've been taught? You made the initial connection with Matthew, nothing can reverse that. I would recommend you use it to contact him while he sleeps. If he believes he's dreaming, he won't become alarmed or be stubborn about revealing his secrets to you."

Col gave Geral a sour look. "My only excuse is the anxiety this is causing." He hesitated a moment, then sent Geral a very searching look. "Geral, are you sure…"

"Col, there's nothing wrong with you. You're a good man. When you work through Matthew's fears, he'll accept you as he's meant to and realize that he's gotten a wonderful mate in the bargain."

Smiling self-consciously, Col twisted his lips and shrugged. Geral laughed out loud. "If you could only see yourself. Any moment now I expect to hear you say, aw shucks."

Col burst out laughing, his depression swept away by his friend's good humor. "I'm just a modest man," he claimed with a grin.

"Bullshit!" came a distant reply.

"Now, Sam…"

Sam came into view on the screen. "You owe me big-time, Col Oldarie. Nurse Arata made us change the sheets on the bed, then she made damn sure everyone knew exactly what we'd been up to. I was never so embarrassed in my life!"

Col chuckled with glee. "So what can I bring from Earth to make it up to you?"

"Chocolate, Belgian chocolate," Sam answered promptly.

"Done," Col agreed.

"Now that you two are through bargaining, get to work, Col. You've been gone too long," Geral told him.

Col nodded his head in agreement. "Thank you, Geral. I'd be lost without your help."

"You got that ri..." Sam began until Geral clamped a hand over his mouth.

"If I let you two get started, you'll never fix this problem with Matthew. Call if you need anything else, Col."

"I will. Bye, Sam."

Sam muttered some incomprehensible reply behind Geral's hand and Col grinned as the screen went blank. He sat for a moment considering the logic of Geral's thinking. With a sigh he nodded and went to his cabin to prepare for a visit with Matthew.

* * *

"Matthew," Col called softly. Matt stirred, a small, uneasy movement. "Easy, sweet man, it's only a dream, only a dream," Col whispered as the connection easily formed between them. In Matt's subconscious, his eyes opened and Col let himself fall into their deep blue depths. For the first time, undistracted by the feel of Matt in his arms, he was able to critically study his mate.

Matthew's face bore a fresh, boyish aura that was enhanced by the pale golden color of his short hair. His lips were full and sensual, and Col licked his own at the remembered feel of them, plump and ripe, when they'd kissed. Matt's nose was straight and a bit on the broad side, marking the presence of an African-American ancestor.

In Matthew's mind, he was naked as always when he slept and Col let his gaze wander the firm hills and valleys of Matt's body. He obviously worked to keep himself physically fit. The muscles in his arms and legs were solid and well developed. There were visible ridges on his abdomen and Col smiled, intrigued at the sight of his outie belly button.

At rest, his cock was still respectably long and plump. Col looked forward to seeing, feeling and tasting every inch of this delectable man, especially that oh-so-tempting part.

Growing aroused, Col sternly reined himself in and concentrated on his purpose. "Matthew, do you remember me?"

"Yes, you're Col and we met this afternoon. I hope this isn't going to turn into a nightmare," he murmured plaintively.

"Why do you think it might?" Col questioned gently.

"Because you scared me. I liked you at first. You smell good and you're really hot," he admitted innocently. "But then, it changed. Why did it change, Col? I've been so careful. I thought I was strong now. I don't want to go back," Matt confessed, growing agitated. "I don't want to go back there. Eric! Eric, help me!" Matt cried out, his voice almost child-like in his need, while his body and mind thrashed against Col's hold.

Alarmed, Col sought to calm him. "Shh, baby, hush, it's all right," he soothed and reached out to stroke Matt's face, not really expecting to feel anything, but unable to stop making the gesture. They both froze in surprise at the warm, tactile sensation of Col's hand against his skin. Instead of growing even more panicked, Matt relaxed under his soft touch.

Col breathed a sigh of relief. "That's right, baby. Just

relax and when you wake, remember this dream, remember the warmth of my touch, but most of all, remember that I will never hurt you," he whispered, softly stroking Matt's forehead and cheek. "Sleep now, Matt. Tomorrow will bring another dream."

"Tomorrow," Matt murmured and drifted deeply into a dreamless slumber.

For the next few nights, Col visited Matthew, and each time he brought only pleasure in the form of soft words and soothing touches. Having discovered that it was possible to touch Matt while he dreamt, and to be welcomed as Matt actively anticipated his arrival, Col gave in to the needs that burned within him. On the third night, he woke Matt in an entirely different way.

* * *

Matt looked at himself in the mirror, his gaze troubled. Each night he went to bed, his thoughts filled with Col Oldarie, and each night Col came to him in dreams, each one more real, warm and comforting than the next. He shook his head, not understanding why. Why would he dream of the man? Col had done something that shook the very foundations of his world; he'd broken through Matt's shields and made him relive the pain, frustration and fear that had haunted his childhood.

Perhaps it was the fact that Col seemed to be trying to help him. It felt as though Col was trying to make amends for that mistake, and yet Matthew couldn't help but believe it was all a delusion, a fantasy of his own making to alleviate his fear and longing. And yes, he admitted to himself, he longed for someone in his life and why those longings suddenly aimed themselves at Col with such an unshakable insistence worried him, made him question his own sanity.

In the mirror, he examined his image dispassionately.

He knew what other people saw when they looked at him. A young man with a nice face and a strong body, a strength they probably assumed was not only present on the outside but on the inside as well. He closed his eyes, bowing his head, one hand scraping through his hair in helpless frustration. How long? How long would this go on, this feeling of emptiness that was overridden only by the constant yearning to feel whole, to feel needed, to feel wanted, to feel as though his life had meaning?

Unshed tears glazed his eyes, his vision blurring as again he gazed at himself in the mirror. It was only when he dreamed of Col that he felt at rest, at peace. When Col held him and talked to him, his hands bestowing soft caresses, his arms holding him tight, only then did Matthew shed the anxiety that colored his existence.

"If only I could live in that dream forever," he whispered and turned out the light. Matt pulled the covers back on his bed, lay down and settled in, rising excitement making him restless until the need for sleep overwhelmed him and he succumbed to its demand.

Not long after sleep claimed him, he woke to another's demand. A guttural groan was torn from his throat as his hips strained upward. His hard, aching cock was engulfed in a warm, wet mouth that worked him with magical precision. His groan was echoed by the throat that suddenly took his throbbing, eight-inch length deep.

"Yes!" he ground out, his back arching, as the vibrations traveled down the length of his cock and ended in the plump spheres of his balls.

Eyes tightly shut, he fisted his hands in the rumpled sheet beneath him. He couldn't stop the rhythmic, primitive undulation of hips that sent his cock sliding in and out of the mouth that worked him. An agile and talented tongue found the ultra sensitive spot on the underside of his thick, vein-wrapped rod, the spot that lay just beneath the mushroom shaped head. Wet and warm, it nudged and stroked until Matt groaned again and felt his balls begin to draw up.

Large, strong hands slid over his thighs, firmly parting them to expose his scrotum, and the twin fleshy rounds were treated to a languidly sensual, yet insistent massage. Matt's labored, panting breaths increased, heat and the musky scent of his arousal oozing from his pores as his heart pounded and his body tightened.

His head slammed back on the pillow when that amazing mouth stroked up and down the solid length of his cock. A wet finger found the tight pucker of his ass and slid in. Matt cried out, his body convulsing and quivering with an in-rushing deluge of pleasure that overwhelmed his senses and sent him spinning into pure physical sensation. Hard, gut-wrenching spurts of hot cream burst from his cock, flooding the mouth that covered and sucked him until he was shaking from the force of his shattering release.

He took deep shuddering breaths and lay quietly quivering while the effects of his climax receded and once again he was able to think clearly. Warm gentle licks at his highly sensitized cock head had him moaning softly at the gossamer-light touches. When the bed shifted, he struggled to open his eyes. Before that feat was accomplished, his lips were taken in a hot, sweet kiss by a soft mouth and a tongue that begged for admittance. He opened and tasted the sweet, tangy swirl of flavors that consisted of his lover and his own essence combined.

Lover, he thought. Opening his eyes, Matt fell into twin pools of deep and tranquil green. Col smiled at him, a smile that set butterflies loose in his stomach and sent a wave of warmth spreading over his skin. "I knew it was you," he whispered.

"Yes," Col replied softly. "It will always be me, Matthew. Sleep now, no questions tonight, just sleep."

* * *

By the fourth night, as much as he wanted to repeat the pleasure of loving Matt, Col had decided it was time instead to address his fears. He opened their link and was able to guide their thoughts in such a way that he appeared to be lying in Matthew's bed while Matt cuddled next to him, his head resting on Col's chest. "Do you remember the day we met, when you became afraid?"

Col felt Matt stiffen in his arms. "I remember."

"Can you tell me what frightened you? Will you trust me with it?"

Matt remained silent for a score of heartbeats. Col was almost certain he would refuse when Matt spoke. "You opened your mind to me. I couldn't shut you out," he explained, his voice filled with trepidation.

"Did you see something bad, something that hurt you?" Col asked, struggling to keep his voice neutral and calm, though this felt like it was the most important question he'd ever asked.

"No, it didn't hurt, but it shouldn't have happened. My shields are strong but you broke through them like they didn't exist. It's been years since that happened. I was afraid I was losing control again."

"Again?" Col asked with surprise. "Can you tell me what happened before?"

Matt snuggled closer as though seeking reassurance and Col tightened his arms around him, then reached up to feather his fingers through Matt's hair. Matt sighed. "When I was born, something was different in me. I had convulsions and they thought I would die, but eventually my physical health improved."

Col made note of the fact that Matt emphasized the word physical.

"What the doctors didn't know and what I was too young to explain was that I could hear thoughts and feel emotions from other people. It was the constant buzz of them in my head that caused the convulsions, but after a while my mind started to find ways to protect itself. The trouble was the process was too slow. When I got old enough, I tried to tell them, but by that time my behavior over the years had been so strange they thought I was mentally unbalanced."

Matt hesitated for a moment. When he spoke again, his voice was low and carefully controlled, but Col could hear the infinite pain that filled it. "When I was five, my parents sent me away to an institution. I was there for eight years."

"Father of us all," Col whispered, his voice echoing Matt's pain. "You're an empath, a full blown empath."

Matt nodded. "Eric is too, but his shields developed early, were possibly in place when he was born, and they were strong. He's only two years older than me. It took awhile for him to figure out what was wrong. Of course, it helped when I was finally old enough that I could share what I was feeling.

"When he did finally understand, he got our mom and dad to let him visit me more often and he taught me how to strengthen my shields so I could block everyone out. Once I'd learned how, I never felt so at peace in my life," he revealed. "Everyone noticed the change in me and before long they let me out. I went back to live with Eric and my parents but when I was old enough, Eric and I moved out.

"Things were never comfortable between me and my parents after that. I think they were almost afraid of me, and

Eric had little success in making them understand. He's never forgiven them for sending me away or forgiven himself for not protecting me, for not realizing sooner what was wrong," Matt finished sadly.

"He couldn't have known," Col commented. "He had no way of knowing that what he was experiencing was so much different than the way the average person's mind works."

"Thank you."

"For what?"

"For saying average and not normal."

"There's no such thing as normal. Everyone has their own quirks."

"Anyway, this brings me to *my* questions," Matt said, raising his head to look down at Col. "How do *you* know? How were you able to get past my shields?"

Col cleared his throat. Though he was grateful to have reached this point, it was still going to be difficult trying to explain. Then Matt surprised him. He reached out and cupped Col's cheek while gazing deep into his forest-green eyes. "Who are the Maleri'?" he whispered and Col's eyes flared in response.

Chapter Two

"The Maleri' are a group of men, empaths, who live on the planet Belthola. From the time they are born and their abilities detected, they are raised to be of service to their world. They become mediators, diplomats, healers and the like, and their skills are made available to other worlds... for a price, usually some service or allowance that will be of benefit to our entire world."

"And you, you're one of them?" Matt asked softly.

Col nodded.

"What if I said I didn't believe you?"

"Then I would say to you, look into my mind. I said I would never hurt you, Matthew. I will also never lie to you. Our bond is there, waiting for you to acknowledge it. You merely need to open the way and this you already know how to do."

Matt considered the possibility, then closed his eyes and went very still. He reached with his mind and found the bond, the path between himself and Col. Picturing it as just that, a path, he walked a short way and entered the realm of Col's consciousness. Images, sounds and smells were there for the taking, and Matt let himself filter through them, finding the truth of Col's claims.

He also found one other thing, a round mass of energy that glowed and pulsed. Tiny fissures marred its surface. A pulsing black opalescent light sought to find escape through the near invisible cracks. Returning the way he came, Matt sat up, his gaze resting on Col. "I believe you. It seems impossible and yet it's all there. It's like writing on a page.

All I have to do is think of what information I need and it's mine. Can you do the same with me?"

"I could, if I wished," Col answered.

"Why didn't you? Why come to me and ask? Why didn't you just take what you wanted?"

"That's not our way, not *my* way. I needed the decision to be yours to share with me. Even though I could, I would never force anything from you. You have the power to shut me out, Matthew. You can do so at will. The fact that you have not is telling."

A slight flush appeared on Matt's cheeks "I wanted the contact with you," he confessed.

"Yes." Col smiled, pleased at his admission.

"But why me? Why did you come here? Why pick me?"

Col too sat up, sitting cross-legged to face Matt. "The Maleri' are a rarity on our world, all of us men, all of us sexually attracted only to other males. Among the population of our planet we are the only ones with this power and this need. As we grow and puberty arrives, we go to live with a mated pair of our brothers. Our physical, emotional and sexual needs are met while the experienced Maleri' teach us the fine points of our powers and limitations.

"The arrangement is... wonderful, magical," Col admitted wistfully. "But the day comes when we must take a mate. To do so, we must seek our mates elsewhere. Some of your people, as you know from personal experience, have natural empathic abilities. A Maleri' must be able to mind-bond with his mate, not only for the pleasure it will bring them, but because his sanity depends upon it. As to why you?" Col shrugged his shoulders. "Why is one person attracted to another?"

Matt shook his head. "But why does your sanity depend on your mate?"

"Did you see anything unusual when you were in my mind?"

"The mass of trapped energy?"

Col nodded. "Our empathy allows us to read people, to feel their emotions and to a certain extent, their thoughts or intentions, but the energy acquired by the process doesn't dissipate. It's stored in our minds, trapped inside that shield. The only way to rid ourselves of it is through our mates. Through the joining of our minds our mate is able to filter the energy, bleed it away, acting as a release valve for that which would eventually drive us mad."

Col gave Matt a considering look. "In a way it's similar to what you experienced when you were unable to keep other's thoughts and emotions from you. We are born with this natural shield that protects us for a finite time, but if the pressure is not relieved, it would burst through the shield and flood our minds, causing a massive overload and complete burnout, resulting in total insanity."

"Your shield is failing," Matthew whispered.

Col acknowledged the truth with a nod.

"How long do you have?"

"I don't know. There have been several incidents when I blacked out while trying to use my gift. I can no longer function as a healer."

"So... what neither one of us has actually come right out and said is that I'm..."

"My fated one, my mate," Col finished.

Matt sat mutely for a moment. "I don't even know what to say to that," he admitted, confusion prominent in his reply.

"Would you consider spending time with me? Perhaps

if we get to know each other better an answer will come to you."

Matt was surprised. Not only at the question, but the tone in which it was asked. Col Oldarie was the very epitome of charismatic alpha-male. He exuded power and control, and yet he asked. He did not demand. Matt was finding it harder and harder to resist the pull he felt whenever Col was near. This was just another point in Col's favor.

He looked into Col's eyes and found a hint of unsure vulnerability. "Come to the house tomorrow at noon. We'll go somewhere for lunch or something. Okay?" he said, then added somewhat shyly, "If this isn't all just some weird dream."

"Okay," Col answered, a big grin on his face. He leaned forward and hooked a finger under Matt's chin while bestowing a soft kiss on his lips. "Would it upset you if I told you I find you to be absolutely adorable?"

"Nooo," Matt drawled. "But don't let anyone else hear you say that. It's kind of sissy. Couldn't you say you found me to be absolutely macho, manly and provocative?"

Col chuckled. "You are all those things and more, Matthew Ashton. I will see you, in person, tomorrow."

Col's image began to fade and Matt halted him. "Wait! Do you know where I live?"

"I could find you with greater ease than a metal detector could find the proverbial needle in a haystack," Col teased.

Matt gave him a skeptical look. "If you say so, Slick. Just in case you get lost, I'm in the phone book."

Still smiling, Col withdrew.

* * *

Matt was unable to settle anywhere. As the minutes

ticked by toward noon, he grew more and more anxious. He'd decided to fix lunch at home. He reasoned if Col didn't show up, at least he wouldn't feel quite so abandoned by having made plans to go out that didn't happen.

Once more he looked at the clock and held his breath when both hands aligned perfectly, pointing to the twelve. At that moment he heard a deep rumble and went to the window. Out in the street, a sleek Harley pulled up behind his car and parked. The big man riding that massive machine dismounted gracefully and removed his sunglasses.

Matt's stomach did a strange twisting flip. Col had arrived, right on time. He turned from the window and went to the front door, opening it before Col had time to knock. Col was smiling as he mounted the front steps and Matt felt his chest tighten. "Oh shit," he breathed softly, his nerves jangling from head to toe.

"Hello, Matthew," Col greeted him.

"Hi, um, come in," Matt managed and stepped back to allow Col inside. He closed the door and turned, unexpectedly finding himself drawn into Col's arms.

Col's mouth descended on his and Matt let go, pleasure and relief making him weak. The kiss was long, soft and sweetly sensual. The exchange of tastes, tongues and breath bound them in a fog of intimacy.

"Have I convinced you I am real?"

"Oh yeah." Matt looked up into his eyes, finding himself fascinated by the ghostly glow that flared within them. "Why do your eyes do that?"

Col shrugged. "No one really knows, it's just something that's brought on by strong emotion."

"Um, well," Matt said, stepping back "I thought I'd fix us lunch here and then maybe we could go for a walk or something?"

"I'd like that," Col answered. "May I help you prepare lunch?"

"If you like," Matt replied shyly, pleased at the offer.

"Lead the way."

Matt went with his original idea of preparing steak hoagies. While the thin steaks were cooking in the broiler, he and Col littered the table with plates and bowls filled with everything from lettuce, tomato and black olives to several kinds of cheese, crumbled bacon and the fresh crusty rolls.

Steaks done, they stood together building their sandwiches and loading their plates with macaroni salad and chips. "I know this isn't the healthiest of meals," Matt said with a grin. "All these calories and carbs."

"But it tastes good."

"Mmm hmm," Matt agreed around a bite of his sandwich.

Matt kept looking at Col as he talked, the words registering, but the whole idea of what he was saying seemed so farfetched, Matt wanted to pinch himself to make sure he really *was* awake. It didn't take long for them to work their way through the food and with the meal finished, they made short work of the cleanup.

Matt wanted to see Col's bike so they went outside. "Would you like to take a ride?" Col asked.

"Could we?" Matt replied, his eyes filled with an admiring gleam.

"Of course."

They spent the next hour or so riding around town and out onto some country roads where Col was able to open the Harley up at speeds that took Matt's breath away. He held on tightly, enjoying the feel of him, so warm and solid in his arms. Eventually they ended up at the park where they'd first met, and it was there they stopped to walk for a time.

They finally settled on a bench near a small duck pond.

"I thought I'd run into a wall the day we met," Matt mentioned with a grin.

"I *am* sorry about that. I was so anxious to meet you, I wasn't thinking clearly. If it's any comfort, you left a bruise," Col teased.

"Now *I'm* sorry."

"For the bruise or that we met?"

"Just the bruise. Col... what exactly is it you want from me?"

"Love? Affection? Sex?"

Matt gave him a piercing look.

"All right," Col conceded. "I want you as my mate. I realize that there's been no mention of love, but the bond that formed so easily proves it's right between us. I can tell you from what I've seen of my brothers that love always follows. It's just a matter of time." Matthew remained silent, giving no hint of what he was thinking as he looked out across the water. "I would also ask that you come live with me."

"Leave Earth?" Matt asked, though his voice held little surprise.

"Yes."

"Col, I'd be lying if I said I wasn't interested. I like being with you. Those nights we were together in my bed with you just holding me as we talked, well, I've never felt so good in my life. I like the way you make me feel. I like you... but... I can't leave Eric," he concluded. "He and I are all we have. Though they're still living, we don't have much if any contact with our parents or other relatives. Eric just went through a very bad experience." Matt's voice grew shaky. "He lost his partner to cancer. Dan was a wonderful guy and we both miss him very much."

Col slid an arm around Matt's shoulders and gave him a rough hug before releasing him. "I'm sorry to hear that," Col replied. "I wish very much that I could hold you now, but I know such wouldn't be met with approval by most people here."

"Narrow minded bigots," Matt replied.

"This is one point in favor of leaving. You would not be faced with such on Belthola. But back to the subject of Eric. I have thought about the fact that you might object to leaving him behind. That's why I contacted my brothers with an idea, an idea they believe has merit."

"What idea?"

"That Eric accompany us."

"Really? Tell me the rest of it."

Col smiled. "You said yourself that Eric too is empathic. It's entirely possible that a mate awaits him among the Maleri'."

"I wonder if he'd go for it." Matt frowned. "You're going to have to help me explain all this to him because if I try it on my own, he's probably going to think I'm nuts. This isn't going to be easy. Not nearly as easy as it was between you and me."

Col nodded. "I realize that, but I think between the two of us we can convince him."

"Let's go back. You're staying for supper and you can help me cook while we come up with a plausible plan."

"Yes, sir," Col replied. "And so it begins."

"What?"

"The nagging and ordering about only a mate can provide."

Col's reply surprised a grin out of Matt. "This may turn out to be fun," he teased.

Col merely groaned and followed Matt's lead back to

the Harley.

Chapter Three

Back in the kitchen, Matt and Col sat at the table while spaghetti sauce gently bubbled in a pan on the stove. They were trying to come up with the perfect words to explain the situation to Eric, when they ran out of time. Col was nowhere in sight when the back door opened and Eric walked in.

"Hey, little brother," he greeted Matt. "Did you see that rad Harley out in the street? I wouldn't mind having one of those."

"That could be arranged," Col replied, entering the kitchen through the other door.

Eric stopped in mid-step. "What the *hell* are you doing here? Matt told you to stay away," he said belligerently, taking a step toward Col.

Though not as tall as Col, Eric was still an impressive six feet four inches of hard muscled man, muscles he earned working construction. He was also not afraid of confrontation.

"Eric, wait! I invited Col here," Matt intervened, stepping between them.

"What about what happened in the park?" Eric questioned obliquely.

"It's all right. We've, uh, come to an understanding."

"An understanding, huh? Not that it's any of my business, if you don't want it to be, but how about you explain this *understanding* to me?" Eric asked, clearly concerned for Matt's welfare.

"Can we all just sit down, please?" Matt asked, looking

from one to the other and sighing with relief when Col and Eric took seats on opposite sides of the table. "All right... this is good," he continued with false cheer and struggled to hide a smile as Col and Eric each gave him a sour look.

Matt seated himself at a neutral corner. "Look, I know this isn't going to be easy for you to believe, but here goes."

Eric sat quietly, saying nothing until Matt finished his explanation, including the part about leaving Earth. Without blinking an eye he looked across the table at Col. "And I'm supposed to believe this?"

"It's the truth," Col replied.

"So what did you drug him with?"

"I did *not* drug him. I would never do such a thing."

"You had to have done something. Matt's normally pretty level-headed. You've obviously fucked with him," Eric accused, the first bit of heat seeping into his voice.

"I swear to you, I did nothing," Col replied adamantly.

"So do something now."

"What do you mean?"

"Do something to prove you're a big, bad alien."

"Such as?"

"How 'bout you shoot me with your ray gun?"

Col's lips twitched. "Only if I can shove it up your ass first."

Eric was having trouble keeping a straight face. Suddenly they both burst out laughing. Matt looked from one to the other, relieved. "You're both nuts," he commented which only succeeded in making them laugh harder.

"I give up," Matt sighed. "Can we table this for the time being, that is if you're both finished playing macho one-upmanship? I don't know about you, but I'm hungry."

A bit more relaxed, but still eyeing one another cautiously, Col and Eric agreed. During the meal, Eric asked

Col pointed questions about Belthola. "You're either a great story teller, a hell of a liar, or you're telling the truth," Eric finally conceded.

"He's telling the truth, Eric," Matt said, taking his plate to the sink to rinse it. "I've seen it in his mind. You know he couldn't lie to me and you know I wouldn't lie to you," Matt concluded, giving his brother a pointed look.

"I know you wouldn't, little brother," Eric admitted, gently reassuring Matt. "But you have to admit, this is all pretty unusual stuff. How many times does somebody walk up to you and say, 'Hi, how you doin'? I'm from another planet.' You've got to allow me a bit of skepticism. I didn't just fall off a hay wagon, you know."

"I know," Matt replied patiently.

"I have a way to easily convince you," Col interjected.

Eric theatrically put his hand up. "No alien mind melds, buddy."

"Hardly," Col answered with a disdainful sniff. He rose from his chair and looked out the window. "It's dark now, but tomorrow I'll show you my ship. Will that be proof enough?"

"I think that would do," Eric answered.

"Good, then I'll..." Col suddenly staggered and went to his knees, grasping his head in both hands.

"Col!" Matt shouted and went to his knees beside him. "What is it?"

"Shield's weakening," he managed, lowering his head, his eyes tightly closed.

"What can I do?" Matt asked anxiously, his arm sliding around Col's shoulders.

"Just give me a moment, baby. The pain's already receding," he replied, relief plainly audible in his voice.

Matt and Eric waited quietly until Col raised his head

and opened his eyes. "The pain's gone," he told them. "There's just one problem. I can't see."

* * *

In his bedroom, Matt helped Col undress. It was several hours later and Col's vision was slowly returning but he was still unable to go back to his ship. Matt insisted Col stay with him. "How do you feel?" Matt questioned as he draped Col's shirt over the back of a chair. Even though he was worried, he still couldn't help but admire the body he was slowly revealing.

"I'm all right, Matt, honestly. Stop worrying."

"Can't help it."

Col groped for the bed and Matt was quickly there, carefully guiding him and urging him to lie down. Seeing Col settled, Matt undressed and stood for a moment, looking at him. His mind made up, he climbed on the bed and without preamble laid himself on top of Col. "Tell me what to do," he ordered softly.

"Matt..."

"Don't even start. This is what you came for, for me, for my help, and I want to give it. So tell me what to do."

Col sighed and wrapped his arms around Matt. "We have to open the link between us. My mentor, Geral, told me it's best if the mated pair are actively engaged in arousing each other. When the shield goes, the energy will be funneled and enhance their sexual activity. It's easier this way instead of consciously trying to direct it out and away from us."

"I think I can handle that," Matt answered with a smile, kissing and licking the skin at Col's throat.

Col shivered and eased his head back, giving Matt room to work. Matt worked his way higher, his lips following Col's jaw line to his chin where he opened his mouth, kissing and lightly biting as he slid his tongue over the subtle indentation there. Col was breathing heavily and Matt could feel the movement of Col's cock as it thickened between them.

Matt's own cock followed Col's lead. He uttered a soft moan when Col's hands slid down his back to end up resting on the firm mounds of his ass. Col kneaded the fleshy mounds, his hips pushing up. He urged Matt to move with him until they established a slow, sensual rhythm.

Matt found Col's mouth and their lips engaged, opening to allow the exploration of tongues to begin. Matt lost himself to the heady taste of Col's slick, wet mouth, and the compelling eroticism of their tongues mating. He squirmed against Col's body, aroused by the heat of his skin and the hard muscles that supported him. The rhythmic rise and fall of Col's chest as he breathed resonated within Matt. His own breathing matched that faster than normal, yet strong, steady pace.

Matt momentarily abandoned Col's lips and again let his mouth travel downward. Soft kisses marked the path he took over Col's rounded pectoral muscles until he found the taut nub of one tiny nipple surrounded by the deeper brown of its nickel-sized areola. He kissed, licked and gently nibbled first one, then the other, enjoying Col's groans before returning to his mouth for a long passionate kiss.

Eager for more, Matt again headed south and followed the center line that moved down between Col's pecs, abs and further still to his belly button, which he experimentally tongued, smiling at the sound of Col's indrawn breath. Fully erect, Col's cock was nudging his chin and Matt lost no time in giving it the attention it craved.

He looked up the long line of Col's body to find Col gazing down at him, his eyes flaring. Wrapping his fingers around the thick length of Col's cock, Matt began at the base and licked upward again and again until the hard pole was slick with saliva. Settling his mouth over the ripe head, he teased the tiny slit while sucking lightly at the clear juice that flowed from inside.

Col's breath was rasping from his throat, his eyes having closed, his head straining back against the pillow. A deep growl rumbled from the depths of his chest when Matt took his cock fully inside his mouth. "Oh *fuck*! Baby, yes, that feels so good. Suck my cock, lover, suck it hard."

Matt groaned, excited by Col's words and he did just as Col asked, loving the satiny soft feel of his skin and the heavy solid weight of him against his tongue. Eventually, Matt let Col's cock slide free until just the plump head rested against his lips. He stroked the long length with his hand, loving the feel of Col's foreskin as it moved up and down. He drew it up until Col's cock head was nearly obscured, then slid his tongue under the loose skin, sucking it up while laving his tongue beneath it to caress the smooth cap.

Col's hips pumped under him and Col reached for Matt, urging him up beside him. Matt engulfed the entire length of Col's cock and managed to stroke up and down several more times before Col interrupted him. "I'm going to come if you don't stop right now," he gasped and Matt took him at his word, allowing himself to be pulled up against Col's body.

Col wrapped his hand around the back of Matt's head and they kissed, long and deep, while Col positioned Matt on his body. Col slid his cock between Matthew's thighs. "Keep your legs together," he ordered, his own legs positioned outside Matt's.

Matt's cock was pressed between their bodies, his pre-come leaking, creating a slick channel for his cock. Taking

Matt's head between his hands, Col whispered, "Join with me."

Eagerly, Matt opened the link between them and slid into Col's mind. He easily found the pulsing mass of trapped energy and metaphysically walked around it. He was momentarily distracted by the sharp pleasure that arced through him when Col moved, gripping his ass, fucking Matt's thighs so that Matt felt the friction against his cock where it lay trapped between them.

Panting and fighting the growing pleasure, Matt reached out and placed his hands against Col's shield. A wild surge of energy poured forth, shooting straight for his groin. His cock lurched and he cried out, actually feeling himself thicken. His cry was echoed by Col who was thrusting frantically, his hips moving hard and fast. Matt felt the climax coming and he knew he couldn't hold out for long. Not wanting to lose the opportunity, he reached out and this time embraced Col's shield, laying his entire body against it.

All hell broke loose. He and Col screamed, their bodies thrashing and slamming together as pleasure, hard and fierce and wild, pumped through them. It was nearly impossible to breathe. There were no coherent words or thoughts or actions, only exploding nerve endings, wrenching shudders and feral, growling groans accompanied by the thick sprays of come that burst from them both. Col's thick cream arced up and gracefully descended, landing with muffled splats against Matt's back and buttocks while Matt released a deluge of thick, warm seed between them, coating their bellies and torsos.

Totally drained and exhausted, they melted into one boneless, aromatic puddle of sweaty, come-covered satisfaction. The room was eerily silent but for their panting breaths of recovery, until a loud pounding sounded against the wall. "It's about time you two shut up! Keep it down, would you!"

Col and Matt chuckled weakly and dozed for a time until Matt moved, the motion pulling at the sticky come that glued them together. "Shower time," Col murmured. "Come on, babe."

He eased out of bed, pulling a sleepy Matt with him into the bathroom where they took a fast shower, quickly dried and returned to bed. Within minutes of turning out the lights, they were both asleep.

* * *

"I'm surprised to see you up so soon," Eric commented as Matt stumbled into the kitchen and poured himself a cup of coffee.

"Mmm," he answered, before sitting down to let the warm steam from his cup drift up over his face. He took a deep, appreciative breath and a cautious sip.

"From the sounds of it, it was a hell of a ride, little brother."

Matt's cheeks reddened slightly and he smiled.

"Nothing to say?"

Matt shook his head.

"Spoilsport."

Col walked through the door and bent, kissing Matt on the top of the head. Acquainted with the kitchen and where things were, he found a cup and poured himself some coffee. "Good morning," he greeted Eric before taking a swallow of the rich brew. "Mmm, damn good coffee, Eric."

"Thanks. I take it you're better now?"

Col had awakened feeling better than he had for months. He felt surprisingly well rested and light of heart and mind. "Much better, thanks to your brother."

"Yeah, I heard his nursing technique," Eric commented sarcastically.

Col grinned. "Are you ready to become a believer today?" he asked, steering the conversation in a different direction to spare Matt any further embarrassment.

"Beam me up, Scottie."

"Let's go," Col answered, his eyes bright with anticipation.

Epilogue

A week later, Eric sat in a thickly padded, oversized chair in the observation room of Col's ship and watched the stars go by. Col had proved his claim and together, he and Matt had persuaded Eric to go with them. It hadn't been as hard as they'd imagined.

Having lost his partner Dan, Eric was ready for a change and willing to take a giant step into the unknown. If things didn't work out, he still had a home to go back to, although he knew he'd desperately miss Matt.

Thinking of Matt seemed to invoke his presence. Across the room, the door slid open and Eric heard Matt say, "I think I left it in here. Yeah, there it is." Their voices were louder as they moved closer, but they failed to notice his presence.

"Good, now can we go to bed?"

"Yeah, but Col, I've never... well, you know... I've never..."

"Been fucked?"

"Succinct but true. Yeah, I've never been fucked."

"Neither have I," Col revealed.

"What! I thought you did everything with Geral and Sam."

"A Maleri' is fucked only by his mate. Sam has fucked Geral, as they are mates, but neither Sam nor Geral could fuck me. Nor could I fuck Geral. We're not mated."

"But you fucked Sam."

"Sam is not Maleri'. He is the mate of a Maleri'."

"That sounds sort of one sided to me."

"It's tradition, Matthew. Our mates do so much for us. It's our way of keeping one part of ourselves for them, and them alone. But to share our mate with another of our brothers brings us great pleasure. One day, if you agree, you and I will offer our home to another of the Maleri'. He will become our third for a time as I was third with Geral and Sam. Would you like that?"

There was a pregnant silence and Eric suppressed a laugh. He could almost hear the wheels turning in Matt's head.

"Umm, the idea has possibilities. Do I have to make up my mind now?"

"Of course not."

"So… what *do* we do now?"

"We go to bed and you fu… you make love to me."

"Make love?" Matt asked, his voice holding a hint of hope.

"Make love," Col affirmed.

They started back across the room. "Are you sure you want me to go first? Shouldn't you?"

"No."

"Why not?"

"Because I said so."

"Well, that's no reason."

"Matthew, my own, does it really matter?"

There was a short silence. "No, only that I make love with you."

The door slid shut and Eric found himself still smiling. He was happy for his brother. Col was not only good to him, but good for him. He was glad to see his brother coming out of his shell to find contentment and from the looks of it, love. Eric sighed and continued to watch the stars, wondering what his own future would hold.

Bonds of the Maleri' 2: Double or Nothing

Kate Steele

Chapter One

Hot, steamy water flowed over their bodies. The stinging spray stimulated and heightened the pleasure of an already erotic shower. Matthew held tightly to his mate's hips as he plunged the thick staff of his cock deep into the clasping channel of Col's ass.

Hands flat against the shower wall, Col growled his appreciation of the move. "That's it, babe. Right there. God, *yes*. Harder. *Harder!*"

Matt took Col at his word. Their bodies slammed together, water spraying between them at each meeting. The ride was hot, wild and endless. Matt gave in to Col's need for a time, fucking him hard and fast. Then he slowed the pace. He looked down, watching the glistening length of his own cock disappear slowly inside his lover. Withdrawing at an equally slow pace, the visual alone had him groaning.

"Ah, Col, you should see this. Feel it. It's so damn *hot*. You wouldn't believe how good this feels."

"I'm right here, babe. Believe me. I know how good it feels. It will feel even better when you speed up," he hinted with a panting groan.

"Not yet. I wanna make it last."

"*Matt.*"

"*No!* Be patient. I'll make you glad you were," Matt promised.

Pushing himself in deep, he draped himself over Col's back. One hand reached around and grasped Col's straining rod, pumping slowly. The motion of his hand matched the motion of his hips.

"*Fuck!*" Col groaned, pushing back into the hard cock that impaled him.

"I am, lover. I am," Matt murmured and began licking the wet, warm skin at the back of Col's neck.

Making love to Col empowered him. Matt was not normally a take charge kind of person. This joining of their bodies, of Col trusting Matt to see to his pleasure, was heady stuff for a recently deflowered virgin. Col was a man of experience. Some might think he would be justified in always taking the lead, but not Col. He'd made it more than clear that he had no intention of allowing Matt to hold second place in any part of their relationship. An attitude Matt could more than appreciate. Especially at present.

Matt lost himself to the feel of his skin sliding against Col's and the growing heat that built between them. Col tasted of fresh water and salty sweat. The pulse in his cock thudded against Matt's hand. With his own cock clasped tightly within Col's body, stroking Col's cock felt almost as though he were jacking himself off.

Matt let his other hand move up Col's hip and over his belly. Searching higher, he found the tight nub of one nipple and tweaked it. Col gasped and growled, bucking forward then back, pushing into the stroke of Matt's hand, then back into the hard thrust of his cock.

His movements were becoming more insistent, near frantic. Col was at the edge. Matt decided it was time to push him over. He released Col's nipple and let his hand fall. Reaching under the thick stalk of Col's erection, Matt found his balls and gently squeezed.

An intense, guttural groan rumbled from the depths of Col's chest. Matt felt the vibration of it reverberate in his own chest. He picked up the pace. Fast, hard and smooth, he pistoned his cock in and out. Col's growling grunts punctuated each thrust. Releasing his cock and balls, Matt again grasped Col's hips and slammed forward. Taut muscles in his ass bunched and released with each hard, ramming stroke of his cock.

The steady slap, slap, slap of flesh meeting flesh grew louder until a final, driving thrust threw them both over the edge. Matt froze for a moment as the first burst of his semen sent an agonizing shaft of pleasure straight through his belly. Convulsively, his hips slammed forward with each subsequent spurting release.

He held tightly to Col, riding the waves, feeling the echo of his pleasure in the rippling shudders of Col's body. The pearly seed of Col's release rained over the shower wall. Warm rivulets and drops slid down to mingle with the water drops that clung there.

Col collapsed against the shower wall. Resting against his back, Matt could feel the pounding of Col's heart racing with his own. Their harsh, panting breaths slowed in unison and Matt smiled when Col yawned.

"Tired?" he asked Col.

"You wear me out, babe," Col replied, his smile evident in his voice.

"Just returning the favor you did me last night."

Col chuckled. "I've never seen anybody pass out so fast after coming."

"You made me come *three times*! That last one did me in."

"And I thought all young studs were supposed to have such inexhaustible stamina."

"You want inexhaustible? Let's try this."

Matt let his shields drop. He easily slipped into Col's mind, taking the path of their mental link. Finding the shield that protected Col from the build-up of psychic energy, Matt mentally caressed the shimmering sphere. Col stiffened and groaned at the electrifying sensation. Touching it enabled Matt to drain away the harmful energy, turning it into sexual release, a process they'd enjoyed many times over the past few days. Even though those energies were now at an all time low, it was still an act that brought both of them great physical pleasure.

"That's not fair," Col gasped.

"No? How's this? Is this fair?" Matt renewed the slow thrusts of his thickening erection.

"*Matt*," Col groaned.

"Do you want me to stop?"

"Hell, *no*!"

Matt smiled. "Let's start counting. This will be climax number two."

* * *

On automatic pilot, Col's ship approached his home planet of Belthola. Automatic signals were sent to the planet below, identifying the ship to the proper port authorities. In addition, the ship sent a status report of the passengers. All three were in perfect health and sleeping peacefully. Satisfied, the duty staff ordered the ship to maintain its orbit.

Aboard ship, one sleeper slowly stirred. Eric Ashton, Matthew's brother, rolled to his back, his eyelids lifting and falling as he fought waking. He'd been having a very sweet dream. A dream in which his now heavy erection was being serviced by a very industrious and appreciative pair of lips.

Groaning, he rolled to his back and pushed away the light blanket that covered him. Eric reached down, letting his hand slide over his torso and belly. Going further still, he felt the first tickle of pubic hair against his fingertips seconds before wrapping his hand around the thick width of his cock. Slowly, his hand moved. The stroke was smooth and deliberate, gradually building his arousal.

Still partially enveloped in sleep and totally relaxed, Eric let his mind drift. His dream resurfaced, the image causing his fingers to tighten around his erection. He grunted with pleasure and increased the pace, but still, something was missing. Something he could feel waiting, just out of reach. Unconsciously, bit by bit, he let his mental shields dissolve.

His mind rapidly and automatically sifted through the impressions that began to seep in. Somewhere nearby, the thing he sought waited. It called out to him, drawing him closer and closer until with a sigh of satisfaction he found it and sank within. Enveloped in an unexpected flash of heat, Eric groaned. His cock pulsed within the stroking confines of his fist, his arousal suddenly magnified and growing.

* * *

Below, on the planet, Greyan Dennon was engaged in diplomatic negotiations. The conference room was carefully appointed. The colors were neutral and calming. The temperature was set at an optimal state. Too warm would make tempers rise; too cold made concentration hard and fostered an increase of impatience to be elsewhere. The butter-soft, leather chairs were padded, geared to cradle and comfort the user.

Greyan was pleased at the progress being made. His two often combative clients were finally in agreement. What remained was merely to formalize the terms and add their signatures to the final product. This process was even now underway. He sat back with a satisfied sigh that nearly morphed into a surprised groan of pleasure.

Reining in the burst of arousal that assailed him, Grey gritted his teeth, forcing himself to remain still in his seat, even as his cock thickened and grew. His thoughts immediately went to his twin brother, Sethian.

I told him I was going to be in conference this morning. Wait till I get my hands on him! Greyan thought silently. He sent his consciousness winging outward. Making the connection with his brother, he mentally shouted, *Seth, you horny bastard. Stop whatever you're doing. Right now!*

It's not me!

Not you? Who else could it be?

I don't know. I've never felt him before, Sethian groaned. *But I sure as hell feel him now!*

Grey suppressed a shudder. *I've got to get out of here before I disgrace myself.* He let the connection with Seth grow slack.

Returning his attention to those present, he found himself the target of several sets of puzzled eyes. Mentally rolling his eyes, he smiled at them. "Gentlemen, I've just received a communication from my brother. A matter of some urgency. As you're all in agreement at this point, I believe my work here is done." He rose from his chair, keeping his jacket carefully arranged to cover the thick bulge at his crotch.

Putting his high-backed chair between himself and the assembled company, he accepted their thanks as sweat broke out between his shoulder blades. The arousal was building faster now. Greyan felt as though he'd just been shoved into an oven. He struggled to still breaths that wanted to turn into pants, but was unable to slow his now thudding heartbeat.

As his clients wound down, Grey thanked them and made his escape. Had it been possible, he could swear there was a disembodied hand stroking his cock. Allowing his breath to explode out in a panting groan, he hurried to his office and raced into the bathroom. His pants were opened in record time, his straining shaft jumping free.

Grey took himself in hand and frantically pumped. The mental link with his brother and the unknown male expanded, drew them in, then threw them together with a violent jerk. They merged. Climax exploded through them. Three cocks simultaneously jerked and expelled wild, spine-wrenching spumes of semen. Greyan threw back his head on a guttural groan and slid to the floor as his knees buckled. Shuddering, he rested for a time, listening to his own heartbeat grow still and steady.

Seth? You still alive? he questioned, sending the thought to his brother.

Barely. Please tell me you made it out of the conference. I don't want to have to try and explain that to the council.

I made it. Who do you think that was?

I don't know. But I sure intend to find out.

* * *

Back on the ship, Eric wiped at the semen that spattered his shoulder and chest. He reached down and felt for his balls, chuckling in dazed relief that they were still in place. When he came, it felt as though they'd been drawn up the shaft of his cock and spit out, so hard was the climax. He'd never felt anything to equal it.

As his body cooled and quivering muscles relaxed, he reviewed the impressions that swamped his mind at the point of orgasm. At first, the presence felt big, larger than life, a magnified version of humanity. Until it split. Right before they'd merged, Eric became aware of two separate entities. And though they were closely similar, each had a different feel, a taste that rested on his mental palate. A taste he found himself savoring.

He rolled out of bed and walked to the large oval porthole that graced the outside wall of his cabin. Far below, a planet slowly rotated. Surprised at first, he thought they'd returned to Earth. Until he noted the land masses. They were in no way similar to Earth and yet, like Earth, each was surrounded by large bodies of water. The planet was all blues and greens, with masses of fluffy, white clouds majestically floating in random patterns.

He closed his eyes, reaching out with his senses. Somewhere below, two waited. Eric wasn't sure what to make of it. But he had to admit to himself, he was intrigued.

Turning away, he went into the small bathroom that was part of his cabin to take a shower.

Chapter Two

Eric carefully watched his brother. Matt was talking with Sam Roth and his Maleri' mate, Geral Pardais. Eric detected a certain tension in Matt that was not completely caused by an encounter with these two men who were strangers. He knew without asking that Matt was disturbed by the fact that both men had had sexual contact with Col. He knew exactly how Matt felt. He'd once met a former lover of his deceased partner and the encounter had been distinctly uncomfortable.

Never one to beat around the bush, Eric decided it was time to stop avoiding the discomfort. He waited for a lull in the conversation, then jumped in. "Col told Matt that you, he and Sam were once a threesome. How does that work? And what's the status of that relationship now?"

Matt turned beet red. "Eric!"

Geral laughed. "It's all right, Matt. Your brother merely wishes to protect you." He nodded his approval. "An admirable trait." He gave Eric his full attention. "When a young Maleri' reaches the age of eighteen, he is sent to live with a mated pair. Contrary to what you might think, we are not an overly promiscuous group. This is done so that the young one not only has a mentor to help sharpen his mental skills, but has an active outlet for his sexual urges. I am sure you will agree, young men are well known for the strength and frequency of their urges."

Eric nodded. "What do they do between puberty and eighteen?"

Geral made a familiar motion with his hand. "What we all did."

Eric laughed, liking the big man's answer.

"We don't feel it would be wise for any of the young ones to engage in actual sex until they are eighteen. Our lives are complicated enough as it is without adding that confusion to the mix. I'm thirty-two. In that time, I've had sex with four men. The bonded Maleri' pair I went to live with when I was eighteen, then my mate, Sam." He gave Sam a smile. Eric could see the love glowing in the depths of his eyes. "And, Col. For us, sex isn't about conquest or racking up numbers. It's about caring and love."

"And now that Col and Matt are together?"

"They're bonded, mated. Off limits to any but each other. In time, they may welcome a budding Maleri' into their lives, but it's not mandatory. Nor may it even be an opportunity that's offered to them. We're not a large group. There are currently fifty-four bonded pairs, eleven single men who are of age to take a mate and seventeen young ones under the age of eighteen. We of the Maleri' are but a very small portion of the population on this planet."

"I appreciate you answering my questions."

"I appreciate your candid attitude, Eric. I assure you, your brother will be cherished by Col."

"Of course he will. Who said he will not?" Col asked as he entered the room.

"No one," Matt assured him, rising to meet him. "Eric was just expressing his concerns about the lifestyle of the Maleri'."

Col wrapped an arm around Matt's waist. "And have your concerns been addressed?"

"Addressed and laid to rest," Eric admitted.

"How's Kiel?" Sam asked, changing the subject. "Were you able to bring him out of the coma?"

"We were. When I left, he was out of bed, walking around and complaining about being under for so long. A few days of physical therapy should set him to rights. After that, he'll get the very great pleasure of returning to the negotiating table. I have to admit, the Yalhandrans and the Kasians have been uncharacteristically patient."

"They don't really want to go to war," Geral commented. "At this point, it's a matter of saving face. And don't you know? That Yalhandran patience has its roots in their queen. She's taken quite a shine to Kiel."

Col's sudden laughter was infectious.

"I take it Kiel is one of the Maleri'?" a grinning Eric asked.

"He is," Col answered. "The poor woman is doomed to disappointment."

"I hope he has sense enough to negotiate the treaty before he lets her down," Geral said fervently.

"Kiel may take chances with his own safety, but he knows his responsibilities," Col answered. "I'm sure he'll handle it well."

"You're right, of course," Geral began.

"But you have to worry about something," Sam interjected. "Col, you know how he is."

Geral rose and went to his mate. "No fair parading my inadequacies in front of company," he said with a smile.

Sam left his chair and leaned into Geral, kissing him lightly. "Inadequacies? There's only the one. Other than that, you're perfect."

There was a concerted groan from Col, Matt and Eric.

Geral chuckled and looked at them. "Do you mind? We're sharing an honest and open conversation here. The room just reeks of jealousy."

"I think we need a bucket and shovel. The bullshit's getting deep in here," Eric grumbled.

His comment brought another round of laughter.

"Come on, all of you," Sam ordered. "Into the kitchen. We promised you dinner. We just didn't tell you, you have to help fix it."

With good cheer, the five of them trooped into the kitchen.

* * *

Eric took a sip of coffee and absently ran his hands over the agate countertop. The light of the afternoon sun picked up tiny, reflective planes and sparkles within the stone. So far, his time on Belthola had been interesting and pleasant. Deciding to accept Col's offer to come so that he and Matt could stay together was turning out to be a very good idea. Although he knew there would be things he'd miss on Earth, there was so much to be discovered here.

Their arrival on the planet had been amazing. Col docked his ship at the Taskin City Port. The place was huge. Like a sprawling airplane complex with no runways. The ships that came and went didn't require them. It was abuzz with people and ships docking and taking off.

Col, because of his position, had a reserved docking space and VIP treatment extended to him when he signaled the Port Authority he was ready to land. A vehicle was waiting for them. There was no driver's seat, only an automated control panel across the dash. Plush seats awaited the passengers. They were placed around a center table with glowing controls. At the push of a button, a variety of drinks and food was available.

As soon as they entered the car, a disembodied voice spoke. The voice was male, lushly deep and sensual. "Good afternoon, Col, dear. Welcome back. Where would you like to go?"

Eric and Matt gave Col a speculative look, Matt's brow rising. Col flushed. "LAT, can the endearments. We want to go to Geral and Sam's."

"Of course, darling."

Col rolled his eyes. "I didn't program that voice."

"Whose voice is it?" Matt asked with a frown.

"As far as I know, it's computer generated."

"It sounds pretty damned human to me."

"Now, Matt," Col began.

"Yes, dear?"

"I said Matt, not LAT."

"*Who* is Matt?"

"Matt is my mate."

"I see," came a chilly reply.

Col rubbed his forehead. "This is ridiculous. My mate and my car are jealous of each other."

Two voices replied simultaneously. "I am not!"

Eric sat back and laughed.

"What's so damned funny?" Matt demanded.

"This."

Col finally sorted out the confusion and introduced Matt and Eric to LAT, his Luxury Automated Transport. At Col's order, LAT set voice recognition for Matt and Eric which would allow them to use the car as they pleased. By the time they'd arrived at Geral and Sam's, LAT was freely bestowing endearments on all three of them. Eric deduced that he wasn't one to hold a grudge.

The evening spent with Geral and Sam had been fun and entertaining. Eric liked them -- especially after the way they treated Matt. Eric had watched his brother blossom under their easy company. Matt was usually awkward in social situations, but Col's friends made both of them feel like family. It was an experience that warmed Eric's heart. He hadn't realized, until that moment, how solitary and insular he and Matt had become.

This evening, they'd been invited to a gathering. Several members of the Belthola High Council would be there. In addition, many of the Maleri' would be attending, as well as diplomats and representatives from other nearby worlds.

Eric shook his head. Rubbing elbows with the planet's movers and shakers was not something he'd expected. Although, he reasoned with himself, he really hadn't known what to expect. This was all very well for a short span of time, but he found himself growing restless. He was a man used to making his way in the world. He wanted to be engaged in something constructive. Lounging around for too long made him edgy.

"Any coffee left?"

Eric turned to find Col sauntering into the kitchen. "Yeah, I just made a fresh pot. Where's Matt?"

"Um, resting," Col answered casually.

Eric grinned. "Hope you didn't wear him out too much."

"I think he'll be recovered for tonight's festivities. Did you find the clothes we left for you?"

"Yeah, they fit great. Thanks. I didn't think to bring formal wear with me."

At his tone, Col gave Eric a look of concern. "Something bothering you?"

"Sorry. I'm just not used to being so sedentary. We were on the ship for a week and though we've only been here a couple of days, I'm starting to go stir crazy."

"Would some exercise help? There's a fully equipped gym downstairs."

Eric's eyes lit up. "That'd be great!"

"Come on," Col said, while checking his watch. "We've got some time before we need to start getting ready for the gathering."

* * *

From his vantage point on the balcony above, Sethian Dennon observed with interest the arrival of Eric, Matt and Col at the very posh Amiston Hotel. A teasing glimpse was all he was afforded before they were escorted inside. He left the balcony, going in search of his brother, Greyan.

The banquet room was enormous and lushly appointed. Tables, draped in white, were set up for the diners at one side of the room and a large space was left open near the balcony for dancing. The night was pleasantly mild. The balcony doors were thrown wide to let in the fresh, evening air. A live orchestra played music that was mellow and relaxing.

Their arrival drew quite a few glances. Those members of the Maleri' that were present wished to greet Col and congratulate him on finding his mate. They also, understandably, wanted to satisfy their curiosity about Matt, as well as welcome him. Quite a buzz started over the arrival of Eric on Belthola. Col reported his return to the High Council, informing them of his success in finding Matt and about the presence of his brother, Eric. Eric's status as an empath stirred more than a little interest. Rumors had immediately started to fly.

All eleven of the single Maleri' who were ready to take mates were in attendance, including Sethian and Greyan. The two of them stood across the room, watching as introductions were made and words of greeting exchanged.

"Which one do you think is Eric Ashton?" Sethian asked.

Greyan kept his gaze on the small group across the room. "The taller one, I think. Yes, look there, Col's put his arm around the shorter man's waist. He must be Col's mate, Matthew."

"This has to be a first among the Maleri'. A mate who comes to the hunter, instead of the other way around. That is, of course, if he's really ours."

"It must be him. What happened to us yesterday coincided with his arrival. And he *is* an empath. We have Col's word on that. He must have unconsciously found the path that will form our link with each other."

"Umm, which means he's strong," Sethian agreed. "He's quite handsome, isn't he?" Seth asked, admiring Eric's trim and muscular body and his blond hair. "I look forward to seeing him out of his clothes."

"Dog," Greyan admonished, shaking his head. "Let's meet him before we strip him naked."

"Don't tell me the same thought didn't run through *your* head," Seth returned sarcastically. "Are you getting anything from him?"

Greyan shook his head. "He's shielding."

"So when do we introduce ourselves?"

"Let's let the initial furor die down. I'd like to do this privately. Then we can claim him quickly."

"I do like the way you think," Seth told him with a grin. "Come on, let's get a drink. We *are* supposed to be mingling with the off-worlders."

* * *

Eric was becoming aggravated. While the gathering was pleasant, the food good and the company better, he was beginning to feel like the only bone in a yard full of dogs. He'd been introduced to many of Col's fellow Maleri', some mated pairs and some singles. The singles were easy to spot. They arrived with a certain expectant air and went away in disappointment. It was enough to give him an inferiority complex.

Was it his fault he didn't fit the bill where they were concerned? It wasn't enough to be a decent looking, nice guy. All of a sudden, there had to be some mystical, empathic connection. Although he'd known this was coming, he wasn't sure if he was relieved or disappointed that the magic didn't happen.

"What's the matter?" Matt asked, leaning toward him.

They were seated at a table, the meal coming to a conclusion. The conversation had been lively, as Sam and Geral were included in their dining companions, but Eric had let his attention drift.

"What makes you think something's wrong?" he asked.

"You're frowning."

"Oh. It's nothing, little brother. I just think I need some air," he hedged and rose from his chair. "I'm going out on the balcony. I'll be back in a few minutes."

Eric wound a path through the tables and circled around the dance floor. Quite a few couples, male and female as well as male and male, were taking advantage of the music. He briefly envied them as he slipped out the balcony doors. He and his partner, Dan, used to enjoy dancing.

The balcony was wide, with a low, outside wall. Potted plants were placed artfully here and there with some comfortable chairs scattered around as well. Eric walked to the wall and leaned on it, looking out over the lights of the city.

"Nice view, don't you think?"

Startled, he turned to face a tall man with dark, chestnut hair. The lights from inside glinted on the shining strands.

"Um, yeah. It's a very nice view."

"I don't believe we've met. I'm Greyan Dennon." He turned and from the dim recesses of a sheltered alcove, another man appeared. "And this is my brother, Sethian."

Eric received his second shock when the two of them stood side by side. Two sets of wide shoulders, trim waists, lean hips and long legs. And from what he could see, despite the concealment of clothing, all those magnificent body parts were well defined by hard sculpted muscle. Pure temptation in stereo.

He held out his hand to Greyan, looking from one to the other. "I guess I'd be safe in assuming that you two are brothers. Hello, I'm Eric Ashton."

Grey took his hand and Eric felt his knees weaken. He swayed, ever so slightly and suddenly, Sethian was there with an arm around his shoulders. "It is you," Seth whispered, his hand cupping Eric's cheek.

Under the double assault of their physical touch, Eric's knees nearly gave out. Before he could utter a protest, Seth lowered his mouth to Eric's and kissed him. Eric moaned as his shields were assaulted, not by a rough, battering presence, but by a gentle, persuasive phantom that promised pleasure and delight.

Seth's kiss was soft silk and hot, molten spice that made his tongue tingle when Eric opened his mouth to him. Any resistance he felt began to melt under the sensual assault. His shields were weakening, growing gossamer thin. Unfamiliar images and sounds began to swirl through his head. Seth released him and for a moment his head cleared. Until Grey stepped in.

With Seth at his back and Greyan before him, Eric was surrounded in their warmth. Grey bent to him. "Let us in, Eric. We're yours and you're ours." Grey's lips touched his and Eric's shield dissolved. Moaning at the ripples of pleasure that shot through him, he let the unfamiliar sounds and sights and smells wash over him. An unbreakable connection formed and forked, twin pathways leading to Greyan and Sethian.

No longer were these two strangers holding him. They were well-known friends on the verge of becoming intimate lovers. Eric saw images in his mind of two young boys running and playing, two teenagers studying and laughing together at some amusing picture in the book before them. He felt their sadness and excitement, as on their eighteenth birthday, they prepared to separate for the first time. Each to live with their own Maleri' mentor and his mate.

The impressions whirled through Eric's mind and swamped his consciousness, before gently draining away, leaving only the pleasure of Grey's kiss. Released from the paralyzing effect of the forming connection, Eric wound his arms around Grey, not only accepted the kiss, but taking over.

His mouth slanted and slid, his tongue slipping in to curl around Grey's. He was rewarded by double moans as the pleasure traveled the triple path of their connection, and rippled between the three of them. Behind him, he could feel

Seth's burgeoning erection pressing between the cheeks of his ass. In front, his own growing erection raced to fullness with Grey's. The three of them ground their bodies together, fast losing touch with the fact that they were in a very public place. Until a voice shocked them awake.

"You three need to get a room."

With a guilty start, their group separated. Before them stood a man of many extremes, among them height and pure, devilishly good looks. Eric's gaze moved upward until his eyes met the stranger's. Eyes of shining silver-gray steel. Eyes that made him squirm like a wayward schoolboy until the man smiled.

"Are these two miscreants bothering you?" he asked with a stern air that was belied by the smile.

"Now, Chase. You know us," Sethian began.

"I certainly do. What do *you* say, sir?"

Eric returned his smile. "No, they're not bothering me."

"Very well, gentlemen, carry on. Though perhaps a private place would be more appropriate, as well as more comfortable. Welcome to Belthola, Eric Ashton, and congratulations to the three of you."

Chase's retreat was followed by thanks from the three of them. "Who's that?" Eric inquired, sitting down on the balcony wall.

Greyan sat to one side of him, Sethian to the other. Seth answered. "Chasetien Kaldor. He's Maleri' and head of the Taskin City Security Bureau. His specialty is policing the Maleri'."

"You two in particular?" Eric asked with a grin.

Grey bumped Eric's shoulder with his own. "*No.* But just because a man is born Maleri' doesn't always mean he's automatically honorable. There have been incidences of misuse of power. Chase is very good at ferreting out such things."

"I see," Eric replied. "So, what happens now?"

"Come home with us and you'll see," Seth answered.

Eric laughed. "You don't waste time."

"Why should I? We all felt the connection form. What Grey said is true. We're yours and you're ours. Is there any reason to question it?"

Eric shook his head. "I don't know. It just seems so anticlimactic somehow. You know? No guess work involved. No dating, no getting to know each other, no uncertainty."

"Oh, but you see, that's where you're wrong. There's plenty of getting to know each other. While it's true we've seen parts of each other's lives as the link formed, we've not interacted on a one to one basis. There could still be conflict and problems as well as pleasure," Greyan assured him. "Just because we know that we're meant to be together doesn't mean it's all handed to us with no work involved. And I can prove it by asking you one simple question. Do you love me?"

Eric looked at him in surprise. "I just met you."

"You see," Sethian pointed out. "There's still lots to do to make this mating work."

"That's another thing," Eric said. "Why both of you? Is it because you're twins?"

They both nodded. "We were born with our own links in place. While we each have our own thoughts, feelings, etcetera, some things just can't be separated. This, apparently, is one of them. Is that going to be a problem?"

Eric stood up, turned and looked at the two of them where they sat on the low balcony wall. The light from inside shone on their faces, and for the first time, he could see that their eyes were sapphire blue. In both pairs of eyes, he could see uncertainty. Despite the link that had formed between them, neither one of them took for granted his acceptance. It was their lack of arrogance in the face of what their gifts told them that decided him.

"Double or nothing," he murmured under his breath, then smiled. "Come on. I want you to meet my brother."

Twin sighs of relief met his words as the brothers rose. With smiles on their faces, they followed their mate back into the banquet room. From out of the shadows, a woman appeared. She watched their progress with interest as a plan formed in her mind.

* * *

Matt watched his brother appear through the balcony doors, followed by two men. Twins, he noted with some surprise. They moved forward and flanked Eric, one on either side. The three of them were fairly equal in height, with Eric possibly an inch or so taller. They made quite a delectable picture as they walked together.

Two heads, topped by gleaming chestnut hair, leaned in close when Eric said something. They made quite a nice contrast against his own shining blond hair. The two pulled back, all three laughing. Laughter that drew more than a few appreciative glances their way.

A thought suddenly struck Matt as they approached. He automatically reached out for Col as he struggled to keep rising tears at bay.

"What is it, baby?" Col asked, his voice laced with concern.

Matt drew Col's attention to Eric and his entourage. "I've lost him."

"Eric?"

Matt nodded. "He's found someone. Two someones, by the look of it."

"Greyan and Sethian Dennon. Could it be?"

Before he could speculate further, the three arrived before them.

"Hello, Col. It's good to have you back with us. And after such a successful trip," Seth said in greeting.

"Seth, Grey, it's good to be home. I see you've met Eric. This is Matthew, Eric's brother and my mate."

Matt reluctantly shook hands with them, his smile a bit strained. He turned his gaze to Eric and found concern filling his brother's eyes.

"Could you excuse us a minute? I'd like to talk to Matt in private," Eric told the other three.

They readily agreed. Eric steered Matt out of the room and across the hall to an empty office that Col pointed out. Once inside, Eric didn't say a word. He just wrapped Matt in his embrace and held him.

"I'm sorry," Matt whispered as his tears fell on his brother's shoulder. "I should be happy for you, but it's all happening so fast." He pulled away and sat down in one of the chairs that were placed in front of the office desk. "First Col appears like a genie out of a bottle. The next thing I know I have a mate, a new home, a new planet and now to pay for it, I'm losing you."

"Matthew Ashton, you are *not* losing me," Eric told him sharply. He took a seat in the chair facing Matt's. "I'm not going anywhere. Except probably to a different house. But I'm still right here. I'm still your brother. We're family and I'm always going to be here for you."

Matt shook his head and angrily wiped the tears away. "I *know*. In my heart, I know that. I guess it's just that, for so long, it was just you and me. All these new people suddenly appearing in our lives has made me a little shaky."

"It's funny you should say that. I was thinking the same thing earlier," Eric revealed. "I think this is a good thing. For both of us. Surely you wouldn't want to give Col up and go back to Earth?"

"Hell no! I'd never give Col up!"

"Well, that's good to know," Col said as the door opened and he popped his head in. "Is everything all right in here?"

"How do you do that?"

"What?"

"You always manage to turn up just when your name comes up in a conversation," Matt answered.

"Psychic?"

"Lucky."

"To have you," Col answered.

"Come in here," Matt ordered.

"Um, there are two guys out here who are a bit worried. Can they come in too?"

Col and Eric turned questioning gazes on Matt. It was his decision, they silently told him.

"Bring them with you," Matt conceded. "I guess I'll have to get to know the guys that are stealing my brother."

Greyan and Sethian heard Matt's last remark and looked at him with real concern. "I'm not," they both began and stopped, looking at each other. "That is, we --" Once again they stopped, giving each other a look of disgust.

"Wait a minute. Can I say something here?" Everyone looked at Eric. "Matt and I have talked it over and Matt has agreed to share me with you. Right, Matt?"

Matt looked at his brother as a huge, crashing wave of love rushed into his heart. "Yeah, I guess I can be an adult and share."

Eric gave him a grin of approval.

"Thank you, Matt," Greyan said.

"I promise we'll take care of him," Sethian added.

"Oh, I know you will," Matt told them. "If you don't, I'll sic Col on you."

"Now, babe, that won't be necessary," Col soothed, before turning his unwavering gaze on the twins. "You know I'll go after them without any prompting whatsoever."

There was a moment's shocked silence before Col's laugh eased the tension.

"What were those words you used?" Seth asked Eric. "Anti-climactic, no uncertainty? This seems to be an endeavor that's fraught with danger. I don't think we're going to languish for want of excitement."

Matt smiled as he saw the light in Eric's eyes when he looked at the twins. A sudden visual went through his head. Three of them? Together? In bed? *No*, he thought silently. *I don't think there'll be any lack of excitement.*

Chapter Three

Not without some trepidation, which fortunately was overlaid by a lot of anticipation, Eric went home with Grey and Seth. Muted excitement and tension filled the vehicle as the three of them made the trip in the twins' LAT. Unlike Col's, their LAT's voice was rather ordinary and not given to passing out endearments. It merely asked their destination and took them there. Eric found himself missing the other LAT's idiosyncrasies.

Unlike the multi-levels of Col's house, this one sprawled out on a single level. At least Eric assumed so, until the car pulled into the long driveway and halted before the house.

There was a deep, low volume noise. "What's that?" Eric asked.

"The garage door opening," Grey replied.

"I don't see any door opening."

"It's under the car."

Eric's brow rose as their vehicle began to tip downwards. A ramp was opening below them and the LAT slowly rolled forward and parked in the underground garage. Lights immediately began to bloom around them, the intensity increasing slowly to allow their eyes to adjust as they got out of the car. The garage was large, with room for at least three other vehicles. Seth led the way to a small elevator.

"There's also stairs, if you prefer," he pointed out before the elevator doors closed.

The trip up took mere seconds and the doors opened into the main living area. "What do you think?" Grey asked.

"This is amazing," Eric commented, leaving the elevator and wandering around the room.

The main living area was on two levels. The largest part was on the same level as the elevator exit. It was furnished with sofas, tables and chairs. A large entertainment system took up a good part of one wall.

Across the room, a pie shaped wedge was formed with one of the room's corners as its point. The floor was raised, making it look like a small stage. The outer edge was curved, and along the upper edge ran what looked to be an elaborate, wrought iron railing. Between the open spaces one could see a large lounging sofa, ultra thick carpeting and a fireplace. The base of the platform was glass enclosed and turned out to be a fully functioning fish tank.

Eric could see several colorful varieties of fish swimming in the crystal clear water. "Are those real?" he asked.

"Yeah, they are," Seth answered.

"Is the entire space under the floor filled with water?"

"No. Actually the tank is only about twenty inches wide. It just curves around the whole platform."

"How do you take care of it?"

"We don't," Grey confessed. "There's a service that comes once a week to do whatever they do to keep things running smoothly. The way I understand it, the filters and air supply are such that this thing is pretty much self-sufficient. The system even automatically feeds them twice a day."

"Very clever," Eric commented, mounting the two, shallow steps up to the platform. His shoes sank into the thick padding and he slipped them off before proceeding.

Grey and Seth emulated him. Eric walked around to the sofa and sat down with a sigh. "It certainly is comfortable. So is this the seduction nook?" he asked with a grin.

"It could be," Grey offered, seating himself next to Eric.

Seth flipped a switch near the mantel. The fireplace came to life, flames crackling over the wood. "We've never used it as such. But I don't see any reason that we couldn't." He approached the sofa and took a place at Eric's other side.

Eric was already kissing Grey, who was moaning under the tender assault. Eric released him and turned to Seth, giving him similar treatment. He pulled away, stood and began unbuttoning his coat. "I don't feel like wrestling you two on the sofa while trying to get your clothes off. Let's do this the easy way, hmm?"

The brothers rose and followed his lead, beginning to strip out of their clothes. They watched Eric intently as more and more of his body was revealed, but no more intently than he watched them. While still half dressed, Seth went to the set of switches near the fireplace. Seth flipped several switches, and all the lights went out except for one, which sent a soft amber-shaded glow over them. It echoed the flickering shine of the fire. Under the gentle glimmer, their bodies were revealed.

Soft music played, accenting the fall of discarded clothing. Eric felt his heart begin to pound as a feast of smooth, muscular flesh was set out before him. He and Grey were the first to finish undressing, with Seth running a close second.

"Just stand there for a moment," he ordered softly. "I want to look at both of you."

A flush of heat swept over his skin. Before him stood two of the most beautiful men he'd ever seen. Their shoulders were breathtakingly broad, their chests and arms firm and well developed. Washboard abs drew his gaze to lean torsos, trim waists, slim hips and long legs. Every luscious part was well defined and sleek with bundles of flowing, delineated muscle.

Two thick and ready cocks eagerly jutted forward from dark nests of hair while resting below hung full and lightly furred testicles. The hard lengths of their cocks were wrapped with several bluish and prominent veins. Both of them were topped by plum-shaped caps that glistened with the sweet juice that dripped from the tiny slits at the tips.

Eric felt his own cock lurch in reaction. Two sets of sapphire eyes flared in response and the three of them came together. As before on the balcony, Seth circled and held Eric from behind, while Eric and Grey wrapped their arms around each other.

Their lips met and melded. Their tongues engaged in a sensual tangle of caresses as they explored each other's mouths. Seth's body was sealed to Eric's, the thick length of his erection nestled in the crease of Eric's ass. With lips and tongue he caressed the back of Eric's neck and shoulders.

When his tongue began to swirl over the whorls of Eric's ear, Eric pulled his mouth free from Grey's, a moan grinding free from the depths of his chest as he shuddered. Grey released him and Eric turned in his arms. Seth stepped into Eric's eager embrace, their mouths sealing together. Grey stepped away, his leaving drawing their attention.

"Where are you going?" Eric panted.

"For lube," Grey replied with a strained grin. "Carry on, I'll be right back."

Eric and Seth smiled at each other and eagerly complied. When Grey returned with towels in addition to the lube, they were on the floor. Seth was on his back. Eric was leaning over him, his tongue delicately lapping the clear, savory fluid from the reddened tip of Seth's cock. Grey echoed Seth's groan when Eric's mouth easily engulfed his brother's full, straining length.

Grey watched, mesmerized as Eric spent several minutes sucking Seth's cock before he looked up, an invitation in his glinting, brown eyes. Grey eagerly accepted. Eric released Seth and at his direction, Grey spread a towel and sat down on the sofa. Eric rose to his knees and placing his hands on Grey's knees, he spread his thighs wide.

He took the bottle of lube from Grey and handed it to Seth. "Think you can handle fucking me while I suck this enormous cock?"

Seth gave him a lascivious grin. "Get ready for the ride of your life, babe."

Eric returned his grin and centered his attention on Grey. "Did that excite you? Watching me suck Seth?"

"Oh yeah," Grey admitted breathlessly, his eyes dark with arousal.

"Then you're gonna love it when I do it to you."

Eric bent, but instead of taking Grey in his mouth, he let his cheek slide the thick length of that eagerly standing column of flesh until he could bury his nose in the skin and pubic hair at its base. He inhaled and groaned in pleasure as the scent of male in rut swept into his nostrils. A chill swept down the length of his spine and he shuddered as his belly tightened.

"You smell *so good*," he growled. "You both do." He raised his head. "And Seth tasted sweet. How do you taste, Grey? Is your honey sweet?" He swept the pad of his thumb over the glistening head of Grey's cock, drawing a moan from him. "Is this thick syrup going to be the most delicious thing I've ever tasted?" Eric examined the crystal smear of pre-cum on the tip of his thumb. Holding Grey's gaze, he brought his thumb to his lips, his tongue flicking out as his lips opened and closed around the tip of it. "Mmm," he moaned. "Oh, yeah. Fresh male honey, rich and ripe," he growled.

Wrapping his hand around the column of male flesh before him, Eric lowered his head, opened his mouth and closed his lips over the plump, red tip. Grey's head fell back as Eric's tongue slid over him, that sinuous organ seeking out every rich drop of pre-cum.

Seth watched and listened, fascinated as Eric seduced his brother. Their mate was no shy flower and for that, he was grateful. He and Grey both had hardy sexual appetites, their mentors and mentors' mates often teasing them about the amount of time they had to spend satisfying those hungers. Up until this time, those hungers were seen to separately. For the first time, they were sharing another male, their own mate, between them. It was an experience, erotic in the extreme.

Seth let his gaze wander the length of Eric's back, his eyes following the sleek, sharp line of his spine. That line led downward to the tempting crease between two taut cheeks. Seth shifted to his knees and urged Eric to spread his legs. When Eric complied, Seth moved between and rested his hands on Eric's back before letting them glide over the warm, smooth skin.

He moved closer, letting his rock-hard cock rest between those tempting cheeks as he bent forward to kiss and lick Eric's back. He smiled when Eric shivered and moaned. Eric's skin was slightly salty and beginning to dampen with sweat. The smell was clean and musky, all male and filled with the spice of growing arousal.

Seth let his hands and mouth caress and taste at will, following the line of Eric's spine and without hesitation, moving down to that beckoning crease. His hands on Eric's ass spread the rounded mounds, revealing the taut pink pucker of his entrance. Seth brushed his thumb over the wrinkled skin. Eric jumped and moaned again.

Lowering his mouth, Seth let his tongue sweep over the tight, rosy opening. His mind clouded with lust as he began to feast. Primal urges lured him in and wrapped him in their drugging embrace. When at last he struggled free, Eric was groaning, his body pushing desperately back into Seth's. His puckered entrance was wet and flushed, the once snug opening relaxed and ready. Seth growled in anticipation and fumbled for the lube.

Coating his fingers, he slowly and patiently inserted first one, then two, then three. Each time he made sure of Eric's comfort and willingness for more until Eric released Grey's cock for a moment and turned to him.

"Fuck me! I want your cock, Seth. *Now!*"

Eric turned back, engulfing Grey once more and, satisfied, Seth obliged by liberally applying lube to his own cock. Placing the fat, red tip at Eric's entrance, he pushed. Eric pushed back, groaning when the head of Seth's cock breached the taut ring. Both of them held still for a moment until Eric broadcast his readiness by once again pushing back. Seth's hands found Eric's hips and held him as he slowly slid into the humid depths of Eric's velvet lined channel.

Fully seated, Seth stopped, his breath racing in measured pants. "*Fuck!* You are so damn tight." Eric pushed back against him and Seth's hands tightened, holding him still. "Don't move. Don't you dare move or I'll lose it before

I've begun." He rested a moment, then slowly, slowly he started to move.

The strokes at first were shallow forays in and out. They grew in length, strength and speed until Seth was thrusting deep and hard. He varied the movements, slowing when he felt his climax approach, rushing full speed ahead to bring it close again. All the while, Eric sucked Grey's cock. The moans, grunts and groans of all three broke the silence, accompanied by the rhythmic smack of Seth's hips against Eric's ass.

Climax was once again approaching fast when he met his brother's gaze. Grey's eyes were dark with strained arousal. Their link flared wide and Seth groaned, feeling Grey's need for release wash over him. Suddenly, unthinking, unreasoning, Seth pulled free of Eric's body.

Leaning over Eric he gasped, "Ride Grey. Ride his cock, Eric."

More than eager to comply, Eric rose and straddled Grey, who held his cock steady as Eric lowered himself to it. The thick rod slid smoothly in place and Eric eagerly rode as Grey thrust upward, hard and fast. Seth moved close. His arms wrapped around Eric's chest, his cock sandwiched between his own belly and Eric's back.

Seth pressed his lips to Eric's ear. "Open for us, baby. Open the link. Let's wring this fucking climax dry."

Seth met Grey's eyes once more as Eric nodded and dropped his shields. The world exploded. Piercing pleasure, so razor sharp it penetrated every cell in their bodies, detonated within them. It twisted and burned, the ache of its brilliance finding release in hoarse male groans and guttural wails that pierced the room and drowned the soft music that played from the stereo.

Three bodies shuddered and shook, muscles tautly bunching. Three cocks erupted. Thick streams of fragrant white seed flowed over bellies and backs, and flooded one dark, clasping channel that eagerly milked the thick rod filling it. Seth collapsed against Eric and Eric against Grey who dropped back to let the sofa support them all.

Their racing hearts and breaths eventually restored themselves. Minds again took up their usual function and they stirred, groaning as previously straining muscles protested these further moves.

Seth was the first to back away. He rose on wobbly knees. "Everybody intact?" he asked with a growing smile that was accompanied by a weak chuckle.

Eric got his feet under him and gasped when Grey's softening cock slid free. He stood and leaned back into Seth.

"You okay?" Seth asked, sliding an arm around his waist.

"I'm good," he replied, his eyes dazed, his voice a lazy drawl.

"Grey?" Seth asked, extending his hand to his brother.

Grey reached up and let Seth and Eric help him stand. "Yeah, fine. What the hell was that?"

"Sex on a grand scale," Eric commented dryly.

The brothers chuckled weakly. "Grand it was. No doubt about that," Seth agreed. "Shower?"

"Shower. *Oh, yeah,*" the other two agreed. The three of them staggered off to the bathroom.

During a hot, relaxing shower in which their senses revived as well as their cocks, Eric, Grey and Seth relieved the new tension by jacking off in front of each other. This exercise was accompanied by teasing comments that degenerated into panting groans and hot looks as each shot another impressive load.

Relaxed and totally sated, they dried themselves and headed for bed. It was then a question arose. "So what are the sleeping arrangements?" Eric asked.

"We were hoping you'd sleep with both of us," Grey answered.

"Do you two normally sleep together?"

The brothers shook their heads. "We each took one of the smaller bedrooms. We've been saving the master bedroom for when we found a mate. Now that you're here…"

"I'd like to see it," Eric answered.

They opened a set of double doors that led from the bathroom into the room next door. The bedroom was enormous. A huge bed dominated the space. Its frame was wrought iron, black, thick and heavy, yet artistically pleasing in the whorls and curves of its shape. The furniture was dark, gleaming wood inlaid and carved with echoes of the shapes from the bed frame.

There were tall, floor-to-ceiling windows and Seth demonstrated how the glass could be darkened to keep out the light and the spying looks of any curious neighbors. Two walk-in closets were built in and a table with three chairs was placed near the windows. As in the LAT, there were buttons which would bring forth a variety of drinks. Coffee, tea, juice or water for the morning or afternoon, something stronger for the evening, if desired.

Eric wandered over and sat on the bed.

"What do you think?" Seth asked.

"It's beautiful. But, I have a question."

"Sure."

"You don't sleep together. Does that mean you don't have sex with each other?"

"No. Don't get me wrong," Seth continued. "I love my brother. Hell, he's a good looking guy," he added with a teasing grin. "He's just not my type."

"You don't exactly turn my knees to pudding either, buddy," Grey shot back.

"All right," Eric interrupted. "And is it true that neither one of you has been on the receiving end of anal sex?"

To his surprise and amusement, both brothers developed a faint blush. "That's true," Seth answered. "It's something we give only to our mate."

Eric grinned. "Well, well, well. This should be interesting. I've never taken a cherry before."

"Cherry?"

"Virgin."

"We're not virgins," Grey protested.

"Anally you are," Eric pointed out.

"That doesn't count," Seth grumbled.

Eric stood and dropped his towel. "Let's discuss it in bed."

"So... does that mean you're sleeping with us?"

"Of course. What more could a guy ask for than to cuddle up at night with a couple of sexy virgins?" Eric teased.

"Eric," they protested.

Eric pulled the covers back and climbed in the middle of the huge bed. He patted a space on either side of him. "Don't worry. You won't be virgins for long."

Seth and Grey rolled their eyes and got in on either side, pulling the covers up over the three of them. Seth rolled to his side. Eric followed with Grey behind. The three of them lay spooning each other.

"This reminds me of something," Eric said with a yawn. "Have either of you heard of a Lucky Pierre?" Both answered in the negative. "You see, it's like this. The guy in front gets fucked by the guy in the middle and the guy in the middle gets fucked by the guy behind *him*. That makes the guy in the middle Lucky Pierre, 'cause he fucks and gets fucked at the same time. I have just become the permanent Lucky Pierre in this relationship," he chuckled.

"Go to sleep, Pierre," Seth grouched. "You haven't gotten lucky yet."

"Yeah, I did. The day I landed on this planet," Eric whispered. He hugged Seth tighter as Grey in turn tightened his own arms around Eric.

"We all did, Eric. We all did," Grey replied.

The three of them sighed with satisfaction and drifted to sleep.

Chapter Four

The next few days flew by in a blur of sensual pleasure. Eric was apprised of the Maleri' need for his assistance in draining the harmful energies that built behind their holding shield. He took the information in stride and used the opportunity not only to drain their mental energy, but their physical energy as well.

On successive nights, he initiated each of his lovers to the ecstasies of anal sex. Grey and Seth decided who would go first by using Eric's suggestion. They flipped a coin. Seth won and it was decided that Grey would retire and leave the two of them alone.

Eric began by slowly stripping Seth of his clothes before urging him to lie on the bed. After ridding himself of his own clothes, he climbed on the bed and started things off with a relaxing massage. With Seth a puddle of male jelly under his hands, Eric turned up the heat, bringing his mouth and tongue into play. He caressed, sucked and licked over the back of Seth's neck, his shoulders and back. Eventually he worked his way down one taut cheek to one leg and up the other, ending between Seth's widely spread thighs.

Parting the tempting crease between his buttocks, Eric teased Seth's tautly clenched pucker until the opening relaxed under the warm onslaught of his clever tongue. It wasn't long, with the use of liberal applications of lube, before Eric was slowly reaming the tight opening with his fingers. Seth was groaning and pumping his hips against the bed.

Feeling he was ready, Eric urged Seth to his back and raised Seth's legs to rest on his shoulders. "You ready, lover?" he asked softly, stroking his own lube covered cock.

"Yes, God yes!"

"Remember what I said. Relax and bear down. I can't wait to be inside you."

Eric leaned forward and took Seth's mouth in a scorching kiss. Rising up, he positioned his cock and eased forward. The thorough preparation paid off. The plump head of his cock effortlessly breached Seth's channel. Eric slowly rolled his hips, screwing his cock in to the hilt.

"Now you're really mine," Eric gasped, slowly stroking himself in and out of Seth's hot clinging depths while Seth moaned and undulated beneath him.

They fucked for a slow, endless time, reveling in the growing heat and smell of spicy, male musk, rising with every stroke. Their bodies grew damp with sweat. The effort speeded their hearts, the blood rushing hot and wild to gather in their cocks, filling and thickening them until the satiny skin was near bursting. When the explosion came, thick, hot semen burst free. Eric's filled Seth, while Seth's inundated the space between their bodies, painting them with the visible result of their lust.

Riding out the climax, they collapsed together and rested for a time. Eventually they stirred. "That was amazing," Seth praised.

"Yeah. But something's missing."

"Grey." They both spoke the name at the same time.

Eric rolled off the bed and padded into the bathroom. Coming back with a damp cloth, he wiped the semen from Seth's abdomen and his own. "Grab that blanket," he said and motioned Seth to follow him.

The two of them walked out in the living room to find Grey lying on the sofa as he watched a sports program on the wide vid screen.

"Busy?" Eric asked as he approached.

"Not really," came the lackluster reply. Grey looked up, his brows rising at the sight of his two naked bedmates.

"Stand up a minute, would you?" Eric asked.

Grey frowned and levered himself off the sofa. His face bore a puzzled frown when Eric took the blanket from Seth to lay it over the cushions.

"Seth, lay down. Not completely. Prop yourself against the side cushions." Seth obeyed Eric's directions and settled himself. "Grey, I want you to lay back against Seth." Still frowning, Grey did as he was told, then smiled as Eric draped himself over both of them.

He captured their gazes. "Seth. All I want you to do is unbutton Grey's shirt and rub his chest and shoulders. You can do that, can't you?" Seth nodded. "You don't mind if Seth does that, do you?" he asked Grey, who shook his head. "Good."

Eric went for the opening of Grey's pants, behind which a thick bulge was already beginning to form. "Mmm, I feel something here. Oh yeah, this is what I'm looking for." He looked up at Grey. "You know what I need, don't you? Some sweet, hot, man honey," he leered, wiggling his eyebrows. His over-the-top performance had the desired effect.

Grey's face crinkled and he shook with laughter. Behind him, Seth was doing the same. Eric grinned up at them both, suddenly struck by a wave of emotion so strong it brought tears to his eyes.

Grey sobered and reached out to stroke his cheek. "You're the most amazing man," he murmured softly.

"I'll second that," Seth added.

Eric smiled. "You're not so bad yourselves. Now, where was I?" He lowered his mouth to Grey's cock and worked his magic.

All the sweetness he desired was his and he drained Grey of every drop. Afterward, the three of them sprawled on the sofa together. They watched the game, swatted comments back and forth and eventually dozed as the seeds of love germinated, winding their tendrils around three steadily beating hearts.

* * *

Eric sat back, watching the scenery as the LAT sped to its destination. Matt and Col's. It had been several days since he'd seen Matt, something he felt not one whit guilty about. Col had declared himself on holiday and was keeping Matt more than busy. In and out of bed. Seth and Grey had also managed to do the same for Eric and he smiled at the memories they'd thus far created. His two lovers were nothing if not inventive and insatiable. On this day, Col, Grey and Seth had been called in by the High Council for a special meeting. Eric and Matt, free of their Maleri' mates, had decided to tour Taskin City.

The road he was on was not a particularly busy one. Seth and Grey had chosen a fairly new section of developed land to build their house on. As the car rolled on, in the distance Eric could see a stopped vehicle at the side of the road. He ordered the LAT to slow down when a woman appeared, waving her arms to get his attention. Eric ordered his own vehicle to stop.

He stepped out and met the woman halfway between his vehicle and hers. "Do you need help?"

"I sure do," the woman replied. She brought her hand from behind her back. In it, she held a small pistol of some sort.

"Whoa, look, lady. I'm new here. I don't have any cash. You can take the car, if that's what you want."

"I don't want either, Eric Ashton. Only you. Put this here," she ordered, handing him a small, flesh colored chip while pointing to her own temple. Eric frowned but did as she directed, pushing the small chip against the skin at his temple. He immediately felt a slight humming disturbance that rippled over his consciousness before it disappeared. "Now please get in my car," she said, motioning him on with her weapon.

"What's this all about? How do you know my name? And what is this thing?" he asked, tapping the small chip with his finger.

"I wouldn't do that if I were you. Once that device is activated, if it breaks contact with your skin before I deactivate it, it will detonate," she told him callously. "It's merely there to prevent you from making contact with your mates. As for your other questions, I was at the gathering the other night. You're the new mate of Greyan and Sethian Dennon, something that reveals you have an empathic gift. I need the services of an empath." Eric entered her car and she followed him in. "Since the Maleri' see fit to ignore my request, I have no choice but to take matters into my own hands. Lives depend on it, Mr. Ashton."

"What do you mean, they've ignored your request?"

"Exactly what it sounds like. The Maleri' don't work for free. My associates and I don't have enough wealth to pay their fee, nor do we have anything they wish to acquire in trade."

"I can't believe they'd do that. Especially if what you say is true about lives depending on it," Eric said, shaking his head. "Surely they wouldn't be so cold-hearted."

"How long have you known these Maleri', Mr. Ashton? A matter of days, weeks? I can put you in contact with others who will confirm what I've told you. But for right now, all I want is your cooperation." She fixed him with a stare, her dark eyes somber. "To ensure that cooperation, I must tell you that I have a man watching your brother."

Eric started in alarm.

"He won't be harmed as long as you board my ship and give me no problems. His continued good health is in your hands."

Impotent anger lanced through him. "I'll do whatever you want. Just leave my brother alone."

The woman nodded and turned away. Eric saw the tightening of her mouth and the flicker of regret that appeared in her eyes for just a brief moment before it was overshadowed by determination.

"Thank you," she murmured. "I'm very sorry about this. I wish there was another way. I hope when we arrive on my home world that you'll understand."

Eric remained silent while he studied her. She was a delicately built woman with elfin features, short dark hair and dark eyes. Her clothing was neat, clean and neutral, as though hand picked to draw no overt attention to her. He smiled sarcastically at his own musings, realizing that was the very reason she wore such unremarkable garments.

The silence stretched between them, unbroken until they reached Taskin City Port. "Remember your brother, Mr. Ashton," she warned, exiting her vehicle.

Eric said nothing, his hands figuratively tied. He followed his captor like a well trained puppy and silently let his anger seethe while letting himself be led on board a small ship. Her departure time already set, she locked Eric in a cabin before piloting her way out of the port. Eric stood in front of the small porthole and watched Belthola quickly disappear.

* * *

Matthew was pacing the floor. Eric was over an hour late and calls to his house received no response. Worried and not knowing what else to do, he opened the link between Col and himself.

Col immediately responded to Matt's troubled thoughts. *What is it, babe? What's happened?*

It's Eric. I can't find him.

Wasn't he supposed to pick you up?

That's just it. He hasn't. I've tried contacting him but there's no answer at his house.

Hold on a minute, Matt. Let me see if Seth or Grey can find him.

Matt waited patiently for a moment. The time seemed to stretch out and out until his nerves were zinging with renewed alarm.

Matt? I want you to stay calm. First of all, Eric is all right.

Oh, my God. What's happened to him?

Seth and Grey have both spoken to him. He's been kidnapped.

What! Why? Who would do such a thing?

We're not sure, but the twins are already on their way to the port and we've contacted the Security Bureau. We'll get him back, Matt.

Col, Matt's mental call was barely audible.

I'm on my way, baby. Hold on.

Scared and sick with worry, Matt huddled on the sofa to wait.

* * *

"You can come out now," she said, standing at the doorway of the cabin she'd locked Eric in.

Eric looked her over. "Where's your gun?"

The young woman rolled her eyes. "It wasn't real," she replied with some asperity. "And take that stupid piece of plastic off your head," she ordered, pointing to the small chip at Eric's temple.

Eric strolled to the door. "Who the hell are you?" he asked, slipping his fingernail under the adhesive to peel the chip away.

"Dr. Janice Deleft. I'm an aquatic biologist. I take it your mates have contacted you?"

"Oh yeah. They're not happy, to say the least. Why the big charade?"

"I told you. We need the services of an empath. The Maleri' turned us down."

"I still find that hard to believe," Eric replied, shaking his head. Before she could speak, he continued. "But just in case it's true, why don't you explain to me why you need me? Or was it my mates you hoped to lure here?"

Janice flushed pink.

"Well, that answers that question. I hope this isn't some plan to hurt them. I won't stand idly by and do nothing," he warned.

"We don't want to hurt anyone. As you suggested, why don't you let me explain?"

She led him to the front of the ship and settled in the pilot's seat, inviting him to take the co-pilot's position. "On my planet, Arela, there's an extremely intelligent species of mammal that inhabits many of our waterways. Something is happening to them. There have been unexplained deaths." She looked down. "They're starting to retaliate and there's a faction in our government that's calling for their extermination."

"What form of retaliation? Are they killing people?"

"No! There's never been one recorded incident in which an Eluran harmed a human. For centuries they've co-existed with us. Our planet's landmasses are riddled with waterways. The Elurans keep the waterways clear and we protect them from so-called off-world sportsmen who have tried to persuade us to allow them to be hunted. We also give them certain places that are theirs alone, free from human contact. They're merely letting the waterways fill with growth, blocking them from human travel."

"Like they're trying to keep something out. Do you have any idea what might be causing these deaths?"

"I have an idea, but it's nothing I can prove. If we could somehow communicate with the Elurans, I'm hoping they might be able to tell us something."

Frowning, Eric nodded. "Have you considered the possibility that their thought patterns might not be readable to a human being?"

"I have. But I don't believe that will be the case. Meet them, Mr. Ashton. Judge for yourself."

"Might as well. We've got at least a two-hour lead on Grey and Seth. And call me Eric."

Janice sent him a smile filled with gratitude and hope.

Once they reached her home world, Janice docked her ship and hurried Eric to a different kind of dock. One that sheltered boats of various sizes and shapes. Hers was a medium-sized craft, which Janice handled with obvious expertise. They followed large, well-marked waterways, then moved deeper inland where the paths grew smaller and less traveled. Stopping the boat, Janice lowered a microphone over the side.

"This usually brings them to me. They like the music," she commented with a smile.

Eric looked around in amazement. "Is this typical of your world?" he asked.

Lush greenery grew from the solid land between waterways and swayed in the gentle breeze. Not far away, a small village on stilts could be seen. Every home had a boat or two tied up to a dock.

Janice grinned. "Yeah, it is. We do have larger cities on the more solid landmasses, but even those are crisscrossed by canals and smaller waterways. We're a very water oriented people."

Before he could answer, there was an eerie muffled hooting sound, and a sleek head broke the surface of the water. Eric stared. The creature was large, yet there was something elusively ethereal about it. The head and face were human-like, though the nose and mouth resembled that of a bottle-nosed dolphin only smaller. A short dorsal fin ran along the middle of its skull and ended at the base of its neck. Its body put Eric in mind of a manta ray. While it had shoulders and arms, attached were wide sail-like sheets that flowed down the length of its body. Pearly colors ran over its skin, seeming to twinkle and swirl in the light.

"Holy shit," Eric muttered under his breath and the creature turned its eyes to him. Large eyes, dark and gentle and filled with a kind of eternal innocence. It shook Eric to his core.

"Do you see what I mean?" Janice asked softly.

Several more of the creatures broke the surface of the water near their leader.

"I do. Will it let me touch it? It might help me to communicate with it."

"Put your hand in the water."

Eric gave her a wide-eyed look. "Are you sure?"

"He won't hurt you."

Tentatively, Eric bent and slipped his hand into the water. With a slight flip of one fin, the Eluran slid closer. Softly, slowly, it lowered its chin into Eric's hand. Eric took a deep breath as a wave of peace slid over him. He fell into the soft encompassing darkness of the Eluran's eyes. Closing his own eyes, he let himself join with the Eluran's emotions, then tried to shape the feelings into a silent conversation. Picturing a waterway as best he could with his limited knowledge, Eric then populated the clear waterway with growth, seeing the passageway close while projecting a questioning feel to the image.

His mind was immediately inundated with feelings of sorrow and pain, a feeling of loss so deep it brought tears to his eyes. He fought to bring the emotions under control and again sent feelings of puzzlement, curiosity and question. An image suddenly appeared in his mind. A boat, liquid being spilled over the side, the water's creatures rushing away from the poison, some making it, others dying before it spread and dissipated.

Eric opened his eyes, meeting the enigmatic gaze of the Eluran. He sent understanding, thanks and reassurance. The Eluran fluttered his fins and hooted softly. The sounds were echoed by his companions. Backing slowly away, it dove deep, the others with it, only to reappear seconds later.

Fins wrapped tight around their bodies, they spun up and out of the water like veiled tops enwrapped in gossamer raiment. Suddenly, they spread their sail-like fins and resembling birds in flight, they soared over the boat. The breeze and their own momentum carried them over and away until they pulled their fins in tight and dove straight down, leaving barely a ripple in the water.

Eric looked at Janice with a wide and wondering grin on his face. "That was the most amazing thing I've ever seen. I wish you could have felt what I did."

"Was he able to tell you anything?"

"Yeah. Do the letters E and S followed by Co. mean anything to you?"

"Edgewood and Sands Co. I knew it! I knew those sneaky bastards were poisoning the waters!"

"How do we prove it?"

"That's just it. You just proved it. You're the mate of a Maleri'. The reputation of the Maleri' is rock solid and incorruptible. If you pass the mental images on of what you've seen to your mates and they swear on it in a deposition, Edgewood and Sands are finished."

"Just like that? The Maleri' are that powerful?"

Janice nodded.

"That's a lot of power for one small group."

"I know. That's why I think it's such a shame that they're endangering their reputation for monetary gain."

"Before I'll believe that, I want to talk to Grey and Seth."

"I'll take you back." Without another word, she started the boat and they returned to the dock.

Eric didn't have to wait long to speak with his mates. They were there on the dock, along with Chase Kaldor, the Maleri' security officer Eric had met on the balcony of the Amiston Hotel. They were apparently arguing with the owner of one of the docked boats.

"How can you follow them when you don't know where they've gone? In case you haven't noticed, water don't hold footprints. You've never been here before, have you?" the man asked reasonably.

Seth opened his mouth to argue when the sound of Janice's returning boat caught his attention. With a grin, Eric leapt up on the dock and in no time was engulfed in the embrace of his two lovers.

"You're really all right," Grey breathed, hugging him hard.

"I told you I was."

Grey released him and turned him over to Seth. "We had to see for ourselves," Seth explained and again Eric was hugged so tightly he found it hard to breathe. It was a feeling he enjoyed.

When he was released, he looked up to see Chase snapping restraints around Janice's slim wrists. "Wait a minute. What are you doing?" he asked, striding down the dock to where they waited.

"This woman kidnapped you. That happens to be a very serious offense," Chase told him.

"There were mitigating circumstances and I'm not pressing charges."

"Are you sure that's wise?"

"I think you'll agree with me when you hear what she has to say." He paused and looked at the three Maleri'. "Especially if what she tells me about how the Maleri' accept their commissions isn't true."

"What are you talking about?" Seth asked, giving Eric and then Janice a puzzled frown.

"Let's find a comfortable place to sit. I need something to drink and this hopefully will come as a shock. At least it will if you're the kind of men I think you are," Eric explained.

"I'm hooked. Unshackle the woman, Chase. She probably knows the best place to go," Grey reasoned.

With the restraints removed, Janice smiled, rubbing her wrists in relief. "Right this way, gentlemen."

An hour later, three puzzled, angry Maleri' were holding a council of war. "That's not the way it's supposed to be," Chase told Eric and Janice. "Yes, our services are used to bring benefits to our planet, but not to the exclusion of helping those who can't afford to pay. That was *never* our agreement. We're supposed to be informed of each and *every* petition for help."

"Apparently, Belthola's High Council has taken it into their heads to change the rules without informing you guys," Eric pointed out.

"The High Council is in for a shake-up," Chase announced and rose. "You three ready to go home? We've got work to do."

Everyone rose from the table. Janice held her hand out to Eric. "Thank you. I'm sorry we started out on the wrong foot. I wish I could repay you."

"Your fee is paid," Grey informed her. "You let us know what's been going on behind our backs. You may have just saved the reputation of the Maleri'. We'll send that deposition and if anyone gives you trouble, let us know."

Eric shook her hand. "I never thought I'd thank someone for kidnapping me, but it was worth it to meet one of the Elurans. They're amazing beings."

Janice leaned in and kissed his cheek. "Come back some time. They actually love to swim with humans."

Eric's eyes widened. "I'll think about it. Goodbye, Janice."

Once they were back on the twins' ship, Chase took the pilot's seat, leaving the others free. Seth, Grey and Eric settled in the observation room. Eric sighed with satisfaction and relief, then frowned at the speculative looks the twins were giving him.

"What?" he asked.

"That girl, Janice. She likes you," Grey observed.

"More than a little," Seth added.

"Don't tell me you're jealous? Nothing happened between us. You know I don't like girls," Eric babbled. "I mean I like girls, I just don't *like* girls. You know what I'm saying?"

"Calm down, Pierre. We know what you mean," Seth soothed.

"Pierre?" Eric questioned.

"Feeling lucky?" Grey asked.

A slow grin spread over Eric's face.

"We thought, when we get home, we'd show you just how lucky you are," Seth told him.

Eric looked at the two handsome men seated across from him. "I'm feeling pretty damn lucky right now. But I won't mind if you show me. Not one little bit."

Epilogue

"That worked out well," Chase observed.

Eric, Grey and Seth, as well as Chase, Geral and Sam were gathered at Col and Matt's home. The five Maleri' males had just returned from a meeting in which the entire contingent of Maleri' had confronted the Beltholan High Council on what they considered the breaking of their agreement.

Their threats to discontinue the use of their powers for the planet's benefit had had the desired effect. The High Council had humbly apologized and given over the records of any unfulfilled requests.

Seth, Grey, Chase, Col and Geral were now in possession of those records. "There's only one problem. We need someone to act as liaison between petitioners, the High Council and the Maleri'," Col explained. "Anyone have a suggestion?"

Seven pairs of eyes turned to Eric. "Me?"

"Why not?" Grey asked. "You said you wanted something constructive to do. If anyone understands the goals of the Maleri', it's you. You certainly proved you could do the job in the way you handled the problem with the Elurans."

"And, you proved you believe in us. In my eyes, that's the most important thing. We need someone who will fight to keep intact the reputation we've tried so hard to build," Seth added.

The others heartily agreed.

Eric flushed slightly at their accolade. Matt laughed with delight. "I've never seen you embarrassed over anything. I didn't think it was possible. You're always so in control," he said, teasing Eric.

Seth and Grey grinned at each other. "He's not always in control. Isn't that right, Pierre?"

"Guys," Eric warned, his blush deepening.

"What are we missing here?" Col asked.

"*Nothing*," Eric answered, giving his mates the evil eye.

"Doesn't sound like nothing," Geral chimed in.

"If you even open your mouths, you'll both be sleeping in the garage," Eric threatened.

"Ah, Lucky, you wouldn't do that to us," Seth cajoled.

Matt and Sam both hooted with laughter as they suddenly got the joke.

"Now you've done it. Matthew Ashton, Sam Roth, don't either of you say a word."

Col slipped an arm around his mate. "Come on, babe, you can tell me."

Everyone chimed in as the bickering and byplay deteriorated into laughter. Everyone except Chasetien Kaldor. He felt a sudden flicker of unease pass like a slowly drifting cloud over his consciousness. Rising, he went to the open, sliding glass doors and looked out into the night. Something was stirring. A wave of eagerness tightened his belly. With a small smile of anticipation, he returned to the company of his brothers.

Bonds of the Maleri' 3: Between Love and Law

Kate Steele

Prologue

Chasetien Kaldor felt a flicker of unease flash like a spark of lightning through his consciousness. Rising, he went to the open sliding glass doors and looked out into the all encompassing night. Something was stirring. A wave of eagerness tightened his belly while a swift rush of emotion arrowed up and out of his control. Swiftly quashing it, a keen smile of anticipation curved his lips for an instant before he returned to the company of his brothers.

From his place beside his human mate, Matthew Ashton, Coltas Oldarie watched Chase cross the room. Excusing himself, he joined Chase who was renewing his drink at the small bar that was part of Col and Matt's living room. "What's up?"

Chase gave him neutral look. "Why do you ask?"

"A second ago you sent out a wave of mental energy that slapped everyone here. It's not like you to be sloppy, Chase. We normally have to pry things out of you."

Chase let his gaze take in the puzzled and expectant looks from the others in the room. His Maleri' brothers and their mates. All empathic to one degree or another. One eyebrow rose, a self-contained smile curving his lips. He spoke to the room at large. "When I figure it out, I'll let you know."

His answer generated several doubt-tinged grunts and a chorus of "sure you will," from the twins, Greyan and Sethian Dennon, mates to Matthew's brother, Eric.

Chase grinned and downed his drink. "I'll see you, Col. Goodnight everyone." Without another word, he left the house and headed home.

Col watched him go. A worried frown creased his brow.

Once outside, a low frequency, proximity identity signal was generated from the tiny chip implanted in Chase's hand, causing the door on his Security Transport Unit to open. Once settled inside he spoke briefly, "STU, let's go home."

"You got it, Chief."

Chase sighed but didn't bother reprimanding the vehicle *again*. Some comedian of a tech had programmed the STU to call him Chief, and no amount of arguing could dissuade it from doing so. During the ride he contemplated Col's words. *We normally have to pry things out of you.*

When did I become so silent and self-contained?

The answer came with little effort. It was a gradual process. With each passing year as part of the Security Bureau and with each promotion, he'd become more cautious, more aware of what an inadvertent slip might cost him or one of his men. He became more emotionally and mentally isolated and lonely. Though he'd rarely admit that part to himself.

The wild burst of feeling that loosed itself earlier had carried the promise of a possibility Chase had all but resigned himself to never having. The possibility of finding a mate. Despite the looming specter of his mental shields overloading, all his responsibilities had kept him from considering the eventual need for a mate hunt. It was something every Maleri' who wanted to retain his sanity would eventually undertake.

His lips twitched. Chief of the Taskin City Security Bureau on a mate hunt? He could only imagine what that would do to his reputation. Who would believe that under his cool, hard exterior a fire burned? Banked and barely smoldering to be sure, but there just the same.

STU slowed and Chase pulled himself from his thoughts, ordering the vehicle to let him out at the front door before garaging itself. Working in security, Chase had inevitably made enemies over the years and he varied his routine even in simple things, like which door he entered his home on any given occasion.

Automatically he checked the obvious security seals from the locked panel at the door, then the hidden extra measures he'd installed himself. Satisfied, he entered the house, ordering those few dim lights in his wake to turn off as he made his way to his bedroom.

Though he was home, Chase still felt tense. Entering the bedroom, he undressed and padded to the bathroom, going straight into the shower/sauna. Setting the controls, he seated himself on part of the bench-like seat that was built into the wall and leaned back with a sigh. Steam immediately started to fill the enclosed cubicle, misting the opaque walls and his skin with moist, heated air.

Chase slowly relaxed, letting his thoughts wander in aimless patterns until they focused on that burst of energy that still resonated within him. He explored the memory. The steady beat of his heart increased, sending hot blood to his groin, causing his cock to thicken and rise.

A low, rumbling growl reverberated in his chest. With eyes closed, he wrapped long fingers around his rapidly swelling erection and pumped. Chase imagined a pair of plump, male lips enclosing his shaft, a hot tongue swirling over the stretched, satiny skin of his cock. The muscles in his abdomen and ass tightened, his hips moving with the rhythm of his stroking hand.

Each shallow breath he took filled his lungs with steamy air. The dark, silky hair on his chest, legs and arms was veiled with gossamer beads of moisture, settling like a warm blanket against his skin. Sweat broke out to run in slow, hot trickles, sending a shiver down his spine.

He tightened his fist, and in the mist-filled silence his guttural groan was muffled, muted. Chase increased the speed of his strokes, lost to the building pressure and pleasure while his balls drew up tight to his body and prepared to unload. Unwilling to let this carnal bliss end so soon, he fought his climax, wrestling it down again and again. Instead of easing the grip of his pumping fist and slowing its speed, he growled his defiance and hung on, riding the wave higher and higher until it crested and he was plunged into the maelstrom of orgasm.

His shout echoed, his panting breaths stirring the steam in white billows that swirled and danced. Thick streams of hot semen jetted from the bulbous head of his cock and rained over his heaving chest and abdomen. The pleasure plunged in like a sharp knife, leaving him feeling replete, drained and temporarily robbed of strength.

Chase eased his strokes, slowly surfacing into awareness enough to open his eyes. He mindlessly gazed at the foreskin of his cock, dappled with plump drops of thickening cum. It moved easily under now lazy fingers that pulled it up over the shiny, wet head of his cock and retreated when he pushed it down.

Sated, he sighed and released himself, pausing a moment to yawn before standing and turning off the sauna. Replacing steam with warm jets of water, he lazily washed and, after drying, returned to the bedroom. The comfort of his bed beckoned and he wasted no time answering its call. Pulling back the covers, he settled in and was asleep in seconds.

Chapter One

Chase walked into the building that housed the Taskin City Security Bureau and immediately headed for the Port Authority offices. Returning the greetings that came his way from several members of the staff, he wasted no time in conversation. He went straight to the Senior Chief of Operations, Beydrun Pomal, who just happened to be his brother by joining.

The comings and goings of every ship, passenger and piece of cargo that passed through any port on Belthola was monitored by Bey and his crew. Through the use of scanners so sensitive they could pick up the presence of a millimeter long reek bug just by its scent, it was safe to bet nothing of note happened without being observed in one manner or another.

Chase found Bey discussing a problem with one of his tech wizards.

"Is that right?" Bey asked the man who was waving a sheaf of spec films under his nose.

"I'm telling you, Bey, if we make these modifications, here, here, and here," he said, pointing out locations on the diagrams printed on the clear sheets he held, "we could tell what every passenger had for lunch and if his body's digesting it all right."

Bey made a grimace of distaste. "Off hand I'd say that was a little too much information, but as long as I don't have to see it unless absolutely necessary, go ahead and make the mods, Daril."

"He's enthusiastic," Chase commented, bringing Bey's attention to him as Daril walked away, talking to himself.

Bey's slightly ill expression turned into a grin. "That he is. Sometimes too enthusiastic, but you can see why nothing gets past us. How are you doing, Chase? Merri was just saying this morning she was going to track you down and make you promise to come to dinner this week. She said we haven't seen you for awhile." He gave Chase the once over. "I thought she was exaggerating, but I can see now she's right. You've had time to grow that," Bey said, indicating the neatly trimmed beard and mustache Chase now sported.

Chase brought a hand to his face, his fingers gliding over the wiry yet soft, dark hair that graced his chin. "Just thought I'd try something different. I think it gives my image an extra boost."

Bey chuckled. "Yeah, like you aren't intimidating enough already. I heard about the smuggler being held in Security who confessed as soon as you walked into the interrogation room. From what I heard, the poor guy couldn't spill his guts fast enough."

"It's not my fault the rumor mills have given me a bad rep... you know I've never abused a prisoner in my custody."

"Hey, I know that, but they don't. And from the sounds of it, that bad reputation is an asset. I wouldn't worry about it, Chase," Bey advised. "Now what brings you to my humble offices?"

"The one thing I've always liked about you. You get straight to the point. What I want to know is, were there any odd incidents reported or unusual travelers coming through the Taskin City Port last night? Specifically around twenty-two hundred hours?"

"Not that I'm aware of. I've checked my morning summaries. There wasn't anything that stood out."

Chase frowned and nodded slightly. "Could you get me a vid chip of all arrivals between twenty-one and twenty-three hundred?"

"Sure, that's easy."

Bey walked to one of his seated technicians and gave the woman a few instructions. In seconds, her monitoring unit produced a milky, opaque square of plastic the size of a thumbnail. Bey took the chip and handed it to Chase. "Here you go."

"Thanks."

"Is there something going on here I should know about?"

Chase shook his head. "I'm not sure. I felt someone arrive last night. Someone who may be of some significance, but I don't know why or for what reason." He looked at the chip in his hand. "I want to review this to see if anything jumps out at me. I'll let you know. Thanks, Bey. Oh, and tell Merri to expect me for dinner next week. I've got a feeling I'm going to be busy for the next few days."

"Will do, Chase."

* * *

Settled behind his desk, Chase inserted the vid chip into the console of his comp unit. The screen immediately flared to life showing a constant parade of arrivals through the various port entrances. So many people gave it the appearance of an insect colony, but Chase was used to the sight. He blanked his thoughts, letting his Maleri' senses analyze the visual data.

Nothing of note presented itself until a certain group of passengers came under his scrutiny. His heart gave a hard thump before settling into an accelerated rhythm while his breath picked up speed. His vision zeroed in on one figure and speared it with his sharpened gaze.

Tweaking the controls at his fingertips, Chase enhanced and magnified the compelling figure. The man was clearly tall, standing centimeters above those in his party. His golden blond hair was very short on the sides, longer on top and sported a spiky tuft of bangs at the front. The fabric of his light linen tunic and trousers caressed and draped the finely chiseled muscle and sinew of his body.

Chase uttered a short grunt of arousal when his cock decided to show its approval of the sight by thickening and filling the limited confines of his pants.

The most surprising thing about the man was the color of his skin. It was a light, all-over bronze that was enhanced by faint iridescent blues and greens. Lightly, it shaded and hugged the contours of his face, neck, and the portion of his arms visible below his mid-length sleeves. The color was ethereal, a gossamer veil showing only when the light caressed it at the proper angle.

Chase was fascinated. Tapping at a second set of controls, he brought up the passenger info on the man. Cazius Rey, native of the planet Metonia, employed by Kogan Delmon.

The name, Kogan Delmon set alarms off in Chase's head. He knew Delmon was a filthy rich entrepreneur/businessman of dubious background, turned patron of the arts. Owner of a large collection of works by artists from many worlds, he sometimes allowed parts of his collection to be displayed in various museums for a time. There were rumors that, just as in his business deals, some of his art was acquired by unscrupulous means.

With a frown, Chase let the vid play on in slow motion, allowing thoughts of Delmon to recede while he watched

Cazius move. He noted the cat-like walk and the aloof expression on his face, struck by the coldness there until Cazius looked directly into the camera monitoring his arrival. For a moment something vulnerable shone through, a hopeless misery that stopped Chase's breath and twisted his heart. He watched while Cazius' eyes widened in understanding when he noted the presence of the camera. Alarm swept over his expression for a split second before it again became blank and shuttered.

Forcing a deep breath, Chase let the vid play out until Cazius and his party were through inspection and gone. "Cazius Rey," he whispered and felt a shudder of excitement tingle down the length of his body. He sat back in his chair, bemused and astounded by this wholly unexpected turn of events.

My mate, possibly in distress and in the employ of Kogan Delmon. One amazingly good point out of three. Time to fix the rest.

With that thought, Chase brought up all the info he could find on Delmon and what had brought him to Belthola.

* * *

Cazius leaned back in the padded chair, his eyes closed while a hot, wet mouth worked over the length of his hard cock. He strove to mentally divorce himself from what was being done to his body, forcing his revulsion into submission. Hovering on the verge of climax, he at once welcomed and repudiated the release that would temporarily free him from the unwanted touch of the man who was diligently sucking him off. When the persistent mouth pulled away, he stifled an angry groan of frustration and disgust.

"Fuck me, Caz. You know you want to."

Caz opened eyes filled with muted blue-green fire. "Get on with it, Delmon, or get off your knees. We've already negotiated this deal."

"But it could hold so much more for both of us. I'm told by many I have a tight and talented ass. Try it, Caz, fuck me."

Caz drew his gaze away from Delmon's bright, greedy eyes and looked down at his waning erection. "If all that many have tried it, it's probably not as tight as you may think," he muttered while his stomach did another queasy roll.

Delmon scrambled to his feet, letting the long tunic he wore fall in place to his knees. Caz thanked the Deity that it covered Delmon's erection a split second before Delmon grasped a handful of his hair, yanking his head back. "For someone in such a precarious position you take chances, boy. I could ruin your family with a word."

"And I could return the favor with that bit of evidence I collected from your office. In this case, precarious is a two-way street."

Delmon's pale blue eyes crinkled slightly at the corners. "That's what I like about you, young Caz. You've got guts. Unlike that spineless father of yours. It boggles the mind how he got the nerve to try and steal from me." He gave his head a slight shake and raised his hand, striking Caz's cheek. The air resounded with the sharp sound of a stinging slap. "But just you remember this," he spat viciously. "I've got the upper hand here, and you'll do as I say until I deem this debt paid. Or it will be paid in ways you'll regret until your dying day."

Caz kept his expression blank though inside he was seething with rage, humiliation, and fear. "Are we through?

I've got work to do if you want the Blaze of Belthola. Stealing a national treasure's not going to be easy."

"But you're such a talented thief. I'm sure you'll have no trouble."

Caz refused to comment.

"Get on with it then. We'll continue our little game later."

With that unwelcome promise, Kogan Delmon strode from the room. Caz rose from the chair, tucked himself back inside his trousers, and walked to the window. The view of the city from the hotel's top floor was magnificent, but Caz stared sightlessly through the clear glass.

He fought the despair threatening to engulf him. Because of his father's folly their entire family was in danger, and not only of being disgraced. Delmon had people watching his family. Caz knew he wasn't above ordering a murder or two. The thought of his mother, sister or brother dead at the hands of Delmon's thugs struck terror into his very soul. Even the anger, still festering at what his father's ill thought out plan had cost him, waned at the thought of him being dead.

His hands tightened into impotent fists. When Delmon said his situation was precarious he hadn't been lying, and there wasn't a damn thing Caz could do about it.

He turned from the window and headed for the bathroom, determined to temporarily rid himself of the stink of Delmon's touch.

Chapter Two

Chase walked into the Trelayan Museum and Gallery with anticipation making his pulse speed just the tiniest bit faster than normal. Dressed in formalwear, his appearance caused more than a few heads to turn his way. He ignored the looks, nodding instead to the guards on duty while searching the crowd for Director Jenskil.

He knew the director would be hovering over Kogan Delmon, and where Delmon was, he was sure Cazius Rey would also be. He wasn't mistaken. He found them in the east wing, presiding over the new exhibit which consisted of pieces from Delmon's extensive art collection.

The room was crowded with well dressed patrons who sipped expensive champagne, imported from Earth, while eating dainty delicacies prepared by one of the city's top chefs. Chase paused in the doorway to scrutinize what at this point could only be called his prey. Cazius Rey was dressed in formalwear like every other man in the room, and yet he did it a justice few could lay claim to.

Chase felt his stomach tighten, but he kept his emotions well in hand as he studied the little group. Director Jenskil was fawning over Kogan Delmon who was looking graciously bored. Delmon was a man of mediums, medium height, weight, and build, with medium brown hair. His one arresting feature was a wicked looking scar that sliced inward from his left temple to end midway over his cheekbone.

Having studied his face in the vid records, Chase wasn't surprised to see the scar. Delmon could easily have had it removed through cosmetic restructuring but he'd opted to keep it. A symbol, Chase felt, to broadcast his ruthless side. Nearby were two of the men who'd arrived with Delmon. Bodyguards the records claimed. *More like hired muscle, enforcers maybe.* And then there was Cazius, putting more and more distance between himself and those in his party as he drifted in a seemingly aimless pattern around the room.

Chase let his gaze wander with Cazius for a time before giving himself a mental shake and moving forward to attract the director's notice.

Director Jenskil observed his arrival with a welcoming smile. "Chase, it's good to see you!" he exclaimed, holding his hand out to be shaken. "Kogan Delmon, this is Chasetien Kaldor, the head of Taskin City's Security Bureau. Chase, this is Kogan Delmon, our gracious benefactor for this beautiful exhibit. I was just telling Kogan that we've never had a loss of any piece from the museum thanks to the security the city provides."

Neutral silver-gray eyes met cool ice blue as Chase let his gaze connect with Delmon's. They exchanged a handshake. The touch of Delmon's skin against his own brought forth a flare of his Maleri' empathic powers, and Chase was hard pressed to keep the distaste from his expression. Though Delmon's hand was warm, Chase had the distinct impression he was touching a slimy silt crawler.

"The director's correct. No thief has ever been successful in liberating anything from the museum," Chase answered. "I hope you're enjoying your stay on Belthola?"

"It's good to know my collection will be safe for the duration of the exhibition. And yes, I'm enjoying my stay immensely. I just wish I could delay my return longer, but we'll be leaving in a few days for home. My business affairs keep me very busy."

"Understandable, considering the size of your... empire."

"Empire? Hmm, I like that term. Bearing in mind your position as head of the Security Bureau, I assume you know quite a bit about me and my business concerns," Delmon probed, his eyes sharp with inquiry.

"It's part of my job to learn all I can about visitors of note," Chase said, skillfully evading the question. From the corner of his eye he saw Cazius casually slip from the room. "Gentlemen, if you'll excuse me, I have some security business to attend to. Mr. Delmon. Director." With a small nod to each of them, he made for the exit.

* * *

Chase crossed the threshold and looked around. Unable to catch a glimpse of Cazius, he had a quiet word with one of the guards who pointed him in the direction of the museum's main viewing room. It was here that Belthola's greatest treasures were displayed, and here that he found Cazius contemplating the Blaze of Belthola.

Walking quietly across the floor, he halted a few steps back and to the left of Cazius. He contemplated the man from the back. His finely shaped ears and his tempting neck were left uncovered by the short glossy golden blond hair that graced his head. Chase could imagine himself nuzzling those ears and kissing the fine, elegant line of that neck.

Cazius' shoulders were broad, tapering down to a slim waist and hips and long legs that even now Chase could feel wrapped around him. Once buried in that glorious body he knew the passion would flare between them and burn them both to ash. His Maleri' senses cried out for the joining, urging him closer, and mindlessly he obeyed until he came to his senses and stopped.

Taking a deep breath, instead of pouncing, he forced himself to speak. "It's a magnificent gem, don't you think?"

Cazius started and turned to find Chase nearly at his side. He took a half step back while muttering a mild curse. "Sorry, you startled me. Um, yes, it is impressive, so much more than the pictures I've seen. It's amazing how that fiery red-orange blazes up out of the center. Thus the name I suppose," he said with a self-deprecating shake of his head.

"It created its own name," Chase answered with smile and held out his hand. "I'm Chasetien Kaldor. Chase."

Cazius reached out to shake his hand. "Cazius Rey. Caz. Pleased to meet you."

When they touched, Chase felt his knees go weak. Caz's eyes widened and he swayed for second before catching himself. He shook his head. "Must be all the travel catching up with me," he murmured and Chase nodded in agreement, not yet ready to reveal the truth.

"You're part of Kogan Delmon's entourage."

"Yes. And you're the head of the Taskin City Security Bureau."

Chase nodded. "Guilty. What is it you do for Delmon?"

Caz's expression remained placid. "I'm sure you already know, but I'm in charge of security while his collection is being transported from place to place."

"You're awfully young to have such a responsible position."

"True. My father works for Delmon so I had an in as far as getting this job you might say."

"And do you enjoy the work?"

"Not really. I don't plan on doing it for much longer."

"That's a shame. But I'm sure you'll do very well at anything you put your hand to."

All during the conversation their gazes remained locked. Though he looked perfectly at ease, Chase could feel the turmoil twirling inside Caz. Hidden behind those blue-green eyes was a mix of emotion swirling and roiling in a confusing mass. Chase sensed fear, speculation, hope, dread, suspicion, and overlaying it all, desire. Caz, no matter the cool face he presented, was struggling with a growing arousal every bit as deep and insistent as Chase's own.

Though this room was not nearly so crowded as the one which housed the new exhibition, there were still more than a few people roaming around. Chase wanted Caz to himself. "I was going to the guard's break room for some coffee. Care to join me? Unless you'd prefer Delmon's champagne?"

"The coffee sounds good."

Chase led the way, and the two of them walked corridors less and less populated until they went through a door labeled "Staff Only." Down a short hallway, past several offices, they turned into a room that housed lockers, tables and chairs, and a small kitchen area with sink, fridge unit, radi-oven, and, most importantly, beverage maker.

A mostly full pot of coffee sat ready on the warmer ring. "Looks like someone made fresh not too long ago," Chase commented, pulling two disposacups from the dispenser, setting them on the counter, and pouring each one full.

Caz accepted his cup and reached for the sweetener dispenser. He dashed a small measure of the sweetener in his cup, some of it hitting the rim and sticking. Artlessly, he wet his finger and captured the sweet crystals on his fingertip. Before he could raise it to his lips, Chase reached out and captured his hand.

Hypnotically holding his regard, Chase raised Caz's finger to his mouth and took the tip inside. His tongue swirled over the sweetened flesh. Silver-gray eyes flashed and met blue-green that darkened to the color of stormy seas. Caz's lips parted, his breath coming in fast, audible pants. The gossamer veil of colors that shaded his skin intensified and shimmered.

Chase was mesmerized by the look, feel, and taste of the man standing before him. He released Caz's hand and laid both of his on Caz's shoulders, pushing him against the wall. Though Chase was taller than average at six feet five inches, Caz matched him in height. There was no awkward stooping or bending. Their lips met and their souls crashed together.

The kiss was hot and hard, steel and velvet, raging and gentle, everything and all. It was filled with the sounds and smells and images of two lives lived, two lives suddenly melding together and becoming one, while two bodies strove to do the same.

Chase felt Caz's arms encircle him and he returned the favor, bringing their bodies fully and completely together. He wanted to shout out the elation filling him when Caz's erect cock ground against his own, not only accepting the touch but returning it full measure.

His tongue found Caz's and was welcomed, seduced when Caz let his own slide and caress Chase's in an enticing dance that ratcheted his desire even higher. The fit and feel of their bodies accompanied the parade of memories and images flowing between them. Their connection formed and opened, the bonding perfect until Caz began to struggle. Chase immediately released him and backed away.

Eyes wide, Caz stared at him. "What in Deity's name was that?"

"Maleri' bonding. You know of the Maleri'?"

Caz frowned and nodded.

"I sensed you the night you arrived. Knew you were mine. My mate," Chase revealed. "What just happened between us is part of the bonding. A joining of our minds. From this day forward, there's a mental connection between us. The bond between mates."

Caz shook his head. "*No*. You can't do this. *I* can't do this."

"It's done, Caz. It can't be undone. I've shared a part of your soul, just as you've shared mine," Chase soothed. "I've seen some of what Delmon's done to you. Let me help you. You're my mate now. Your troubles are mine."

"Just like that? You decide I'm yours and so you take without asking what *I* think or what *I* feel? You're no better than Delmon," Caz hissed. "Stay away from me, *Maleri'*." He turned on his heel and strode away, leaving Chase to stare in dismay at his retreating form.

* * *

Caz went straight for the museum entrance and walked out into the night. Blinded by anger and confusion he walked, unaware and uncaring of where he was going.

"Arrogant *hanulth*!" he muttered sharply, spitting the particularly vile curse and aiming it toward Chase. It was a word he'd used time and again to curse Delmon, and yet something inside him cringed at applying the same term to Chase.

He stopped abruptly and closed his eyes for a moment, taking a deep breath in an effort to calm himself. When he opened his eyes, he noticed a small park laid out with a fountain at its center. Caz crossed the street and found an unoccupied bench, letting the sound of the water soothe his troubled thoughts.

From the moment he'd been pulled into this mess Caz knew he could expect nothing but trouble, and the feeling had intensified when he'd studied the dossier on Chasetien Kaldor. The vid chips he'd seen had shown the big man taking part in a raid on Bliss dealers. Chase apparently wasn't the kind of man to sit blithely behind a desk while his men took all the risks.

What he hadn't been prepared for was the longing and pure lust that assailed him at the sight of Chase. The vid chip showed an extremely tall, broad shouldered man whose body was well proportioned, obviously muscular and fit. For so big a man he'd moved with surprising grace. Caz had practically drooled over Chase's body, not to mention the finely chiseled features framed by gleaming dark hair and accented by the deepening shadow of a beard and mustache.

Caz knew it was nearly inevitable he and Chase would meet, something he'd looked forward to with anticipation and dread. A man of Kogan Delmon's reputation would garner Chase's attention. But this, this *bonding*. Caz shivered and took another deep, calming breath. When Chase had taken his hand and slipped his sweetener coated finger into his mouth, Caz went under. He gave in to the instant attraction he'd felt, wanting to choose and not merely be forced to accept the attentions of another.

Why did he have to do that? Why couldn't he tell me instead of forcing the bond? Caz thought desperately. His mind spun with the images he'd been fed of Chase and the impressions fitting those images. He knew now, without a doubt, Chase was an honorable man. A man who put great stock in honesty, loyalty and the law.

The gossamer veil of colors blazed on his cheekbones at the thought of what Chase had seen in return. Caz had already stolen twice for Delmon. He knew Chase had seen it. His own mind had forced the images forward, unlocking his guilty secret for Chase to share. Not only had he shared images of his thievery, but of his physical degradation at Delmon's hands.

Caz dropped his head in his hands and groaned. "I'm a thief and he thinks I'm a whore," he moaned bitterly. "I've just shown every sordid detail of my life to the Chief of the Taskin City Security Bureau. Deity, how much worse can it get?"

He shook his head, willing the reality gone but knowing he had no choice but to move forward with his plans. If he didn't steal the Blaze of Belthola, his family would die. Caz knew life as he'd known it was over, but he hadn't believed it would get this bad.

Wearily, he rose to his feet and flagged down a passing automated vehicle. Giving instructions to be taken to his hotel, he disciplined his thoughts and ran over his plans for the night.

Chapter Three

Chase sat alone in his darkened living room, silently cursing himself for what seemed to be the hundredth time. *I should have kept a handle on it. I should have stayed in control! How could I have been so stupid?* The words rang in his head over and over again. The answer merely served to make him angrier at himself. It was anxiety and fear. The fear he'd lose the one man in all the universe who would complete him before he had a chance to win him.

And so he'd blithely kissed him, opened the connection between them without asking him, without warning him, without a thought of what Caz might feel about it. Just as Caz claimed, in this instance, he was as bad as Kogan Delmon.

Chase shook with rage when he recalled Caz's images of Delmon on his knees and the shame and revulsion filling him at Delmon's touch. Chase wanted to strangle the man. He knew Delmon had some hold over Caz and was forcing him to do things Caz would never have done had he been given the choice. His fear for his family had been very much apparent in his thoughts.

Fighting down his murderous urges, Chase made himself think with the cool head that had caused the downfall of many a would-be law-breaker. Putting what knowledge he had to use, his first order of business was decided.

He rose from the large padded chair he'd thrown himself into and headed for his home office. Once there, he placed a call to his counterpart in the city of Varknia on the planet Lamarra. It was Lamarra Kogan Delmon called home, and there Caz's family resided. Chase was determined to take Caz's family out of harm's way. Delmon's downfall was next on his list, and hopefully earning Caz's forgiveness after that.

He contacted the Varknian Security Offices. "This is Chief Chasetien Kaldor of the Taskin City Security Bureau on Belthola. I want to speak with Chief Nazkarion as quickly as possible."

Assured his call would be put straight through, Chase sighed and relaxed back into his chair. This was what he needed. Action. Brooding wasn't in his nature. When there was a problem to be solved, he wanted it solved without delay.

A familiar face came on the vid screen. He grinned and went straight to the point. "Bron, how'd you like to take part in bringing down Kogan Delmon?"

A shrill whistle met his words. "Tell me this isn't a joke, Chase."

"No joke. I've got something that'll send the son of a slime crawler away for a long, long time."

Chase went on to explain his plan. At the end of their conversation, Bron whistled again. "You don't know how happy you've made me. If you weren't as ugly as a mud woggler, I might bend over for you myself. Though I don't think my wife would appreciate that," he joked.

"Save your ass, Bron. I've found my mate."

"Really? Anybody I know?"

"Our coerced thief."

Bron burst out laughing. "I should have known. Well, good luck, Chase. We'll have things covered on this end."

"Glad you're with me on this. I'll let you know when I've got Delmon in custody."

Now all he had to do was get Caz to cooperate, something he knew wasn't going to come easy. He headed for bed. Lying there naked and wide awake, he toyed with the idea of trying the link with Caz, but knowing how disgusted Caz would be, he put the thought aside. At least he tried, until the link opened from the other end.

Chase nearly groaned aloud at the pleasure their joining brought. He sat up, clearly feeling Caz in his head, feeling the reciprocal pleasure even tinged as it was with shame.

Seeing through Caz's eyes, it suddenly struck him that Caz was outside the museum. Phantom words whispered in his head. *Watch me.*

"Caz, no," Chase ordered softly, but no answer was forthcoming. He watched in helpless fascination as Caz began his work.

With the use of some device Chase had never seen before, Caz carefully created a loop in the security feed. When the door he stood at was totally unprotected by any alarm, he easily defeated the locking mechanisms. Gliding in on silent feet, he headed for the main viewing room and stopped when the footsteps of a patrolling guard sounded from down the corridor. Instead of running for a place to hide, Caz melted back against the wall.

From his position inside Caz's vision, Chase saw a shimmer of blue-green. From the outside, Caz had become merely another shadow among many. Somehow, that gossamer veil of color was allowing him to blend in with his surroundings. Chase held his breath as the guard passed by and breathed with Caz when he moved again. Circling the display holding the Blaze of Belthola, Caz employed his device. Chase could see the readings and realized it was mimicking the security system.

The device picked up all the readings being monitored and fed them back to security. Instead of breaking through the security system, the device was sending its own signal, using it to meld with the security system. The piggybacking signal eased its way seamlessly into the flow, keeping the readings steady, even as Caz reached for the huge amber gem and slipped it into the small pack strapped to his chest.

Caz's device spit forth a small chip which Caz placed in the gem's stead. The chip, with its limited power, continued to mirror the feed as Caz slipped his device into another pocket on his pack and backed silently away. Cat-footed, he stole from the room. returning the way he came. Just as he reached the street, the museum's alarms went off, but Caz was again a shadow slipping easily into the surrounding darkness.

The images Caz fed him abruptly stopped. Chase inhaled deeply, not realizing he'd been holding his breath. He levered himself out of bed and grabbed a robe, pacing while he thought about this unexpected turn of events. He'd planned to talk to Caz, to persuade him into testifying against Delmon. But now, this. How was he going to clear up this mess when Caz had just stolen the Blaze of Belthola?

Chase tried to contact Caz but was summarily blocked out. He continued to pace, again and again running a hand through his hair in agitation. Was he going to be forced to hunt down and arrest his own mate? Cursing roundly, he headed for his office but was stopped by the buzz at his front door, signaling the arrival of a visitor.

His Maleri' senses immediately intuited who was there, and a wave of relief went through him when he went to the door to find Caz looking straight into the vid screen. He opened the door. Caz stood silently for a moment, then held out the small pack Chase had seen him use to hold the

Blaze and the device he'd used to break in. Chase took the pack, moved to the side, and with a gesture invited Caz inside.

The two of them stood looking at each other for a moment until Chase softly swore. "Why did you do it? I told you I'd help you. You've just complicated things."

Caz shook his head. "I had to. If I didn't, Delmon would have killed my family. That's why I'm here. Now it's public knowledge the Blaze has been stolen. It gives you time. Delmon knows I've done the job. You've got to protect them. I don't care what happens to me. Just help them."

"It's already done."

"What do you mean?"

"I *mean* that I've called Chief Nazkarion in Varknia. He's got men watching your family right this minute. If any of Delmon's thugs makes a move on them, they'll be stopped."

Caz looked at him in disbelief. "Why would you do that without my asking? I'm a liar and thief, not to mention other things."

"You are *not*," Chase denied with quiet vehemence. "When our connection was made, I saw what you'd done. I also experienced what you felt while doing it. You were forced to act against your will. You did what you had to do to protect your family. Those are the actions of an honorable man."

Caz shook his head, his eyes glittering and his expression hard. "You make me so angry."

"Why? Because I see who you really are?" Chase asked softly, his voice tinged with puzzlement. "Caz, I'm sorry I inflicted the bond on you without your permission. I…"

"Stop it! Just stop," Caz ground out. "I guess I should be grateful. I suppose you think I should bend over for you. I told you I wouldn't be taken against my will. You don't know what it's like! You don't have the *least* idea!"

"No, I don't."

"Maybe it's time you find out just how contemptible I am."

Without waiting for Chase's reply, Caz ripped the pack from his hand, threw it to the floor, and slammed Chase back into the wall. Effectively trapping Chase between his body and the wall, Caz smothered Chase's lips with his own. He savagely nipped at Chase's lips, forcing him to utter a protest which allowed his demanding tongue entrance. Brutally, he took possession of Chase's mouth, ravaging the warm, wet cavern while sucking at and fiercely subduing his tongue.

After long moments of hard, ruthless kisses which left both men panting for air, Caz pulled back slightly. "Fight me," he urged.

"No."

"You like this then, don't you?" he sneered.

"No."

"Then fight me."

"I said no."

"Why not? I know you're not afraid of me."

"You're right. I'm not afraid of you. But I'm not going to fight you because you need to do this."

"I need to abuse you and so you're going to let me?"

"Yes."

"How very, very generous and open minded you are. Let's see if this will change your mind."

Caz grabbed Chase by the shoulders and spun him, again slamming him into the wall. Chase turned his head to the side and grunted with the impact, groaning when Caz cruelly ripped his robe away. Two hands callously gripped his hips, bruising fingers holding him in place while Caz rocked against him.

"I'm going to fuck you, Chase. Hard and rough. Are you ready to stop me now?"

Chase shook his head, then heard and felt Caz opening his pants. Roughly, Caz kicked at his feet, forcing him to widen his stance. Using one hand, he exposed the tight, crinkled opening of Chase's asshole. Holding his cock with the other, he rubbed his leaking cock head briefly over Chase's entrance, then pushed. Chase froze for a split second, then struggled to relax. A cry of pain tore from his lips when Caz breached the tight ring of muscle. Both men froze.

Breathing heavily, Caz dropped his forehead against Chase's temple. His breath misted against Chase's cheek, causing him to shiver. "You'd do it. You'd let me do it. You'd let me rape you."

Caz withdrew as gently as possible and turned away. With shoulders shaking and tears running down his face, he thoroughly cussed Chase out. "Why won't you hate me?"

Chase gathered Caz into his arms, Caz's back solid against his chest. "There's nothing there to hate. The shame and anger and guilt are eating you alive. All that's happened is not your fault. Let it go, Caz. Let it go."

Caz sagged in his arms, half formed sobs torn from deep inside. Chase turned him and held him tight. "It's all right, baby. It's all right now."

The vid unit on a nearby table in the living room blared a signal into the room, announcing an incoming call.

"Fuck! That's gotta be someone from my unit," Chase cursed. "Here, babe, sit," he ordered softly, helping Caz to a chair. He picked his robe up off the floor and shrugged into it, wrapping it around him.

Caz grabbed his arm, self-consciously wiping at the tears on his face. "What are you going to tell them?"

"Not a damn thing. At this point we've got to let them think the Blaze is still missing. I want Delmon to believe you're still cooperating with him."

Caz nodded and stayed silent while Chase took the call. He watched Caz lean back in his chair, his eyes closing while exhaustion slid over his features. He listened calmly as the situation was explained and gave instructions to the officer in charge of the investigation.

Ending the call, he went to Caz and urged him to his feet. "Come on, you need to rest for a bit and so do I."

Picking up the pack that held the Blaze, he led Caz to his bedroom and encouraged him to undress by unbuttoning a few of the buttons on his shirt. Not protesting, Caz took over and was soon naked and sliding under the covers Chase had pulled back for him.

"Mind if I join you?"

Caz shook his head and Chase followed him in, pulling the covers over them both. Caz turned on his side, away from him, and Chase sighed in resignation, making no move to touch him. "Get some sleep. We'll keep Delmon in suspense for a time, and then I think I have just the plan we need to put him away."

Caz muttered a muffled thanks and was quiet.

"You're welcome," Chase replied, and with a weary sigh closed his eyes. Tension made way for fatigue, and they were both soon asleep.

Chapter Four

Chase woke to the feel of a body, warm and weighty, partially wrapped around him. The early morning light, muted but still visible through the bedroom window shields, shimmered in the blond hair that tickled his lips. In his sleep, Caz had shifted and squirmed until he found Chase and, finally content, settled against him.

Chase remembered waking briefly when Caz's body lightly collided with his during the night. Caz had thrown an arm and leg over him, pressing in tightly and holding on with a kind of desperation that revealed itself even in his sleep. Chase had gently rubbed his arm and back, murmuring soft, soothing words while Caz slowly relaxed, the tension flowing out of him.

Content and sleepy, Chase closed his eyes and dozed off. The next time he woke it was to the feel of a large, firm, and slightly callused hand roving over his chest. He moaned when clever fingers swept over one nipple, then stopped to lightly pinch the hardening tip. His eyes fluttered open to find Caz, awake and solemn faced, leaning over him.

"Is it all right if I do this?" Caz asked, letting his fingertips continue to sweep lightly over Chase's hard nipple.

"As much as you like," Chase replied and groaned when Caz again gave his nipple a light tweak.

Caz leaned down and briefly settled his lips against Chase's again and again, each time remaining longer, each time deepening the kiss. His tongue lightly slid over the seam of Chase's lips and Chase opened for him. Two moans accompanied the meeting of mouths and lips and tongues that petted and caressed each other in a seductive swirl of motion.

The heat under their cocoon of blankets increased. Warm air wafted from beneath, bringing the combined scents of two males surrendering to rising testosterone. The smell was musky yet tart and oh so alluring. Chase could feel Caz's cock, hard against his thigh, and his hips nearly left the bed when Caz's hand drifted low and closed around his own cock.

"Ah, God!" Chase groaned.

"I'm sorry," Caz whispered, his hand stroking Chase with a slow, easy rhythm.

"For touching me? Don't be."

"Not for this. For earlier. I'm sorry I hurt you. I want to make it up to you."

Chase placed a hand over Caz's where it rested on his cock, stopping the motion. "Is that the only reason you're doing this?"

Blue-green eyes and silver-gray locked gazes for a silent space of time while their chests rose and fell with the pace of their accelerated breathing. The colors on Caz's cheeks intensified, and he finally blinked and shook his head. "I saw you on a vid chip before we came here. I wanted you the minute I saw you. I knew we'd meet because of Delmon. I never expected this. When you caused that bond between us, I hated it because you saw me. You saw who I was and what I'd done. I hated *me*. I never hated you. I wanted you before and I want you now. Even if I don't deserve..."

"*Stop!* Don't say it, don't even think it. Caz, when you said I saw you as the bond formed between us, you were right. What I told you before, I meant every word. The things you did or had done to you, they weren't by choice. They weren't you. I know that. And so do you, if you'll just admit it to yourself." Chase reached up and let his fingers trail over the gossamer veil of color on Caz's cheek. "Sometimes victims erroneously blame themselves for whatever's happened. Let's put the blame back where it belongs."

The color under his fingertips flared and Chase widened his eyes in surprise. "What is it?"

"My father," Caz murmured and pulled away, lying back on the bed. "My father's to blame."

Chase rose up on his elbow and leaned over him. "How so?"

"He developed a water purification method specifically aimed for use by terra-formers. The process is simple and unique, but he needed financial backing to fully develop it. He went to Kogan Delmon despite the protests of my mother and myself. He didn't believe a project like his would warrant Delmon's undue attention." Caz grimaced. "Turned out he was wrong. Delmon provided the financial backing, the technique was perfected, and then he stole it, completely cutting my father out of any recognition or financial benefit."

"So what did he do?"

"He tried to break in and steal proof of Delmon's duplicity. He developed the device I used to steal the Blaze but he got caught. He doesn't have some of my more subtle talents."

Chase trailed his fingers over the blue-green veil of color that could barely be seen highlighting the contours of the muscles on Caz's chest. He felt Caz quiver at the touch and noted the heat filling his gaze. "You're Metonian. I read up on it when I first saw the vid of you coming through the port. You're able to blend into your surroundings, somewhat like the chameleons of Earth."

"Part of my heritage from my mother. She's full Metonian, I'm half."

"So your father was caught in the act, and your services were the bargaining chip that got him off the hook?"

"Yeah."

"Your father may have behaved foolishly, but it still comes down to Kogan Delmon. He's at the heart of all this. The one to blame for the entire situation. I think you need to cut your father some slack. He must be feeling pretty low about now."

"I know he is and I really want to."

"Then do it."

Caz smiled and Chase felt his heart stutter. "You're such an uncompromising man. You see a situation that should change or something that needs to be done and there's no hesitation. You just do it."

Chase shrugged. "No sense wasting time. Speaking of which, we need to go over the plan I've hatched but first, since we're both in agreement about wanting each other..." Chase leaned down and kissed Caz hard and deep, drawing a groan from him. "I think we should do something about it."

Caz nodded. "I definitely agree with that."

"Good. I want you to fuck me."

"What! After what happened last night? *No!*"

"Settle down and listen to me," Chase soothed. "I've been thinking about this. I don't want any more misunderstandings between us. You were right when you said I should have told you that the bonding was going to take place. I should have given you a chance to accept or refuse. I took without asking."

"Chase, it's all right."

"Sure, now it is, but that doesn't matter. What matters is that I want to give something to you... me," he confessed, his cheeks reddening slightly under the concealing brush of his neatly trimmed beard.

Caz struggled to control his smile while Chase gave him a self-conscious glare.

"Look, I'm not a virgin. I've had my share of sexual encounters, but Maleri' males only get fucked by their mates. I don't want to take from you. I want to give."

Caz gave him a thoughtful, considering look. "How about instead of taking or giving, we share?"

"Sharing sounds good," Chase agreed with a smile.

"Good. Now where's the lube?"

Chase laughed and reached over to the bedside table, opening a drawer. He came back with a capped tube. "Right here."

Caz took the offered tube. "On your stomach. Let's do things right this time."

Chase obeyed and rolled on his stomach, his body anticipating Caz's touch. His breathing ratcheted higher when Caz straddled his thighs and his hands settled on Chase's shoulders. Instead of going straight to work on his ass, Caz started at the top and worked his way down with slow, maddening strokes that left Chase aching with need.

Firm hands and fingers possessing sensual, tactile strength caressed Chase's skin while massaging muscles that loosened and relaxed under the insistent pressure. Caz worked his shoulders, arms and back, moving at a lazy unhurried pace. Chase tensed when those same hands slid over the cheeks of his ass and groaned in disappointment when they merely skated over his flesh and ended at the back of his thighs to continue the massage.

"Patience, *reabbah*," Caz murmured, moving down his body.

"What does that mean?" Chase asked, his voice hoarse with arousal.

"Lover."

"Mmm."

Caz leaned down and kissed both rounded cheeks of Chase's ass. "*Reabbah*," he whispered against the warm skin under his lips.

Chase groaned again and forced himself to lie still under Caz's hands. Hands that massaged his thighs, calves and feet before returning to the place he wanted them most. Back on his ass. Caz massaged the firm mounds, then parted them, revealing the taut entrance to Chase's body. Leaning down, he blew a warm breath of moist air across his skin. Chase automatically tightened and growled when he heard Caz chuckle.

Before he could say anything, a slick warm tongue connected with his puckered opening and his open mouth produced a rolling, "Ahhhh."

Caz chuckled again and went earnestly to work. His tongue slid over Chase's quivering flesh again and again, stopping only to prod insistently at the slowly relaxing ring of muscle. Just as Chase felt his body skillfully invaded, he felt phantom touches at his mind and dropped his shield. Their connection flared wide and Caz's consciousness slid sinuously in. Chase cried out, embracing the mental connection just as his hole relaxed and yielded to the hot tongue that plunged inside his body.

Caz's tongue probed and impaled the compliant opening, then seamlessly withdrew to make way for a lube-wet finger. Chase welcomed both invasions with equal enthusiasm. His hips ground against the bed, increasing the pressure on his hard, aching cock even as his consciousness quivered at the warm caress of his mate's mental touch.

More, reabbah? Caz whispered into his mind.

Yes. Deity, yes, more.

Caz complied, sending a second finger to join the first and then a third, easing the tight muscle, stretching Chase open with easy, rhythmic strokes. Chase pushed back into the steady in and out plunge, groaning a denial when Caz withdrew.

Caz draped himself over Chase's back, his mouth finding his ear to lick and softly nip. "Roll over. I want you to ride me."

Gut clenching at the thought, Chase turned over to find Caz stretched out, his upper body propped against several pillows and the headboard. His eyes widened in surprise. Caz's lube-slick fingers were wrapped around his own cock, sliding up and down the long, thick length. Luminous blue-green color infused the satiny skin.

"Is that normal?" Chase asked, staring at Caz's cock.

"For me, yes. Like I said, I'm half Metonian. You object?"

"Fuck no, I don't object. It's actually beautiful, not to mention big and thick. Just the way I like."

The colors on Caz's cheeks intensified as a bashful smile curved his lips. Chase moved in, straddling his thighs. "I want you in me now," he growled and leaned down to seal their lips together.

When Chase sat up, Caz took hold of his own cock and held it up while Chase lowered himself down. The head, plump, ripe and leaking, made contact and nuzzled in. Chase gave his hips a slight circular undulation and pushed down, groaning when he was impaled and the thick shaft slid in several inches. Panting, hands resting on Caz's shoulders, head thrown back and eyes closed, he concentrated on their joined flesh, silently willing himself to relax.

His hole convulsively gripped and released, fluttering around Caz's cock and drawing a moan from him. Chase opened his eyes and brought his gaze to Caz's. With agonizing slowness, he lowered himself, feeling every thick, hard, pulsing inch of Caz's cock fill him. Caz's eyes held a kind of desperate pleasure, his panting breaths loud and mingling with Chase's own.

When finally fully and completely seated, Chase let his head fall forward, again closing his eyes, wanting nothing more than to concentrate on the feelings sweeping through him. He could feel the rhythmic pulse of Caz's cock deep within and everywhere they touched skin on skin, heat and moisture formed, sealing them together.

A touch on his face brought Chase's head up, his gaze caught and held by Caz. "Are you all right?"

Chase nodded. "I just want to savor it for moment."

Caz groaned. "I wish you'd move, *reabbah*. Deity, you're so tight." He convulsively pushed up. "I need you to *move*."

"Unnhh," Chase groaned, responding to Caz's plea.

Acquiescing to Caz's need, Chase rose up, then slid down, a slow, shallow move that increased in speed and length until he was rising up and down, driving the full length of Caz's cock deep into his welcoming sheath. Caz rested one hand on the bunching muscles of Chase's thigh, his other sliding down the length of Chase's cock to cup his full, round testicles. His fingers caressed and gently kneaded the heavy balls, drawing gasps and groans from Chase.

The steady slap of flesh against flesh sounded in the room as Chase's buttocks slammed against Caz's thick thighs. "Touch me!" Chase ground out, his throat tight, his voice husky and deep. *"Here."*

Mentally he guided Caz to the inner shield wall that held the build up of energies his Maleri' senses had acquired. Caz followed his lead and wrapped his essence around the pulsing shield. The energy gleefully took the path offered and discharged a bolt of pure sexual electricity. Both men hoarsely screamed as climax exploded deep within, the power of their release rushing up and out in waves of punishing pleasure and spumes of white hot seed.

Buried deep and held in a vise-like grip, Caz flooded the smooth, dark channel that milked him. The backflow leaked past the tight seal of their joining, mingling with and matting his pubic hair. The first shot from Chase's cock landed with a warm wet splat on his chest while a subsequent burst decorated the straining muscles of his abs and stomach.

Slowly their convulsive movements waned until muscles once elastic and energized were inundated with a sated weakness that left them trembling. Chase collapsed forward into Caz's welcoming arms, disengaging Caz's diminishing erection. The two of them rolled to their sides. Face to face, they lay together, eyes closed while taking deep breaths laden with the combined musk of their mating.

Chase opened his eyes to find Caz smiling, his eyes still closed. "What's so amusing?" he asked with a hoarse growl.

"When you decide to give, you don't fool around."

Chase chuckled. "You're young, you can handle it."

"Why do you keep bringing up my age?" Caz asked, opening his eyes. "I'm twenty-three. You can't be that much older than me."

"Twenty-eight."

"Whoa, ancient. I'll try to take it easy on you from here on in."

"Fuck you."

"Oh, I hope so. You looked like you were having a good time."

"I was. Now I know why my mentor's mate, Jamie, liked getting fucked so much. What's your preference?"

"Don't know. Never been fucked," Caz confessed with a rueful smile.

"No?"

"Most guys take one look and automatically decide I'm a top. Besides, I never met anyone I'd trust to fuck me."

"And you have now?"

"Oh, yeah."

Chase grinned and rubbed a large hand over one cheek of Caz's ass, squeezing lightly. "You've just made it very hard for me to keep my mind on business, but this'll have to wait." He lightly smacked the flesh under his hand and struggled up into a sitting position. "We've got a crook to catch."

Chapter Five

"Where have you been?"

Caz entered his hotel room followed by one of Delmon's thugs. The man had been stationed in the lobby, instructed to wait for Caz's arrival and escort him upstairs.

"Evading the TC Security Bureau, as if you didn't know. For your information, I almost got caught," Caz answered, his voice filled with exasperation and anger.

"Let me see it." Kogan Delmon rose from the chair in which he'd been seated. He caught the pack Caz tossed to him. "Watch it, whelp."

"Watch it yourself. I'm done with this, Delmon. I've more than paid my father's debt. Enough is enough."

Delmon made no comment. The Blaze of Belthola glimmered in his greedy hands, and he reverently caressed the amber gem while gazing deep into the fiery blaze at its center.

"Did you hear me? I said I'm through," Caz repeated, pushing for a response.

It wasn't long in coming. "Do you honestly think you can dictate to me, young Cazius? You think the jobs you did here, on Selmora, and Ahveinth are enough to pay your father's debt to me?"

"They're more than enough."

"No. Not *nearly* enough. You'll continue on or you'll pay the consequences."

"Consequences. I've heard a lot about consequences. Why don't you spell them out for me? Just what are the consequences?"

"You'll be mourning a death in your family, and I'll be the one to choose who dies. Is that exact enough for you?"

"Taskin City Security!" someone yelled a split second before the door burst open. Chase and several of his men rushed in.

"That's more than exact enough," Chase answered. "Kogan Delmon, you're under arrest for coercion, conspiracy to commit murder, grand larceny, and a host of other charges we'll discuss back at the Bureau."

Despite the weapons aimed at him, one of Delmon's thugs chose to draw his own. Seeing the path of the weapon zero in on Chase, Caz jumped the man just as he fired. They were immediately surrounded by security men who disarmed the man and slapped him in restraints.

Caz stood and sought out Chase, who'd thrown himself out of harm's way. At least he'd tried to. The blast from the weapon had caught him on the upper arm, burning through the fabric of his uniform to scorch and score the flesh beneath. Blood oozed sluggishly from the shallow wound.

"Chase! Deity, are you all right?" Caz yelled, pushing his way through the security men to Chase's side.

"I'm fine, Caz. It's a graze. It's nothing."

"Let me see," Caz insisted and examined the wound close up. Satisfied, he looked into Chase's eyes. "Some loena cream and an aid strip should take care of it. Don't do that again," he threatened, his tone serious, his gaze unwavering.

Chase smiled and put a hand on his shoulder, lightly shaking him. "I'll try to avoid it in future. Come on. You've got statements to give, and I have a prisoner to house. A nice comfy cell should do him a world of good while we sort out who gets to prosecute him. Now that he's been toppled from his throne, I have a feeling claims are going to come in from more than just Selmora and Ahveinth, not to mention our own claim. Delmon's going to be a busy boy."

Caz slid an arm around Chase's waist and squeezed, watching as Kogan Delmon was led from the room in restraints. He nodded silently.

Chase turned to face him and slung his uninjured arm around him, hugging him close. "It's over, baby. Come on. Let's get the rest of this squared away so we can go home. My head's filled with a vision of the most fuckable ass I've ever seen, and I can't wait to get a taste of it."

Caz grinned and snorted a laugh against Chase's shoulder. "I've got to call my parents."

"To tell them I want to fuck your ass?"

"No, *nuava cuil*. To tell them they're out of danger."

"What's *nuava cuil*?"

"Don't ask."

"I know how to use a computer, you know."

Caz released himself from Chase's embrace, his cheeks flashing with heightened color. "So?" he asked, walking out the hotel door.

Chase followed. "I can access a translation program for Metonian."

"It's not Metonian."

"What is it?"

"Forget it."

"Tell me."

"No."

"Caz."

* * *

Five hours later, fresh out of the shower, Caz and Chase landed on the bed with a thud. "Finally! My balls hurt waiting for you," Chase confessed with a growl.

"How many hours in a Beltholan day?"

"Twenty-two."

"It hasn't been a day since you last emptied these," Caz teased, reaching for the balls in question.

Chase moaned with pleasure. "I know, but I kept getting erect watching you at the Bureau offices. I've fought down half a dozen erections in the past few hours. All that rising and falling had to have some kind of pumping action that filled my balls more than usual."

Caz rolled to his back and burst out laughing.

A smile curved his lips as Chase watched, entranced and fascinated by his mate. Those gossamer, thin, blue-green colors swirled and seemed to dance over Caz's skin in celebration with his laughter. Caz's face, so relaxed and free of tension, took on a boyish, carefree cast that was gratifying to behold. Chase had thought him handsome before, but now he was pure devastation.

Wiping tears of laughter from his eyes, Caz let his gaze find Chase's. "Thank you."

"For what?"

"For bringing laughter back into my life. It's been so long since I've laughed."

"You should do it more often, it looks good on you."

Caz pulled him down and initiated a heated kiss. Pulling free just far enough that his lips brushed Chase's, he spoke in a strained undertone. "There's another thing I'd like to do often, starting right now. Fuck me, *reabbah*."

"I've never wanted anything more," Chase answered, then kissed him deeply.

On his knees with Caz on his back, he pushed Caz's ass up to rest on his thighs. With lube slick fingers he opened him, using firm yet gentle movements. Through it all he played with Caz's body. Chase stroked his free hand over Caz's chest, arousing his tiny male nipples to hard buds.

Leaning forward, drawing them into his mouth, he sucked and nibbled the taut little points.

Caz squirmed under him, moaning incessantly, the sounds driving him wild. Moving higher, Chase took his mouth in a deep, scorching kiss, his tongue winding around Caz's, while seducing it with sinuous caresses. He drew back again, concentrating on the tight hole that was loosening with every passing minute.

Drawn to the thick, waving pole of Caz's erection, Chase maneuvered himself back far enough so that he could comfortably bend down. Wrapping his fingers around the hard, pulsing shaft, he lowered his mouth to Caz's cock and licked at the sweet clear fluid bubbling up from the tiny slit centered in the plump cap. His tongue probed the little opening before his mouth closed over the head, sucking while his tongue swirled over the tight, silky soft skin.

Blissfully, he explored the veined contours of the flesh that filled his mouth while his fingers stroked what his mouth and throat couldn't accommodate. Chase swallowed heavily, drawing a guttural groan from Caz whose nonstop moans had increased in volume. His body undulated under the onslaught of Chase's sensual touch. Not wanting him to come before the main event, Chase let Caz's cock reluctantly slide free.

Growing impatient, Chase added more lube and scissored two fingers in deep, stretching Caz's snug opening. Drawing back, he sent three fingers in to the knuckle, pushing hard while rotating them, screwing them in as deeply as possible.

"Deity, *yes!*" Caz groaned, his head tossing on the pillow. "Now, I'm ready now. Fuck me, Chase. Fuck me!"

Taking him at his word, he eased his fingers free and pushed Caz's thighs back. "Hold your legs for me," he instructed, and Caz did as he was told.

Taking his thick cock firmly in hand, Chase guided himself to Caz. Reveling in the feel of flesh against flesh, he ran his cock head, leaking with pre-cum, over the blushing, ready entrance several times before aiming true and pushing forward. His cock breached the tight muscle and slid balls deep.

"*Reabbah!*" Caz screamed, his body going rigid beneath Chase before slowly relaxing.

"Are you all right, baby?" Chase gasped, grinding his teeth against the need to move. "Does it hurt?"

"No, no, no. Doesn't hurt. Feels good. So good, Ah, Deity, so good."

"Let's make it even better."

Chase started to move, pulling nearly free before powering slowly forward, stroke after stroke, until his cock was moving freely. He grasped Caz's cock and pumped in rhythm with his thrusts, watching more clear pre-cum leak from the tip of Caz's cock to smear on his belly. Releasing his cock, Chase leaned forward, his hands planted above Caz's shoulders on either side of his head. His mouth found Caz's, kissing him hard and deep while his hips undulated, the muscles in his buttocks bunching and releasing with each dominating thrust.

He eased back but continued stroking his cock in and out of Caz's hot welcoming sheath. Ripples of movement greeted each deep slide as Caz's body sought to hold him inside. He watched Caz's face, the play of mindless pleasure washing over his features, his lips swollen and red from their shared kisses. Sweat formed on his forehead, throat, and chest, making his skin glisten and shine, while shifting shimmers of blue-green played over his straining muscles.

"Look at me, baby," Chase ordered in a husky overtone.

Caz's eyelids fluttered, his blue-green eyes revealed. Their expression reflected the pleasure riding his body and mind. *"Nuava cuil."*

Tell me, baby, please, Chase's mental whisper drifted between them.

Heart mate, Caz revealed and wrapped his legs tightly around Chase pulling him closer still.

A spike of adrenaline rushed through Chase's body, electrifying him. He slammed forward deep and hard, exploding in a fiery rush of hot semen and pure gut-wrenching pleasure. Sandwiched between their bodies, Caz's cock swelled and pulsed, thick spurts of creamy ejaculate spewing forth to fill in any small space left where flesh did not touch flesh.

Their roars of pleasure mingled and were muffled when Chase grasped Caz's head, holding him still while he gently but thoroughly plundered his mouth with lips and teeth and tongue. Reluctant to let go, he moved back slightly and found Caz staring at him, his expression unsure and questioning.

Chase felt a smile tug at his lips while he blinked at tears that refused to stop stinging his eyes. Leaning forward, he kissed the warm satiny skin of Caz's chest, the spot directly over his heart.

"Heart mate. You almost killed me there."

Caz grinned. "You're young, you can handle it."

"You're almost right. *We* can handle it. Together."

"Together," Caz agreed.

Exchanging another long, stirring kiss, they settled in each other's arms talking quietly, touching intimately, and finally drifting off to sleep.

Epilogue

"Does anybody know why Chase called this meeting?" Eric Ashton asked the company at large.

Silent shakes of several heads and succinct denials were his answer.

"I'm sure he has a good reason," Jamie Richards said, shyly speaking up for the first time in the gathered group. His hand found that of his mate and slipped into the sure, comforting grasp.

Despian Rulf gave his mate a reassuring smile. "Chase will have a good reason. He's not one for wasting anyone's time."

"Eric didn't mean to question Chase's motivation," Sethian Dennon spoke up, defending his mate. "We're all just curious. Chase isn't exactly the kind to initiate a party."

"That's true," Grey Dennon agreed.

Col Oldarie laughed. "Everyone be patient. If I'm not mistaken, here's Chase now."

"I'll get it," his mate, Matt, offered, heading for the door.

All eyes were zeroed in on them when the door opened, and Matt stepped back to admit Chase and the tall, blond man at his side. Urging Matt to lead the way, Chase and his companion followed and waited for Matt to seat himself next to Col.

"Everyone's here I see," Chase observed, solemnly looking from man to man.

"Yeah, so what's going on?" Geral Pardais asked impatiently. His mate, Sam, pinched his thigh, causing him to jump.

"Give the man a chance to explain," Sam scolded, drawing a laugh from those gathered.

"Thank you, Sam," Chase acknowledged. "I'll come straight to the point. Remember the other night when I said I'd let you know?"

There were thoughtful nods all around.

He turned to the man at his side. "My mate, Cazius Rey."

His words were greeted with an explosion of well wishes, laughter, and expressions of pleased surprise. He and Caz were surrounded and congratulated. Drinks were passed around and toasts made. An impromptu party was soon underway. Various members of the party began preparing food in Col and Matthew's well stocked kitchen under the watchful eyes and sometimes interfering hands of well meaning mates.

Col was finally able to exchange a private word with Chase. "I can't tell you how happy and relieved I am."

"Relieved?" Chase questioned.

Col nodded. "You'd withdrawn from us, Chase. I'd begun to worry about you."

Chase acknowledged his words with a nod and a sigh. "I let my responsibilities rule my life. I didn't leave any room for fun or friends or laughter."

"And now?"

"You see that man across the room?"

"Yeah."

"He gave me his heart and set me free. How could I not be happy?"

Col smiled, his gaze finding his own mate. "We're of like minds, my friend."

"Of course," Chase answered with a smile of his own. "We're Maleri'. Brothers." Chase's gaze returned to Caz, and Col could feel the slight overspill of emotion Chase sought to keep under control. "Would you excuse me, Col?"

"Of course," Col agreed and watched Chase cross the room to Caz.

Chase slipped an arm around his waist. Caz leaned in, whispered something in his ear, and a wild surge of desire slammed into every man in the room. There was total shocked silence for a moment until Col started to laugh.

"Caz, maybe you should take Chase home and help him practice keeping his shields up. Although it probably won't be as easy as getting his pants down."

Laughter rang out and the tension receded as Chase was good naturedly teased. "Thanks a lot, *brother*."

"Anytime, Chase, anytime. Welcome back," Col offered with a grin.

Chase just shook his head and let his gaze return to Caz. "You gonna make good on that promise?"

"You know I will, *reabbah*," Caz replied, smiling while sheer blue-green color shimmered on his skin when the light caught his face at just the right angle. "But can we stay for awhile? I like your friends."

Chase nodded. "I'd like that too," he said and realized it was true. He had his friends, his brothers, and most importantly, the mate of his heart. He was content.

Bonds of the Maleri' 4: Ride 'Em Cowboy

Kate Steele

Prologue

Lights from the computer screen flickered over the round, boyish curves of Zebian Bakar's face. His fingers flew over the keys, adding to the data that flashed before his silvery blue eyes. So intent was he on the work before him, he didn't hear the knocking that sounded several times at his door.

It was only when the door slid open and a hand settled softly on his shoulder that he pulled his attention from the screen. Without looking, his Maleri' senses told him immediately it was Kiel Omontri, his guardian.

"Rick says you've not eaten since first meal, young one. Come share the evening meal with us, Zeb."

"I'm not hungry." Zeb felt a swift twinge of resentment which he quickly pushed aside, knowing it was unfair to aim such feelings at Rick.

Rick Mason, Kiel's human mate, was concerned for his well-being. It was a feeling many others had expressed for Zebian since the death of his parents. Orphaned and alone at the age of twelve, he was an object for concern and pity. Zeb hated it, and so he retreated. Computers and facts and figures had no sympathy to offer. They merely bestowed knowledge and distraction and a surcease of pain when his unruly thoughts skipped back to the happy days before the accident. The accident that took his mother, his father, and his heart.

"Zebian, I know losing yourself in this work brings you comfort, but come eat. Rick will think you don't like him."

Zeb's brow crinkled. "That's not fair. You know I like him."

"I know. And you're smart enough to know I'm using this excuse to get you to join us. I also know you have a heart filled with kindness and compassion. You'll come, if for no other reason than to put Rick's mind at ease."

A long sigh passed his lips before Zeb rose reluctantly from his chair. His eyes met Kiel's and found affection and concern. Kiel and Rick had made a place for Zeb in their home. Together they'd held and comforted him through his tears, anger and confusion. In the many months he'd been living with them, they had become his family, a fact that oftentimes frightened him. What if something happened to *them*? Losing one family had been hard enough. He never wanted to go through that again.

But Kiel was right. He didn't want to hurt Rick and so he'd go, eat the evening meal with them and keep his barriers in place. There was a line drawn before his heart and no one -- *no one* -- would ever be allowed to cross it.

* * *

They were having sex. *Again*. It sometimes amazed Zeb just how often his two mentors indulged. Though he couldn't hear them, the past six years of living with Kiel and Rick had been enough for him to have established a peripheral link to them both. Now that he was eighteen, they no longer bothered to shield him from the mental vibrations of their play. He could feel the faint echoes of their pleasure as they touched and loved each other.

Zeb lay back on his bed, naked, his cock erect and aching as he moved his hand up and down in a leisurely stroke from the base to the tip. Eyes closed, he let his arousal build with theirs. Frequent spikes of pleasure drew audible groans from his lips. The hand at his cock moved faster while the other glided the length of his slim torso. His free hand slid over his nipple, pinching the tiny nub as it hardened.

Their emotions were so strong at times like these. He could almost feel the heat and the slick slide of skin on skin as Kiel's cock breached Rick's entrance and slid deep within. Zeb convulsively tightened his grip on his own cock, phantom touches of Rick's silky sheath surrounding him, urging him to thrust deep into the tunnel of his own fist.

Zeb let himself sink into the growing sensation. His senses were alive with spectral touches, sounds and heat. The link blossomed open. Rick and Kiel invited him to partake of every aching pulse of pleasure that beat seductively through their veins. Sweat broke out on Zeb's body. Incorporeal tongues swept over his skin and he groaned aloud, shivers rippling down his spine.

The need for release grew stronger. Rick and Kiel's arousal was a wild, demanding thing that pushed them and him over a towering precipice and sent them careening through the air. Zeb's cry of completion echoed theirs. He came to his senses with his hand still lightly stroking his fading erection. Thick streaks and smears of semen decorated his hand, cock and torso.

He lay still for a time, until his breathing eased, before rising to clean himself. As he settled in front of his computer, longing made a fleeting appearance in his mind before he pushed it away. He was eighteen now. Kiel and Rick had told him six months ago, on his birthday, that he was welcome in their bed. They allowed him to feel their pleasure when they made love instead of carefully shielding him as they'd done when he was younger. It was the way of the Maleri'. He longed to join them but refused to take that final step.

Young Maleri' of eighteen were sent to live with a mated Maleri' pair. The pair acted as the young man's mentors. They helped him in his transition from student to part of their exclusive brotherhood. Maleri' were born empaths, men who were trained to help other people and other cultures. In return, they received benefits for the people of their home planet, Belthola.

The mated pair saw to their charge's every requirement, including his indoctrination into all things sexual. Maleri' males had an instinctive need to seek one man, a mate with empathic powers who would provide not only love and companionship, but who would ensure their very survival. They were not by nature a promiscuous bunch but, as with all living creatures, their bodies demanded an outlet for their physical desires. The young, unmated Maleri' had his needs met by his mentors until he was ready to seek his mate.

Zeb knew he had to leave. Because of his circumstances, orphaned at twelve, he'd been living with his mentors for the past six years. Six years in which they'd become a necessary part of his life. If he gave in to the demands of his body, sought to fulfill his sexual urges with them, he knew he was doomed. The love he'd held at bay would spill over and there would be no denying it. No ignoring it. No way to cut himself off from the pain if something should happen to either one of them.

And so he took the way out that had been offered.

* * *

"He's only eighteen, Councilor Ruran, much too young to be put into service."

"I understand your concern, Kiel, I really do. But Zebian will not come into contact with outsiders. His job will be strictly research, data and computers. The boy has an amazing gift. It would be a shame to waste it unnecessarily."

Kiel paced the council chamber. Running a hand through his long, dark hair, his agitation was more than apparent. "You consider his emotional growth unnecessary?"

"Of course not! To what are you referring? Explain." Councilor Ruran gave Kiel his undivided attention. He was a man known for diplomacy and fair play.

"Councilor, the reports you've read concerning Zebian all deal with his intelligence, his studies, his aptitude for the job you wish to assign him. They don't deal with his emotional state."

With a frown, Councilor Ruran studied the reports on his computer screen. "His psych exams are here as well. According to them, he's very well adjusted. You and Rick have done an excellent job with him these past six years. I understand your attachment…"

Kiel held up his hand for silence. "Please. It's not just that. Despite the fact that he appears to have recovered from the death of his parents, Zeb has built walls around himself. He won't let anyone in. Even though my mate and I have established a link with him, he will allow just so much contact before breaking away. It's been more than six months since his eighteenth birthday and he has yet to come to our bed. Have you heard of any Maleri' male who turned from his mentors in this way? In most cases, it's a struggle to curb the young one's enthusiasm and make them wait."

Councilor Ruran cleared his throat. "What you say is true, male sexual urges being what they are. Perhaps there's some disharmony of some sort?" he asked tentatively.

"No, the three of us get along very well together. Zeb takes advantage of his link with us when we make love, but he doesn't join us physically. He's keeping himself from becoming too involved. He's hiding behind those walls he's built. Sometimes I see it in his eyes and feel it so strongly when he looks at me or Rick. It's a longing so sharp it near brings me to my knees. He's hurting and he's afraid. I don't know how to free him from this fear."

There was silence between them for a time. Councilor Ruran sighed. "But what is there to be done about it, Kiel? We can't force the boy. This isn't an exercise of the intellect, something Zebian is so aptly talented for. It's an emotional issue. Perhaps some time apart from you and Rick will bring his need to the surface, make him unable to deny the fact that you two are his family and that he loves you."

"I only hope you're right. What I truly fear is that Zebian will succeed in burying his heart for good. If that happens, what will be his fate when he finally needs to seek a mate? Will he even try?" Kiel sat heavily on the chair in front of the Councilors desk, his eyes filled with worry.

Again there was silence between them. Each knew the answer to Kiel's question. For an unmated Maleri' male there was only one fate. Insanity and death.

"We will watch him closely. I want you and your mate to continue to have contact with him. If, after a suitable passage of time, we still feel there's a problem, we'll have to devise a plan to shake things up. Let's give the boy time to find his way."

Kiel nodded his agreement. "Perhaps you're right."

"Time will tell, Kiel. Time will tell."

Chapter One

Six Years Later

"But, sir, I'm not a field agent. I really don't think I'm the right person for this assignment." Zebian stood before Councilor Ruran, his stomach in knots. It wasn't often that he left his computers for face to face meetings with any of his fellow Maleri', especially not one with so exalted a position.

Councilor Ruran smiled kindly and gestured from behind the big desk that separated them. "Please sit down, Zebian." Zeb took the chair the councilor indicated. "You've been with Division Seven for six years now, is that right?" Zeb nodded. "By my calculations that makes you twenty-four. As you know, all of the Maleri' brotherhood are dedicated to helping those who have need. And all of us, at one time or another, have worked with people of other planets and cultures. It's high time you joined your brothers, Zebian."

"But, sir..."

Ruran held up his hand. "Let me fully apprise you of the assignment before you voice further objections."

Zeb held his tongue and waited. Best give the man his say, then back out as graciously as possible. Surely he'd be able to make the Councilor understand that sending him anywhere but back to his research would be a mistake. Zeb settled back in his chair, his confidence returning.

"The planet Casithia is, compared to many others in that sector, a very under developed and mostly rural planet.

Casithia's sister planet, Erogos, assumes guardianship of Casithia, providing defense from outsiders. Because of the system's development, it is there that the bulk of the system's food stuff is produced. While visiting here, the Erogian Minister was treated to a meal of Earth produced beef. To say the meal was a success is an understatement."

Councilor Ruran locked gazes with Zeb. "The Erogians want beef and they've shared what information they have about it with the Casithian High Council. The Casithians want to know how the ranches of Earth operate, what's involved in the everyday running of a ranch, the care of cattle, breeding procedures. Everything. The people of Casithia would profit a great deal from this. It would open a whole new trade for them with their sister planets in the system and beyond."

"So what has this to do with me?" Zeb asked, although he had a terrible suspicion he knew without asking.

"You, Zebian Bakar, are an expert at gathering and collating data. Your job will be to go to Earth and learn everything there is to know about ranching."

"Councilor Ruran! You can't be serious!"

"Oh, I am quite serious, young man. Arrangements have already been made for you to stay on an actual ranch on Earth in a place called, hmm, let me see..." Ruran flipped through several screens on his computer. "Ah yes, here it is. Wyoming. Interesting name, don't you think? Free Plains Ranch owned by a partnership of three, two silent partners and the man who runs the place, one Jace Fremont. Think of it, Zebian, a real Earth cowboy!"

"Cowboy?"

"Have you never watched any of Earth's entertainment vids?" Ruran asked, his expression incredulous.

"No, sir, I haven't."

"Then that's one of my first orders for you. You leave in three days, and to prepare I want you to watch at least three Earth vids about cowboys. They call them Westerns. I also want you to spend the next three days with Kiel and Rick. Rick will be a fount of information about this part of Earth's culture."

Zeb squirmed in his seat. Ever since he'd moved out, he'd managed to spend a minimum of time with Kiel and Rick, never staying more than a day with them and rarely two. Still, there was a lot of research to be done before he left. Perhaps he could avoid those feelings, both emotional and physical, that threatened to overwhelm him each time he found himself in their company.

He felt he had to try once more to wiggle out of this wretched assignment. "Sir, don't you think I would be of more use here? You could send someone else, let them send me the necessary data and I could collate it for the Casithians."

"No, I want you there. With your keen mind, you'll ferret out every iota of information needed. That's my final word on it, Zebian. Now go. Spend the next few days with Rick and Kiel. Rick is going to help you get outfitted with the proper clothing. I've informed them of your assignment and your pending arrival. Arrangements are already being made for your arrival on Earth. You will have a complete identity in place. No one will know you are from another planet."

Resigned to his fate, Zeb rose from his chair. "I'll do my best, Councilor Ruran."

"I never had any doubt of that Zebian."

* * *

Zeb stepped off the airplane and followed the other passengers to the terminal. A Beltholan ship had transported him to the surface, cloaking itself against detection. He was deposited near an airport in a place called New York and, according to plan, boarded a plane bound for Wyoming. Once there, he was to be met by an employee of Free Plains Ranch. His arrival was orchestrated to look normal should anyone be curious as to where he'd arrived from.

His background and credentials were in order. His presence endorsed by two of the three partners who owned the ranch. The third, Jace Fremont, had been very vocal in his objections. Zeb understood his reluctance, considering the fact that it was Jace who'd be responsible for looking out for him. Still, he resented the implication that he'd be unable to take care of himself. How hard could ranching be?

He'd talked extensively with Rick and viewed the Western vids with him and Kiel. It seemed silly. A bunch of grown men riding horses and chasing cows all over great stretches of open land. What hadn't seemed silly was the fact that they wore weapons and spent a great deal of time shooting at each other. It was an overwhelming relief to him when Rick explained that the weapons and the shootings were things of the past. Modern day cowboys did not carry six shooters. Still, it seemed that Earth men, at least this breed of Earth men, were a rather rough bunch.

Zeb tightened his grip on his carryon bag. He was here. There was nothing to do but go forward. No matter how much he longed to call the ship to come for him.

Once inside the terminal he looked curiously around. There were gates like the one he'd arrived at with people coming and going. A huge open area was filled with seats for passengers awaiting their flights. Smells from several food stands assaulted his nostrils, and he smiled to himself at Rick's admonishment to stop at some eating place symbolized with yellow arches. He was instructed to have something called a cheeseburger. Oh, yes, and fries. Rick said they were delicious.

At this point his stomach was less than enamored at the thought of food and so he walked on, coming to the place where the passengers from his plane had gathered to retrieve their luggage. He stood still, letting his gaze wander the crowds. In a sea of cowboy hats, one stood out. Not for the hat, itself, but the body below it -- a man who literally took his breath away. A larger-than-life, modern day cowboy.

The man was tall, lean and lanky, his six-foot-three-inch frame sleek with wiry muscles. Zeb could see them clearly outlined by the fit of his clothes. A button-down shirt hugged his torso, muscles subtly rippling when he reached up to tip his hat to an elderly lady who spoke to him in passing. His cream colored shirt was tucked into tight blue jeans that lovingly clung to slim hips, and long legs that seemed to go on forever. A pair of well worn cowboy boots encased his feet.

When the man resettled his hat, Zeb could see his hair was dark brown and from his current position it looked as though the cowboy's eye color matched, also a deep, rich brown. The man's face had a finished, commanding look about it. Angular planes consisting of a strong jaw line, high cheekbones and a clean well-defined brow gave his visage a sharp edge. The cream color of his shirt set off the dark, golden tan of his skin to perfection.

He appeared to be searching the crowd for someone when those brown eyes locked with his. Zeb felt himself drawn to the man, walking straight to him as though lassoed. He stopped a few feet away. The urge to speak was strong, but the words he needed were just plain missing and so he waited silently. He didn't have to wait long.

"You Zeb Bakar?"

"Yes," he answered with a nod, relieved that his tongue had finally decided to cooperate.

"Mmm. Jace Freemont." He held out his hand to Zeb.

Zeb shook hands as he'd been taught. No one told him about the surge of heat that accompanied such a gesture. Surely that wasn't normal, was it? Especially when it zinged straight to his cock? He released Jace's hand, fingers curling around the fading flash.

"You got more luggage?"

"One suitcase."

"Let's grab it and go, Zeb. I got work waitin' at home."

Zeb nodded and went back to the baggage claim, finding his case had been taken off the belt by one of the airline employees. He grabbed it up and walked back to Jace.

"Truck's this way."

Jace turned and led the way out the double bank of glass doors and across the passenger unloading zone. A wave of warm air enveloped them, noticeable after the artificial cool of the airport's interior. Zeb let his gaze take it all in. There was a lot to see. The terminal, people coming and going, planes taking off, vehicle after vehicle parked in the huge lot. And Jace's backside. He kept winding up with his eyes glued to the man's ass, fascinated by the firm rounds of flesh that moved under tight, faded denim.

Zeb's heartbeat increased, his breath sped up and the palms of his hands began to sweat. *It's the heat. Just the heat.* Never mind the fact that his cock was stirring, a subtle throb making itself felt with the slow infusion of blood that plumped his flesh.

Jace stopped beside a dark blue pickup truck. "Throw your bag in the back," he instructed, keying the door locks and settling himself behind the steering wheel.

Zeb lifted his suitcase into the bed of the truck, opened the passenger door and climbed in. He settled his carryon bag at his feet and sat back, taking a deep breath. A subtle scent, rich and masculine, invaded his nostrils. His cock jerked, acknowledging the pleasing aroma. He squirmed a bit in his seat, grateful for the tunic that covered his lap. *This is ridiculous! And totally unacceptable.* His body seemed to disagree and Zeb tried breathing through his mouth to avoid the temptation of Jace's scent.

It was then he noted the fact that they were still sitting motionless in the lot. He looked over at Jace. Jace was looking back with one eyebrow raised. "What?"

"Seatbelt, kid. Don't want to have to pay a fine cause you're not wearin' your seatbelt."

"Oh. Sorry." Zeb felt his cheeks flush. He should have remembered that. It was part of Rick's lessons.

Why, after all this time, was his damn libido coming out of hibernation and messing not only with his body, but his mind? Where was the control he prided himself on? Hadn't he resisted Kiel and Rick's allure for *three days*? And they were enough to make the cock on a dead man rise. What was so special about this man? Sure he was tall, sleek, gorgeous and belonged to that masculine, tough and somewhat mythical breed of men called cowboys. So what?

Zeb rolled his eyes and suppressed the wry smile that tugged at his lips. So all right, there was a lot about him that was special.

Jace started the truck and steered it out of the lot. They left the airport behind and merged onto a four lane highway. Nothing was said for a time, but it wasn't a comfortable silence. Zeb could almost feel the tension radiating from the man at his side. He fleetingly wondered if the reason for it was the same as his own and was disconcerted at the disappointment he felt when logic assured him it couldn't possibly be so.

Surprising himself, he spoke up. "Why don't you go ahead and say whatever's on your mind."

Jace gave him a quick glance before returning his gaze to the road. "I'm all for plain speaking, so here it is. First off, nothing personal, but I didn't want you here."

"I know. I also know it probably won't help for you to hear this, but I didn't want to come here."

Jace snorted. "Well, looks like we both got bushwhacked. You know how to ride a horse?"

"No."

"Know anything about ranching, about cattle?"

"No."

"I knew it. A complete greenhorn."

"Greenhorn, I know that term. A friend explained it to me." He wasn't about to tell Jace that it was Rick who'd explained the term while they'd been watching a Western vid. "And yes, according to the definition, I'm a greenhorn but I learn quickly. That's what I'm here to do. Learn."

"And just why is that, Zeb? You got a hankerin' to be a cowboy?"

"They didn't explain to you why I'm here?"

"Yeah, they did. But I want to hear it from you."

Zebian sighed. "I'm here to learn ranching techniques so I can pass the information on to the people of an underdeveloped nation. They want to raise cattle and provide beef to the people of their country and those nearby."

"Mmm hum, that's what I was told. And just where is this underdeveloped nation?"

"In Africa."

"Africa."

"Yes, Africa."

"And just how are these people, if they're so poor, gonna be able to afford breeding bulls and heifers to start a herd?"

"They have the financial backing of a more powerful nation."

"I see. And that's what hooked my partners. They made a big-assed deal to sell one hellacious bunch of cattle to these people. These people who know absolutely nothing about cows."

Zeb gave Jace a patient look. "They will know. When I'm done here."

Jace gave him a speculative look. "I'll say one thing for you. You don't lack confidence in the job you *do* know. I hope you brought more appropriate clothes to wear than what you've got on. They definitely don't look like they'd stand up to what you're gonna be doin'."

Zeb looked down at his pale gray tunic and dark gray slacks. The material was light with a linen-like weave and entirely unsuitable for the rough work he'd seen cowboys doing in the Westerns. "I have jeans and tee shirts in my suitcase. My superiors researched as carefully as possible to make sure I was prepared for this task."

"Well, that's good. At least I won't have to take you shopping for clothes. I hate that shit. But I'll tell you, Zeb, clothes won't get the job done. You've got some hard days ahead of you. I hope you're ready."

"So do I," Zeb answered, letting silence fall between them.

* * *

Jace took the exit off the highway that led to the ranch. The further he drove, the less populated the area became until it was just miles and miles of fenced in range with pockets of cattle scattered across it as far as the eye could see. This was his life and he smiled as the tension eased out of his shoulders. He hated going into the big town. Too much hustle and hurry, and for reasons that just didn't seem to make much sense.

He'd take the quiet of the ranch anytime. Early mornings with a hot cup of coffee in hand, watching the sunrise. Being covered in dust and dirt after a hard day's work. Nights with the occasional lowing of the cattle and the constant, musical chirruping of the crickets. Stars so bright in the night sky a man could almost reach up and pluck a handful. Now that was living, even if it did get a bit lonesome sometimes.

Yeah, he had the company of the hired hands working with him, good men all of them. But there was no one waiting for him at the house when he came in hot and tired. No one to fix supper with or watch television with. When he'd taken the money he'd saved and the legacy from his granddaddy to buy a third share in Free Plains, things had changed.

He no longer lived with the hands. It wouldn't be proper or fair to the men to have him living with them. Too restrictive to have the boss man constantly under foot. He maintained enough informality to be invited to poker games and Rusty, the foreman, came up to the house for their Wednesday night chess game, but he'd lived alone in his house. Until now.

The greenhorn kid was staying with him. Jace glanced over at his passenger. Zeb was looking out the window, eyes shining, a small smile on his lips. And nice lips they were too, full but not pouty. *The bottom one looks downright edible.* Jace frowned. Where the hell did that thought come from?

Jeez, Freemont, how long's it been since you had your ashes hauled? You need to get laid.

Thinking about it, Jace realized that it sure as shit had been a good, long time since he'd gone looking for company. Men were his preference. He was thirty-seven and had never been married. Hell, he'd never bothered to hide his sexuality. It was an accepted supposition by most that he was gay. No one commented on it and Jace didn't flaunt the fact. When he played, it was out of town, though there had been offers more than a time or two from hired hands over the years.

Those offers he didn't accept. It made for too precarious a situation. It'd be fine as long as he and the other guy were gettin' along, but what happened if he decided to break things off? A jilted lover living practically in his back pocket? No thank you.

Jace let his mind wander back to Zeb. Much as he'd objected to the kid coming around, this deal was going to make the ranch his. He hadn't exaggerated when he told Zeb that a contract for the sale of enough cattle to supply every steak house in Texas had been drawn up between Free Plains and the backers for that underdeveloped country.

For finally giving his permission and giving up his share of the profit in that deal, the ranch was being signed over to him lock, stock, and barrel. All his. No more silent partners to deal with. No more talking himself blue in the face, trying to make sophisticated city types understand why the purchase of a prize bull was necessary to keep the bloodlines clean or why more fields needed to be planted with hay to keep them well supplied through the winter.

The decisions and the consequences were all his. While the decisions had pretty much been his anyway -- the partners usually came around to his way of thinking -- the consequences would have been split three ways. Now, profit or loss, it was all on him. The ranch operated in the black for all the years Jace had been foreman and for the three years he'd been part owner. Barring some disaster, there was no reason to think it wouldn't continue that way. Jace knew ranching and it showed.

He also knew he'd watch out for the kid. Wasn't his fault he'd been sent here. Jace's sense of fair play came to the fore, but he still puzzled over a few things. Like the kid's name. Zeb, now there was a down-home sounding name. But Bakar? What was that, Greek? And what the hell was the kid wearing? Jace had seen city types in suits but this was something else. Kid must be one of those, whaddya call 'em, yuppies.

"Where you from, Zeb?" Jace asked, curiosity getting the better of him.

"New York."

"Oh, that explains it."

"Explains what?"

"Your clothes."

"What's wrong with them?"

"Nothin'. I was just wonderin' where people wore stuff like that. New York City, well, that explains it."

When Zeb frowned and shrugged, Jace felt a smile tug at his lips. The kid was cute, no doubt. He was distracted from further observation by their arrival at the ranch. "This is it, Zeb," he said and even Jace could hear the pride in his own voice. They turned down a two lane road and drove under a tall archway that proudly proclaimed this land to be Free Plains Ranch.

Home.

Chapter Two

Jace pulled up in front of the house, got out and watched Zeb pull his suitcase out of the truck bed. "This is the main house, my house. You'll be staying here with me." Zeb nodded and followed him up the steps to the front porch. They turned and looked out over the property.

"This is amazing. Everything's so big," Zeb commented in awe.

Up close, there were several large barns, some smaller buildings and what appeared to be a second house. The fields close to the barns held horses and a few cattle. Further out was the open range dotted with pockets of cattle as far as the eye could see. Beyond that, in the distance, were mountains. They rose cool and majestic, their tops wreathed with clouds. The sky was one unending blanket of pure, clear blue.

Jace felt a grin tug at his lips. *Yep, kid, lots of big things around here. Even some you can't see.* Out loud, he agreed with Zeb's statement. "That's why I like it. Lots of room for a man to stretch out." And didn't that just bring another wild thought to mind. Jace subtly adjusted his cock. Damn thing was gettin' ideas, plumpin' up like it was. *Down boy or you're gonna get a thump. Boss man can't be walkin' around with a blue steeler in his britches for the world to see.* "Come on in the house. We'll get you settled in and then see about your first horseback riding lesson. There's some damage to a section of fence I want to check out."

Jace led the way in. To the left was a dining room, and beyond, the kitchen. To the right, the living room, his office and further down the hall, a bathroom. Straight ahead, the stairs led up to three bedrooms -- two on one side, the bath and master bedroom on the other.

Jace stopped at the first door. "This'll be your room while you're here. Bathroom's across the hall, that's my room beyond. The other bedroom's empty. In case you're wondering."

"You live here alone?"

"Yep. Change your clothes, kid. I'll wait downstairs for you."

"All right, and by the way, my name is Zeb, not kid."

Jace shot him an unrepentant grin. "How old are you, Zeb?"

"Twenty-four."

"I'm thirty-seven. To me you're a kid. Your greenhorn status just makes it that much more apparent. You show me you got some smarts and backbone, and I'll elevate you to man status."

"That's the most ridiculous thing I've ever heard," Zeb replied, his voice tinged with puzzlement and irritation.

"Probably won't be before your time here's up. But that's my opinion. Get changed."

Without waiting for a reply, Jace clattered his way downstairs to wait. The kid didn't keep him waiting long and Jace did a double take as he came downstairs. Well now, hmm. Out of that loose-fitting suit, the kid's body was nice. Though not particularly tall, Zeb's five-feet-ten-inch frame was nicely proportioned. His navy blue tee shirt set off his dark blond hair and made his frosty blue eyes seem darker. It also emphasized the fact that the kid had some muscle definition to his upper body.

His jeans, obviously new but laundered soft, clung to thigh muscles that bunched with each step. They weren't skin tight but tight enough to prove it was a man who wore them. The kid had a nice bulge behind that zipper and Jace felt his stomach do an unaccustomed flip at the thought. Zeb had a leather strap over his shoulder that went diagonally across his chest. It held what looked like a small leather saddle bag.

"What's in the pack?" Jace asked when Zeb took the final step down.

"My FGDL."

"And that is?"

"Field Grade Data Link. While I'm out with you I can input data that will go directly to the computer I set up in my room."

"I see," Jace commented, his gaze coming to rest on Zeb shoes. He wore black athletic type shoes. "No boots? You bring a hat with you?"

Zeb shook his head. "It didn't seem right." His gaze met Jace's, his look open and sincere. "It felt like putting on a uniform I didn't earn. I'm no cowboy."

For some reason, Zeb's admission struck a cord within Jace. The kid was earning points fast. "I think I got a hat you can use. You're gonna need it, Zeb. Sun'll fry your brain and that pale skin of yours is gonna suffer unless you put somethin' on it."

"I'll be okay."

Jace shrugged. "Don't say I didn't warn you." Jace went to a closet down the hall and came back with a billed cap that read 'Brown's Tractor Supply.' "Here ya go. Try this on for size." Zeb put the hat on and his head was immediately engulfed. Jace snickered. "Seems to need a bit of an adjustment." He took the hat and reworked the snaps at the back. "There, try that."

Zeb took the cap and it settled on his head just right. "This is good."

"All right. Let's get to it."

Jace led the way outside and pointed out various barns, out buildings and fields as they crossed the large expanse of ground from the house to the horse barn. There were a couple of men here and there. One was working on a tractor, two more were unloading bags of feed from the back of another pickup truck. They yelled out greetings to Jace that he returned.

"I'll introduce you to everyone at the bunkhouse tonight. For right now, this is the most important introduction you need." They entered the cooler, dim recesses of the horse barn and walked along a row of stalls before exiting out the back to a fenced in corral. "This is Miss Molly and Whirlwind. Guess which one you're riding."

Miss Molly was a sedate bay mare with two white socks who walked up to Jace and Zeb, her nose questing over Jace's pockets for treats. Jace pulled a carrot out of his pocket and held it out to her. Molly crunched it down and looked for more. "Here," he handed Zeb a carrot. "Hold your hand palm up, fingers straight out. Wouldn't want her accidentally nibbling off something you need."

Cautiously, Zeb did as he was told and was rewarded by the velvet soft brush of Molly's nose against his palm as she delicately took the carrot from him. "Oh, she's so soft." Hesitantly, Zeb reached out to touch.

"Go ahead, you can pet on her. Molly's a doll baby. You'll be riding her. And I'll be riding that yahoo over there. Get your butt over here, Whirly." The tall, rangy buckskin-colored horse Jace spoke to gave him a disdainful look and shook his head, his long mane flying. "He's pissed cause he didn't go out with the rest of the boys this mornin'." Jace approached his horse, clucking and promising carrots. Whirly's ears pricked forward and he deigned to let Jace feed him a couple of treats before following him to where Zeb and Molly waited.

"Let's saddle up. You say you learn fast?" Jace asked.

"Yes."

"Let's test that. You watch while I get Whirly saddled and bridled, then you can give it a try with Molly. A man needs to know how to saddle his own horse." Jace went about the business of getting Whirly ready with Zeb's gaze resting intently on him. Whirly's halter was replaced by bridle and bit. The saddle blanket, saddle and cinch followed. When he was done, Jace turned to Zeb. "Your turn," he said, indicating Molly's tack.

Zeb followed Jace's example. He was slower, his actions a bit more tentative and cautious, but he managed the feat with competence. Jace examined Molly's tack, tightening the cinch before turning to Zeb.

He gave him a nod. "Not bad. You do learn fast. Now let's see if you can stay in the saddle. You don't look soft like a good many city folk I see."

"I go to my local heath center every other day. Just because I sit behind a desk is no reason to be soft, as you put it."

Jace moved to Whirly to demonstrate mounting. "Left foot in the stirrup, haul yourself up, right leg over and plant your foot in the other stirrup. Go to it." Again Zeb emulated Jace's example. "Good," Jace praised.

He went on to explain the use of heel and reins, and the two of them left the barn at an easy walk. Jace carefully watched Zeb. The kid was taking to riding with ease. He kept a firm grip on the reins but wasn't putting undue pressure on Molly's mouth. He also had good balance and a natural seat. Actually, a nice, tight, round little seat that hugged the saddle like it was made to fit there.

Jace's fingers flexed on his own reins for a moment, hands itching to cup those tempting cheeks. He uttered a quick curse under his breath while his cock came to life. Saddles and hard-ons were unforgiving bedfellows and he gave his cock a surreptitious thump to make it behave. A grimace crossed his face just as Zeb and Molly dropped back beside him and Whirly.

"Did I do something wrong?" Zeb asked, clearly concerned that the grimace was directed at him.

"No, Zeb. I was just thinking about something," Jace assured him. Damn glad the kid had no idea just exactly what was going through his head. "Let's try a slow lope. You up for it?"

Zeb nodded and they took off across the open fields.

They rode for a couple of hours, Jace checking various stretches of fence until he came to one with red pieces of cloth tied to it. The fence had been repaired by his men. The tracks of several trucks were impressed into the grass and dirt. Jace stepped down off Whirly and bent to examine them. Zeb followed his lead. Some of the tracks followed the fence line coming from the direction of the ranch. Another set came from off over the range.

"Damn," Jace snarled.

"What is it?" Zeb asked.

"Cattle rustlers."

"What? I thought that was only in vids, um, movies." He'd taken out his FGDL and was tapping away one handed at the keys.

Jace stood and gave him a serious look. "Wish it was. See those tracks?" He pointed out the second set. "There's a road about a mile away. These bastards drive in, cut through the fence and take down as many head as they can carry. They shoot 'em and butcher 'em right out here in the field, and truck the meat out to sell."

"But who would buy stolen meat?"

"People who don't know it's stolen. They take it across the state and sell it out of nice, small, innocent looking refrigerated trucks. Sell it on street corners. Just a good ole boy givin' a good deal on prime beef."

"Does this happen often?"

"Now and then, but it's escalated," Jace explained. "Between Free Plains and the other ranches in the area, they've taken near a hundred head in the last six months."

"With all the cattle you have here," Zeb gestured to the cows dotting the landscape, "how do you know how many you've lost?"

Jace gave him a look, one brow raised. "They leave behind the parts they can't use. Like the heads."

"Oh." Zeb's cheeks flushed and Jace noticed he was also starting to burn.

"Yeah. If we had a clue where they might strike, we could put an end to this but with this much land to cover..." Jace shook his head. "Impossible. Come on, Zeb, it's late. Sun'll be goin' down by the time we get back."

They mounted up. Jace became aware of the fact that Zeb didn't seem to have as much spring as he did when they'd first headed out. *Greenhorn kid's gonna be sore tonight.* He shrugged. Nothin' he could do about that. His bosses sent him and the kid was gonna pay the price.

By the time they got back and settled Molly and Whirly in their stalls, the sun was slipping down toward the horizon. Jace stopped at the bunkhouse to get a report from Rusty, and to introduce Zeb to him and the rest of the boys. Zeb shook hands all around and was polite, but Jace could see he was tired and hurting so he made it quick. By the time Zeb got the house, he was walking gingerly.

"Sore?" Jace asked when they got inside and hung their hats on the hat rack by the front door.

"Yeah."

"Go on up and run yourself a hot bath and soak. I'll use the shower down here."

Zeb started upstairs and paused, turning back. "I'm sorry I'm taking up your time. I know you have better things to do than escort me around, but I do appreciate it. I… I liked Molly and the riding. I guess it'll take me a while to get used to it. Probably by the time I do I'll be leaving but, anyway, thank you. I appreciate your patience."

Jace looked up at Zeb, taking in the tired set of his shoulders, the lines of pain around his mouth and the sunburn glowing on his skin. He felt a slow smile spread across his lips and a wave of warmth within. "You got balls, Zeb. You're a good man. Go on up and soak. I'll have supper ready in about an hour. That suit you?"

Zeb smiled back and nodded. It was a shy smile accompanied by another hint of a blush. Jace felt his innards clench. Zeb turned and continued his slow pace upstairs. Jace sucked in a deep breath and softly swore to himself. *Fuck. The kid's gonna keep me hard the entire time he's here.*

He headed to the downstairs bathroom. Jace stripped off his clothes and got into the shower, standing under the hot spray, letting it soothe his taut muscles. The only thing that wouldn't relax was his cock. It stood straight and stiff, fully aroused, refusing to relax. Jace soaped himself and took a firm hold of his rigid cock. Slow, deliberate strokes drew a moan from his lips as they parted.

Heat surrounded him, the water sliding over his skin in a constant caress. He closed his eyes, his free hand planted against the shower wall as he pulled and stroked himself. Under the sound of the water he could hear his own breaths, faster and harder than normal. The undulations of his hips drove his cock through the tight tunnel of his fist, the pace matching the thudding pulse he felt against the palm of his hand.

He slid his thumb over the fat tip and groaned, his head falling back with the pleasure that swept up his spine. His body on automatic, he let his thoughts wander and found them filled with a pair of ice-blue eyes in boyish face topped by dark blond hair. The thought of Zeb's shy smile and trim body revved his engine. The thought of him naked in the tub upstairs brought the revving up to a scream. When he thought about bending him over, parting those sweet, plump cheeks and burying himself to the hilt, he popped a wheely and exploded.

"Son of a bitch," he growled, hoarse and low, semen spilling over his hand to land with a splat against the shower wall.

He slowed his stroke, easing out the final spurts as waves of pleasure shuddered over him. Knees near to buckling, he leaned against the shower wall until his strength returned, then quickly finished his shower and dried himself. He took a swipe at the steam clouded bathroom mirror with his towel and looked at his reflection while heaving a huge sigh. "S'pose it'd be a miracle if the kid swung my way."

He gave himself a self-deprecating grin and shook his head while wrapping the towel around his waist. Climbing the stairs he noted the closed bathroom door and heard a muffled splash. Zeb was in the tub. Naked. Jace paused for a split second, then forced himself to go on to his room. Once there, he dropped the towel and traded it for a soft pair of black sweats and a thin white tee shirt. Barefoot, he headed back down to rustle up supper for the two of them. If he paused at the bathroom door a second time, he didn't acknowledge it, even to himself.

* * *

Zeb gingerly heaved himself out of the tub and patted himself dry with a towel. While the soak had helped a great deal with his sore muscles, his inner thighs were still tender. He opened the bathroom door and started across the hall to his room, halting at the faint sound of a voice. Jace was singing as he prepared supper. Zeb listened intently and realized there was music as well.

He smiled and took a deep breath, his stomach rumbling at the delicious smells that wafted up the stairs from below. Entering his room, he dropped his towel and took out a pair of navy colored pants Rick called sweats. They were soft and light, something he knew his abused thighs would appreciate. Donning a light blue tee shirt, he fleetingly thought of shoes then shrugged. He never wore them while at home, and Rick and Kiel didn't either. Maybe Jace would be all right with him being barefoot.

When he entered the kitchen, he discovered he needn't have worried about the shoes. Jace, too, was barefoot and dressed almost exactly the same as he was, the only difference being their choice of colors. Jace's back was to him and Zeb used the time to admire the man. All day his awareness of Jace had grown, and despite his body being tired and sore, his cock still wanted to stand up and beg.

Snapping his attention from Jace's tight ass, Zeb cleared his throat. "Anything I can do to help?" he offered.

Jace looked around and grinned. "Hey. Feeling better?"

"Yes, almost normal."

"Good. There's iced tea and lemonade in the fridge if you want to fill our glasses. I'll have the iced tea. I fixed some fajita meat, steak. There's tortillas and I've got cheese, salsa, sour cream, refried beans, lettuce and tomato to throw on 'em. It's not fancy, but it'll fill you up. There's some chocolate cake in the fridge and ice cream in the freezer if you want dessert."

"It looks good. Smells good too." Zeb poured the drinks, trying a sip each of lemonade and tea before deciding he liked the tea. "I heard you singing from upstairs. You have a nice voice."

Jace chuckled. "Thanks. Guess I can carry a tune well enough to keep the coyotes from howlin'."

Zeb smiled, pleased when he realized he'd made Jace blush for a change. The man was so confident, so in charge. It was nice to know he had some vulnerability. Made it easier to accept his own shortcomings.

Jace placed a bowl filled with the steaming hot, seasoned pieces of steak on the table and gestured. "Have a seat and dig in."

Not sure where to start, Zeb hung back a bit and emulated Jace as he built his fajita. His first one had everything on it and Zeb devoured it like a starving man. It amazed him how a day of fresh air and exercise had affected his appetite. His second and third fajitas he fixed sans beans, deciding he didn't care for the taste of them. His fourth was basically just meat, cheese and sour cream, and after eating it he was sure he'd had enough until Jace tempted him with chocolate cake.

Together they cleaned up the remains of their meal. Zeb put things away in the fridge while Jace rinsed the dishes and stacked them in the dishwasher. "Are you planning to do anything specific now?" Zeb asked Jace as he closed the dishwasher and started the cycle.

"Nope. Just thought I'd laze in front of the television for a while, maybe watch a movie then go to bed. You got something in mind?"

"I was wondering if we could talk about ranching techniques. I could get my FGDL and start gathering the data my, um, clients need."

Jace shrugged. "Sure. Go get it. I'll be in the living room."

Zeb nodded and hurried upstairs as quickly as his sore legs would let him. During the meal they'd begun to ache and grow stiff. He ignored the pain, grabbed his FGDL and joined Jace on the sofa in the living room. They talked for a couple of hours. Jace answered all his questions and offered things that Zeb wouldn't have known to ask about. He ended up with stream after stream of info going into his computer and felt for the first time since he'd arrived that maybe, just maybe, his presence really was necessary here.

Eventually they wound down and Jace turned on the television, telling Zeb he wanted to catch the news. They sat in silence, watching. Zeb was saddened by all the unrest and killings that seemed to plague Earth. While he didn't understand their reasons, it seemed like such a waste for so many people to die in these wars their leaders seemed so fond of saying were necessary.

Now that they were quiet, Zeb became hyper-aware of the man at his side. Jace's scent, warm, musky and subtle drifted to him in teasing wafts. It was exciting and yet comforting as well. Zeb found himself relaxing, drifting, his eyelids fluttering closed as the drone of voices on the television continued.

"Hey, Zeb. Time to wake up and go to sleep as the Three Stooges always say."

"Huh?" Zeb blinked his sleep heavy eyelids.

"Never mind." Jace chuckled. "Time for bed."

"Oh, all right." Zeb started to rise and dropped back down on the sofa with a hiss and a groan. "Oh, damn that hurts!"

Jace gave him a sympathetic grimace. "Your legs?"

"Yes, and my skin is burning."

"I tried to warn you about that," Jace told him. "Sit still a minute and let me get some stuff from the bathroom. I'll be right back."

Zeb stayed seated, stretching his legs out and wiggling his ankles, working his calf muscles and generally trying to ease the kinks out. He frowned in concentration, grimacing with every twinge. It felt like his thighs were still wrapped around Molly, the muscles strained and aching.

Jace came back with a large towel, a damp washcloth, a bottle of brown liquid and tube of something else. He placed everything on the floor, spreading the towel out, then held his hand out to Zeb. "Lemme help you up."

Zeb took his hand and with a groan but with surprisingly little effort on his part, got his feet under him. Jace was clearly very strong. "Thanks. Now what?" Zeb asked.

"Now you drop your drawers." Jace replied, his brown eyes twinkling with suppressed mirth.

"Drop my drawers?"

"You know, strip."

A shiver slid down Zeb's spine. "And why am I doing this?"

"Cause I can't rub the liniment on your legs or the aloe gel on your sunburn with your clothes on."

"Oh."

Feeling a little lightheaded and very self-conscious, Zeb stripped his tee shirt over his head and dropped it on the sofa. Keeping his eyes downcast, he slipped his sweats down, wondering what Jace would think of his lack of underwear. With an effort, he stepped out of them and sent them to join his tee shirt. Was it his imagination that made him think he heard a small groan? He wasn't sure. He couldn't hear very well over the pounding of his own heart.

"Okay, um, lay down on the towel. Face down."

Gingerly Zeb complied and let loose another groan once he settled and the pressure was off his legs. He felt Jace settle at his side, heard the rustle of his clothing and the top being taken off the liniment bottle.

"The smell of this stuff'll make your eyes water but it'll make you feel better. I guarantee it."

Zeb closed his eyes and forced himself to relax. At the first touch of Jace's hands, warm and wet with liniment, he was unable to suppress the small moan that crawled from deep inside his chest. Jace's hands settled on the back of his thigh and massaged the tight, tender muscles until they grew loose and pliant. His hands moved down the length of Zeb's leg and spent some time on his calf muscles as well, his fingers digging in and loosening the knots.

Zeb sighed with growing relief and growing arousal. With the pain being massaged away and his muscles going lax, his body was concentrating on tightening another part of his anatomy. His cock was filling and he lifted slightly to ease the ache and give it room before settling back on the towel. Embarrassing as it was, there was nothing he could do about it, at least not at the moment. So he merely concentrated on the heat and comfort Jace's hands were bestowing.

Jace moved to his other leg and started at the calf this time, working his way up. As his hands moved higher, Zeb could feel his arousal climb up his spine like mercury in a thermometer. It was all he could do not to start humping the towel.

Jace's hands had reached the back of his thigh when Jace spoke, his voice husky and strained. "Spread your legs for me, babe."

Both of them froze.

Chapter Three

"Spread your legs for me, babe, um, Zeb." Jace corrected quickly and started silently cursing himself for being every kind of a damn fool at the slip.

It was just, damn. Damn! Ever since he'd first laid eyes on the kid there was something about him that had drawn Jace like a bee to honey. He was cute and kinda shy, yet there was a determination about him, a toughness that shone through when it was something he believed in, like the job he was doing. He wasn't afraid to express his opinions or stand up for himself despite the vulnerability that was so evident in his eyes.

In the short time they'd spent together, Jace had felt an almost overwhelming need to reach out to Zeb to… to… hell, he wasn't sure what. Part of it was to comfort, to offer his friendship and understanding, and part of it was just plain physical need. He felt something in Zeb drawing at him, luring him, arousing him until now, with his hands on Zeb's body, all he wanted to do was ride him. All night long.

His cock had gone rigid when the kid stripped his clothes off and laid down on the towel. How could he not get hard at the sight of Zeb naked as the day he was born? It was obvious Zeb worked to keep himself in shape. His muscles were firm and well defined. They moved with fluid grace when Zeb shifted his position. And his skin. Double damn! Like pure Chinese silk under his hands. And warm. And smooth, just inviting him, addicting him to the touch.

Was there any need to mention his ass? Good Lord. He'd known it was nice from the shape of it under Zeb's jeans, but, well, fuck! Those two firm mounds were just the most beautiful things he'd ever seen. Full, perfect curves accented by manly dimples at the outer top of the curve. Who could blame a man for wanting to lean down and run his tongue over those sweet indentations?

Jace knew, too, that he wasn't the only one aroused. Though he'd tried to be unobtrusive while doing it, Zeb had lifted his hips a couple of times and did this tiny little wiggle that nearly drove Jace out of his mind. The kid was trying to give his cock room the stretch out. Jace could clearly see his balls, sleek and smooth, drawing up closer to his body. He was excited and the excitement was visibly rising.

Gritting his teeth, Jace continued the massage, gently working Zeb's inner thighs while trying to avoid two things: applying too much friction to his slightly reddened, sensitive skin and touching his balls. His fingers came really close a couple of times. Zeb was temptation on a stick and it took the devil's own determination not to reach down and cup those tender orbs in his hand.

Trying desperately to get a grip on himself, Jace knew he'd done all he could do while Zeb was on his stomach. It was time to face the music. Or in this case, Zeb's cock. "Turn over, Zeb. Let me do the front." He could see Zeb visibly tighten up and decided there was no reason to be coy about it. "Look, Zeb, I know you're hard. Hell, I am too. Touching and being touched has a tendency to make that happen. It's normal. I'll ignore it if you will. Deal?"

Zeb lay quietly for a moment then answered. "All right."

He rolled to his back and shimmied his body over so he was centered back on the towel. His eyes were closed and Jace was hell and gone grateful for the fact. Did he say he was going to ignore Zeb's hard-on? He'd certainly made a liar out of himself. He couldn't take his eyes off it. Zeb's cock was fully erect and lying against his belly. It was a thick ivory column wrapped with plump veins, the smooth cap flushed and glowing with an inner heat. And right before his eyes, a clear drop of succulent, male honey oozed from the tip, teetering for a few aching seconds before sliding in a slow, mesmerizing trickle over the satiny skin of that plump head.

Jace swallowed hard. His breath, his growl, his need. Like an automaton, he poured more liniment into his hand and warmed it while struggling to make his mind blank. Jaw clenching, he laid his hands on the top of one of Zeb's thighs and proceeded with the massage. By the time he was done, Zeb's muscles were relaxed and loose under his hands. His breath was coming a bit fast, small moans passed his lips a couple of times and his cock was leaking a steady stream of pre-cum but by God, he would be able to walk without pain.

Jace, on the other hand, was wound up so tight he felt like running out into the night and howling at the moon. After maybe a five or ten mile jog. He used the damp washcloth to wipe the liniment off his hands and reached for the tube of aloe gel.

"Sit up," he ordered gruffly and rolled his eyes at the tight, rough timber of his voice. He cleared his throat. Zeb sat up and their eyes met briefly before Jace looked down at the tube in his hands. Zeb's eyes were wide and a bit wild. Jace opened the flip cap and squeezed some of the gel onto his fingers. His need to reach for Zeb's cock was so great he was surprised and grateful his hands weren't shaking. "This'll help with the sunburn. You got burned on the back of your neck. Let me get that since you can't see it, and you can reach the rest yourself."

Zeb turned slightly so Jace could reach and rub the gel gently into his reddened skin. When he drew his hand away, Zeb was watching him. His blue eyes had gone dark, no hint of the normal frost pale color left. There was something there, something in his eyes that drew Jace closer. It was desire and fear and need. Pure uncertainty and lust all rolled into one. Jace felt a smile tug at his lips, momentarily distracted by the glowing red at the tip of Zeb's nose.

"Your nose is sunburned," he murmured softly.

"Where?" Zeb asked, his eyes crossing in an attempt to see it for himself.

Jace laughed. "Didn't your momma ever tell you not to do that? Your eyes'll get stuck that way, mine always said."

"My mother and father died when I was twelve."

"Well, now…" Jace felt his heart clench in sympathy. "I'm real sorry to hear that, Zeb. Damn hard for a boy to lose his folks at that age. Here, let me put some aloe on your nose."

Jace reached up and gently brushed his gel coated fingers over Zeb's skin. First his nose, his cheeks then his chin. His gaze met Zeb's once more and he was transfixed by the emotions there until Zeb closed his eyes. Jace knew he was lost. He leaned in and settled his lips over Zeb's.

The kiss was sweet and gentle. Their lips came together and fit like two pieces of a puzzle long overdue at being put together. Twin moans of pleasure and need issued forth and were exchanged as their lips parted and each accepted the push of the other's tongue. Jace slid his arms around Zeb and pulled him close, gratified by the feel of Zeb reciprocating. Zeb wiggled in his arms, struggling to bring as much of them together as possible in their current position.

Never breaking the kiss, Jace pushed firmly, easing Zeb down on his back until they were laid out against each other. It was only then he began to notice the odd pressure building in his head. It was joined by a phantom swirling movement and he vaguely thought, *I'm gettin' dizzy.* Jace struggled to break free from the kiss, to take a breath of air, but the whirling and pressure came faster and harder. With a suddenness that took his breath away, orgasm burst over him, leaving his mind opened and exposed.

His life literally passed before his eyes and not only *his* life but Zeb's. Somehow he knew that the sounds and smells and images that came roaring into his head were real. They were all connected with Zeb, and Jace had never been so shocked in his entire life. Zeb wasn't human. He wasn't from Earth. Jace saw his arrival and seeing it, seeing everything connected with Zeb, gave him the strength to tear himself free.

He flung himself away from Zeb and sat staring at him. With five feet of space between them, Jace could see that Zeb's eyes were dark and opened wide with shock. His breath heaved in his lungs and fine tremors ran over his body. Jace relaxed slightly. Zeb was just as affected as he was by what had taken place, perhaps even more so. It was a crazy comfort of sorts.

Zeb's arm lifted and slowly his hand came up to his mouth, his fingers just touching his kiss-swollen lips. "What did you do?"

Jace felt his own eyes widen. "What did I do? I'm not the alien here. What... who are you?"

"I'm exactly who I said I was. Zebian Bakar. The only difference is I'm not from where I said I was from. I'm not from New York."

"No shit. I saw that for myself."

"Oh, God, you saw it too?" Zeb started rocking slightly back and forth as though in the grip of panic. "This can't be happening. This can't be happening."

Jace felt a frisson of fear slide down his spine. Funny thing was, he wasn't sure if the fear was for himself, Zeb, or maybe both of them. All he knew was that whatever had happened it was causing Zeb to panic. Not knowing why had his own insides tied in knots.

"Zeb, get a hold of yourself." Jace moved closer and drew Zeb's gaze to his. "Talk to me. Tell me what's going on."

Zeb took a deep, shuddery breath and nodded, the shock receding from his eyes. He swallowed hard and took a couple more breaths, each one seeming to give him another measure of calm. "I'm from a planet called Belthola. I was sent here for exactly the reason I told you, although it's not a country on your planet that's purchasing the cattle. It's the people on a planet called Casithia."

Jace found himself nodding. What else could he do? There was no way to deny what he'd seen and felt in his own head. Somehow he knew Zeb was giving him the straight story.

"I'm Maleri'. I'm just as human as you are, Jace. But I and my Maleri' brothers have special gifts. We're empaths. We use our gifts to help people from other worlds in exchange for profit and concessions for the people of our own planet. Eventually our powers cause a build up of energy in our brains. An energy that, if not drained, will eventually cause insanity and death."

Zeb's gaze fastened to his and Jace suddenly knew what was coming as though it were spread out on a chalkboard in front of him. "When the time comes, we seek a mate. A man whose mind resonates with ours, a man who has some empathic ability of his own. Many of my brothers have found their mates here on Earth. All it takes is one kiss between compatible mates and a mind link is formed. Like the one growing between us," Zeb finished, his voice a near hoarse whisper. "I'm so sorry. I didn't know this would happen. I didn't think you would kiss me. I just didn't... when you touched me, I just stopped thinking."

Hearing Zeb's words, Jace knew without a doubt that everything he said was the truth. The link was growing stronger by the minute, he could almost feel an intangible part of himself opening and accepting that same illusive part of Zeb. Instead of being repulsed by the idea and the feel of it, something deep inside accepted and found pleasure in what was happening. He was honest enough to admit to the attraction he'd immediately felt for Zeb. This was just more of the same, only more intimate, more intense.

No matter how pleasant, it wasn't all sweetness and light. Here he was, a man of thirty-seven, deeply in love with his life, the ranch, the land. And there was Zeb, a kid of twenty-four with a life of his own on a planet God only knew how far away. All in all, it was a pretty fucked up situation and Jace didn't know how the hell they were going to straighten it out. As though suddenly saddled with the weight of the world, Jace slumped under the load of exhaustion that pressed in on him.

"Look, this is a lot to handle in such a short period of time. I need time to think and I'm betting you do too," Jace said. Zeb nodded. "I think we both should sleep on it."

"I agree," Zeb told him and rose. He reached for his sweats and pulled them on. His erection had deflated -- a sure sign of Zeb's stress. Jace could sympathize completely. His own cock had gone limp with shock, his libido having run off to hide.

Silently, Jace gathered up the towel, washcloth, and the bottle of liniment. He pressed the tube of aloe gel into Zeb's hand. "Put this on your arms and anywhere else you feel burned. Go on up to bed. I'll be up in a minute." Jace paused and considered how his words sounded. "What I mean is... oh, hell. Just go to bed, Zeb."

Zeb gave him a quick look. Saying nothing he headed for the stairs.

"Zeb," Jace called softly. "I want you to stay close to the house tomorrow. No riding. Give your muscles time to adjust."

"All right," Zeb agreed and slowly climbed the stairs.

Jace walked away, silent curses ringing out in his own head. He'd seen the wounded look that swiftly came, then was hidden in Zeb's eyes. What was worse, he'd felt the quick stab of Zeb's pain. He didn't want to hurt the kid but he needed, had to have, time to think about all this without Zeb near and clouding his thoughts.

He sighed heavily, dropping the things he carried in the bathroom then headed upstairs. This time there was no pausing outside Zeb's door. Jace went straight to his room, stripped and crawled into bed. There was only a fleeting thought of how much better it would be with Zeb in his arms before his waking senses deserted him and he drifted to sleep.

* * *

Zeb sat in his room in front of his computer. Normally his fingers would be flying over the keys, but not today. Today he sat and stared blankly at the screen in front of him. He had a mate. A sexy, kind, caring, strong and mature man who'd rejected him. He bit his lip and winced at the thought. It seemed fate wanted to play a twisted game, and once more it had chosen him as its focus. Zeb shook his head. He knew he had to go. And soon. Staying here, masking his growing need for Jace, would just be too difficult.

He finally forced his concentration to the work before him, his mind sifting through all the things he'd seen and learned. He added bits and pieces to the information on the screen when Jace's words about cattle rustlers ran through his mind. *If we had a clue where they might strike, we could put an end to this.* Zeb considered the words for a moment, then grabbed up his FGDL and went in search of one of the hands.

He found the foreman, Rusty, doling out orders to a couple of the men. Standing nearby, Zeb caught his attention before Rusty strode out of the barn to some other task. "I was wondering if I could ask you a few questions."

"Sure, Zeb. Jace said to give you anything in the way of information you need. What's up?"

Zeb smiled at him. Rusty was even older than Jace. He was a roughhewn man with auburn hair. Freckles danced across the bridge of his nose. He may have had a fair complexion at one time, but years out on the range had given his skin a toasty glow.

"I'd like to ask about the cattle rustling. Could you give me some information about where the different thefts took place? When and where and approximate times? Any details you can give me will help."

"Sure, I can do that. Come on over to the bunkhouse. I've got records of every incident that took place here on Free Plains."

"That would be very helpful," Zeb said and followed Rusty to the bunkhouse.

The two of them spent the next hour or so in the office while Rusty detailed each incident. Where on the ranch it took place, what the terrain was like, the nearest access road, what day of the month and on and on. Zeb recorded every little detail. When they were finished, Rusty headed back out to his duties. Zeb wandered out of the bunkhouse, his eyes glued to the screen of his FGDL.

It was only a shout and the wild clatter of hooves that drew his attention. He looked up in shock to see Jace on Whirly, galloping toward him from one direction and half a dozen cows bearing down on him from another. Jace reached him before the cows and placed Whirly directly in their path. The big buckskin reared and pawed the air, bringing the cows to an abrupt halt.

Jace clung to the big gelding as though this was an everyday occurrence. There was shouting as a couple more ranch hands on horses came galloping onto the scene. Zeb stumbled, his heel catching on a divot in the yard. He sprawled back, his ass hitting the ground with an abrupt and muffled thump and just managed to keep his FGDL from hitting the ground. From his position, his shocked and wide-eyed gaze moved up and up and fastened on Jace and Whirly as the horse settled back on all fours.

"God damn it, Zeb! You gotta watch where you're goin'! You coulda got yourself killed!"

Zeb scrambled to his feet. "I'm sorry. I didn't... I wasn't."

"Our fault, Jace. They got away from us," one of the hands spoke up. He was giving Zeb a look of sympathy.

"Doesn't matter. Zeb still shoulda been watching out. If you can't keep your nose outta that... that thing when you're walkin' around here," Jace gestured wildly, "then get your ass up to the house and *stay there!*"

Zeb clamped down on the flare of hurt that burned through him. Pivoting on the ball of his foot, he strode away to the house. He didn't say a word, didn't look back and refused to feel the faint echo of regret that battered his shields. He now knew more than ever that he was leaving as soon as possible. He'd set himself one last task, and as soon as it was accomplished he was gone.

* * *

With his heart pounding, Jace watched Zeb march away. Fuck! Why the hell did he have to let his tongue run away like that? Because he was scared, he realized. Scared for Zeb. When he'd seen those cows bearing down on him and Zeb just crossing the barnyard like he was taking a Sunday stroll in the park, Jace's stomach had done a flip that damned near made him lose his breakfast. If anything happened to Zeb, well, it didn't bear thinkin' on.

Then again, maybe it did. He'd known the kid for what, two days? In that short time Zeb not only had his cock constantly standing at attention but his emotions were tied in knots as well. How the hell was he supposed to ignore this? How was he supposed to pretend that nothing was happening? How the *fuck* was he supposed to handle it when Zeb walked away and went not just half a world away but out there somewhere to a place Jace never had a chance of reaching?

What am I gonna do? What can I do? I can't hold him here and I can't walk away from the ranch and my life. So where does that leave us? Nowhere. Absolutely nowhere.

Jace wheeled Whirly around, sending the big horse galloping away like the hounds of hell were on his heels. A couple miles away he slowed Whirly to a walk and realized the truth. There was no way to run from his thoughts. No way to run from the realization that finding the right man meant everything was gonna be good. It was just the opposite. A prize had been dropped in his lap and just as quickly it was going to be taken away, and there wasn't a damn thing he could do about it.

Eyes on the range, his expression bleak, Jace rode on.

It was near dark when he rode into the barnyard at a slow walk. He took good care of Whirly, giving the big horse an extra half measure of sweet feed. He groomed him and praised him for the day's work, then gave in to the inevitable and headed up to the house. To his surprise it was completely dark. There were no lights shining anywhere. Surely Zeb wasn't sitting there in the dark?

Jace quickly took the front steps and opened the front door. "Zeb!" He flipped on the lights in the living room then headed in to the kitchen, turning those lights on as too. The room was empty. Jace turned back, then took the stairs two at a time. Zeb's bedroom door was open. His things were still there which gave Jace a measure of relief, but Zeb himself wasn't there. He wasn't anywhere in the house.

Frowning, a frisson of unease twisted his stomach. Jace returned downstairs and went outside, heading across the yard to the bunkhouse. He knocked at the door and waited impatiently until the door was opened by Bill, one of the hands. "You or any of the other boys seen Zeb this afternoon?" Jace asked, coming straight to the point.

"I didn't see him," Bill answered. "Come on in, Jace. We'll find out quick enough if anybody did."

A couple of the men were sprawled in the living room, watching television. Another was in his room reading and Rusty was in the kitchen fixing popcorn. None of the men had seen Zeb.

"Maybe he went for a walk," Rusty suggested.

"I'm gonna check the barn. See if he's visiting with Miss Molly."

"You want me to come with you?"

"Naw. I'll let you know if there's a problem," Jace promised and headed out across the yard to the barn where the horses were stabled. He turned on one light switch so as not to unduly disturb the horses and made his way down the row of stalls. "Son of a bitch." Molly was gone. "Zeb, what the fuck are you up to?" In answer to his question, he felt a touch in his head that was rapidly becoming familiar, needed.

Jace, can you hear me?

Jace froze and closed his eyes. *Zeb? What the hell?*

Yes. It's the link, Jace. It makes it possible for us to talk to each other this way.

Well, good. Where the hell are you? I'm gonna ring your scrawny neck for worryin' me! Jace could almost hear a short, strained laugh.

That'll have to wait. Right now I'm looking at a bunch of cattle rustlers. I need your help.

Curdled milk and grits! Where the fuck are you? An image came into his mind and Jace knew immediately where Zeb was. *Hold on and stay low. I'm calling the sheriff, and me and the boys are on our way. You hear me, Zeb? Zeb? Zeb!*

There was no answer. Jace took off at a dead run, his heart in his throat.

* * *

"Well, what have we got here?"

Zeb froze as a flashlight was shoved in his face. So much for his imitation of a rock. He'd hoped by staying silent and still he might be overlooked in the darkness.

"Who the hell are you and what are doin' out here, boy?"

Zeb squinted and blinked his watering eyes. He started to raise his hand to shield them. "Don't move, kid. There's three rifles trained on you."

Taking a deep breath, Zeb slowly lowered his arm.

"Smart move. Now once more. *What* are you doin' out here?"

"I'm visiting Free Plains ranch. I went out for a walk and got lost." Zeb had left Molly tethered to the fence about a half mile back.

There was laughter and Zeb could make out at least four distinct vocal patterns. The man speaking hadn't lied. There were three others with him. This was a totally unexpected turn of events. After running the data Rusty had given him and adding in the terrain and the proximity of entry from nearby roadways, the computer had given Zeb three likely locations for the rustlers' next raid.

Smarting from Jace's earlier reprimand, instead of waiting to present him with the data, Zeb had taken Molly and ridden out to check the viability of the places himself. Trouble was, it had taken a lot longer than he'd thought it would. And who would have guessed that by the time he reached the third spot it would be getting dark and he'd see headlights from a truck bouncing across the range? He'd done the one thing he could think to do, open the link to Jace and call for help.

"Greenhorn," a voice sneered from out of the dark.

"You picked the wrong place and the wrong time, kid," said the first man. "Tie him up." Without ceremony, Zeb was shoved to the ground. His hands were tied behind his back and his ankles bound together. Even though it was dark, a blindfold was wrapped around his head. "This blindfold's gonna save your life. We're gonna light this field up and you *don't* want to see our faces."

Zeb kept his mouth shut and prayed that Jace and his men were on their way. Fear made his stomach queasy and his chest tight. The short breaths he was able to take weren't filling his body's needs and his control was starting to fray at the edges. From behind the blindfold, he could see bright lights go on. There were several sharp reports as the rifles barked. He jumped and flinched, hearing the sound of heavy bodies dropping even as hoof beats pounded the ground. The cows not hit were lowing in panic and running off into the darkness.

The sounds of the cattle stampeding away receded and Zeb could hear movement as the shooters walked out to their kills. The truck they used started up and moved further into the field. Its engine died and the door opened and shut. Just as it did, another blaze of light lit the field from somewhere behind Zeb.

"This is the Sheriff speaking. You boys can freeze and drop your weapons. We got a shit load of men and guns trained on you. You're all under arrest."

There was a tense moment when everything went still. To surrender or fight hung in the balance. The rustlers chose to surrender. Zeb could hear cursing and the faint thuds of their weapons hitting the ground. Heart in his throat, Zeb struggled against the ropes holding him. The unreasoning panic he'd kept at bay at being tied up and helpless started to overwhelm him. He felt a scream building in his throat and managed to hold it in, only a small whimper escaping from between his tightly clenched jaws. Suddenly a scent he knew filled his nostrils. Jace. He sagged with relief.

A hand squeezed his shoulder. "Hush now, it's all right. Hold on, let me cut you loose before you hurt yourself."

Zeb nodded and felt the tension on the ropes loosen as Jace cut him free. He reached up and pulled off his blindfold.

Jace was squatted down, his expression calm, his eyes filled with concern. "You all right?"

"Yeah," Zeb replied, his voice a little shaky. He drank in the sight of Jace. The man always looked good to him but for some reason, Zeb couldn't take his eyes off him. All he could do was take deep breaths and stare while his heartbeat struggled to return to normal.

"That's good. Where's Molly?"

"About a half a mile down that way. By the fence." Zeb gestured in the general direction of the ranch house.

"All right. Come on." Jace stood and reached out his hand to Zeb. Zeb took it and was pulled upright. "Go get in the truck, Zeb. I'll be there in a minute."

Zeb frowned at the calm in Jace's voice. Surely the man should just about be foaming at the mouth now? "What about Molly?"

"I'm gonna see to her. Go." From Jace's tone, he'd clearly brook no argument.

Zeb went as quick as his shaky legs could carry him.

* * *

Jace watched Zeb until he was safely inside the truck, then turned back to the sheriff and his men finish rounding up the rustlers and their weapons. Once their truck was back through the fence, his boys quickly began putting together a temporary repair. They'd have to come back out in the morning and do the job up right. Not to mention take care of the cows that had been shot.

For some reason, he felt surprisingly calm now that he knew Zeb was safe and unharmed. He sought out Rusty. "I'm gonna take Zeb on home. Can you handle this all right?"

"Sure, boss."

"Have one of the boys get Molly. She's about a half mile down the fence line."

"Sure thing. I'll see to it myself. It's a nice night for a moonlight ride."

"Rusty."

"Yeah?"

"I won't be gettin' up early. Don't come lookin' for me."

Rusty grinned and clapped him on the back. "Sure thing, Jace."

Jace grinned back. "Good man."

Chapter Four

Jace hauled himself into the truck and after casting a quick look at Zeb to be sure he was wearing his seatbelt, he started the truck, put it in gear and headed home. Zeb sat quietly, at first still and unmoving, but slowly his tension became visible. From the corner of his eye, Jace could see him start to fiddle with his fingers. Little twitches and touches of one finger over another. Then his foot started to tap, a soft, barely there movement that accelerated. By the time the made it to the ranch, Zeb's knee was jiggling up and down like mad.

Jace pulled the truck to a stop in front of the house, turned off the ignition and looked over at Zeb with a raised brow. Zeb was looking at him in return, his eyes questioning and anxious. "Nervous?" Jace asked, looking down at Zeb's knee.

Zeb immediately stopped the movement. "No. Um. Yes. Um…" He bit his lip. "Why aren't you yelling at me?"

"I'm not really sure. I feel very calm and serene at this point. Come on in the house, Zeb," Jace invited softly.

Jace stepped out of the truck and was hit by a sudden wave of emotion. It rushed over him, the force of it nearly causing his knees to buckle. Panic, anger, relief and pure fiery lust flowed hot and wild through his veins. Taking a deep breath, he closed the truck door and mounted the porch steps. Keeping his expression blank, he held the door for Zeb.

Zeb eyed him warily but stepped through the doorway.

Jace closed the door and pounced.

He pushed Zeb against the closed door with enough force to wring a grunt from him. It was only Jace's hand cradling the back of Zeb's head that kept it from hitting the wood with a crack. As it was, Jace figured his knuckles would be bruised from absorbing the impact. It was his last coherent thought for awhile.

His mouth slammed down on Zeb's in a hard, punishing kiss. Instead of being stunned or fighting him, Zeb went every bit as wild as Jace. He wrapped his arms around Jace and climbed his body, ending with his legs wound around Jace's hips. Jace grabbed two handfuls of tight, firm ass and ground his hips against Zeb's. Both of them were hard, hot and ready for whatever came next.

Zeb's sweet moans and whimpers were pushing into his mouth and Jace drank them down like nectar. His invading tongue was welcomed with desperate touches and sensual slides, Zeb's tongue quickly becoming an apt seducer. The feelings that had been growing between them coalesced and boiled down to one sure and undeniable thing. They needed each other.

Jace pushed hard into the cradle of Zeb's thighs, his hips undulating to force their cocks together. The pressure was good and hard, the caress of fabric a rough rasp against his skin. He knew he could come, could bring Zeb off with him this way, but he wanted skin, silky skin and heat and sweat.

The memory of Zeb's naked body under his hands made his fingers dig harder into Zeb's ass, his heart pounding harder. Turning them away from the support of the door, he crossed the space from the door to the sofa in quick, sure strides and lowered the two of them down. Jace came to rest on top of Zeb, pulling back from the kiss and leaning up to give himself room.

Brown eyes met blue with an intensity that burned. "Don't ever do that to me again!" His hand slipped the button of Zeb's jeans and quickly but carefully lowered the zipper. "Do you have any idea what it felt like when you stopped talking to me?" Zeb squirmed under him helping Jace to free his cock from jeans and briefs. "I thought they hurt you. I thought you were... thought you were..." Jace couldn't finish his sentence. He paused and stared down at Zeb to see the helpless fear and the shocking need he felt mirrored in Zeb's eyes.

"I'm sorry. I'm so sorry." Zeb held his gaze but never stopped moving. He tore open Jace's jeans, his hands shaking while he pushed and shoved them down. "They found me. I couldn't think. I was... I was scared. But I knew you'd come. I knew it."

Zeb reached up and desperately pulled at Jace. Jace went with a groan. His mouth once more found Zeb's, searching for his tongue. His invited Zeb's in and captured it, sucking softly. Needy moans and hoarse whimpers vibrated against his palate making his head swim. The sensation of their cocks lined up together and rubbing, was fierce and sweet. Jace met the frantic humping of Zeb's hips with his own eager, urgent movements.

Their cocks were leaking. The slick fluid, already warm, added to the steamy heat building between their bodies. Jace rolled slightly to the side and slid a hand between them. Long, callused fingers wrapped their cocks, squeezing them together, pulling hard and fast.

"Oh, oh, fuck, Jace!" Zeb gasped.

"That's right, baby. Look at me, Zeb. Wanna see you look at me when you come," Jace ordered. Zeb's eyes had gone a stormy blue and heavy-lidded with need. Jace hissed at the sight. "So sexy, so hot. Come on, baby, give it up. Right in my hand so I can lick you up."

Jace swept his thumb over the plump heads of their near bursting cocks. Zeb's eyes widened and his piercing shout sounded out as wet heat spurt between them. Jace kept stroking, pumping hard, his own orgasm following on the heels of Zeb's, another powerful and fragrant spume of male seed coating their bellies and abdomens. Jace buried his face in the crook of Zeb's neck, his growl of completion a hard, guttural rasp.

Beneath him, Zeb's body shuddered and jerked with the aftershocks, then slowly relaxed. Jace pulled his hand away and captured Zeb's gaze as he licked their combined cream from his fingers. His expression dazed, Zeb's mouth opened like a baby bird's waiting to be fed. Jace slid one of his fingers between those parted lips. Zeb took it in, sucking and licking it clean.

Jace groaned. "Mmm, fuck. That's beautiful. Gonna make me hard again, babe."

Zeb released his finger. "I hope so."

"Somebody's hungry," Jace laughed, happiness crawling up his spine as sweet as you please.

"I was hungry when I got here," Zeb admitted. "You just made me realize how much."

Zeb's admission made him feel good, like a randy bull. "Come on upstairs." Jace levered himself up and off the sofa and tucked himself back in his jeans. "I bet I can satisfy that hunger right quick." He laughed. "Actually, I had slow in mind." Zeb had gotten his feet under him and was pulling his jeans back up. Jace slid his arms around him and cupped the cheeks of his ass. "When I get between these sweet cheeks I'm takin' my time. Gonna love on you till you scream for me."

Zeb jumped and his cheeks flushed. "Jace, I... I never, what I mean is..."

A small knowing smile curved Jace's lips. "Zeb? Baby, are you a virgin?" The thought of being Zeb's first. Well now, that was fine, really, really fine.

"Don't say that," Zeb retorted.

"Why not?"

"It makes me sound, I don't know..."

"Sweet, innocent, cute as a bug's ear?"

Zeb reached out and lightly cuffed him on the arm. His cheeks had gone scarlet, his body taut and his feet were shuffling on the carpet in discomfort. He looked away.

Jace reached out and hooked a finger under his chin, bringing Zeb's gaze back to him. "Everybody has a first time, Zeb. You're a prime young bull and this old stud wants you in his bed." Jace brought their lips together, teasing soft and light. Zeb moaned and relaxed against him.

When Jace let him go there was a smile on Zeb's lips and a teasing light shining in his eyes. "So you want to gore me with your horn?"

His words surprised a bark of laughter from Jace who popped him on the ass. "Get upstairs. I'll show you horns."

Zeb grinned and went, his feet light on the stairs. Jace followed, enjoying the sight of the tight little ass that was about to be his. At the top of the stairs, Zeb sent him a questioning look. "My room, babe," Jace answered. He caught Zeb around the waist and led him down the hallway. "We gonna need condoms?"

Zeb shook his head, "I'm perfectly healthy and immune to anything you could give me. If you had anything."

"I don't. I've always used protection and it's been awhile since I was with anyone. My last physical was eight months ago. Everything tested clean. I figured if your people were smart enough to get you here, you probably had advanced medical technology too."

Once in his room Jace didn't waste a minute. He wasn't going to give Zeb time to grow scared. He immediately took him in his arms and started kissing him. Slow, languid kisses that aroused and drew soft moans of need from Zeb. Jace's hands stayed busy, running over Zeb's back and the curve of his ass. Their kisses were interrupted long enough to discard both their shirts and Jace felt his breath hitch in his lungs as their naked chests came together.

He sent his fingers questing over the light ripples of Zeb's abs and up further to tease a hardened nipple. Zeb pulled his mouth free from Jace's and gasped. "Jace!"

Jace smiled and whispered against his lips. "Mmm, there's a hot spot. Let's see if you like this." He bent and slid his tongue over the taut kernel before sucking and teasing it with his teeth.

Zeb's hips bucked against him, slamming their cocks together. Jace groaned and blinked at the stunning impact. In a rush that left Zeb speechless, he stripped them both and tipped Zeb back on the bed. Jace crawled over him and plastered his body against Zeb's.

"Now, where was I," Jace growled. "Oh, yeah. Right here."

Once again he found Zeb's nipple and went to work, licking and sucking the tender flesh. Zeb moaned, one hand landing on Jace's shoulder, the other clutching his hair. With teeth and tongue and lips, Jace teased and explored Zeb's body. He loved all the lines and curves and hollows of Zeb. The scent of their need intensified as the heat grew between them. Moisture broke out on Zeb's skin, and with relish Jace took in the taste of his lovers tart, salty musk.

He licked the moisture laden hollow at the base of Zeb's throat and the sensual curve of his neck and shoulder. He let his teeth tease the skin, pulling up a blood red spot on the side of his neck. *Fremont's brand*, Jace thought through the haze of lust and need filling his head. *You're mine.*

Jace made love with his entire body and no part of Zeb was left untouched. By the time his hands and lips moved lower, Zeb was pushing up against him, his cock rigid and ripe. Jace sifted his fingers through the dark blond curls at the base of Zeb's cock. He wound his fingers around it, stroking a time or two before lowering his mouth to its beckoning heat. He blew a warm mist of breath over the flushed plump, head and watched a bead of clear fluid form at the slit, the bead growing fatter and rounder.

With infinite care, Jace delicately swiped his tongue over the head of Zeb's cock, capturing the tempting drop. The taste was sweet and compelling. It seized his attention not with a bang, but with soft tendrils of flavor that seduced his taste buds. It wafted over his palate, mesmerizing him and holding him as surely as any cell with bars and locked doors. Totally enraptured, Jace closed his eyes and took every inch of Zeb's hard cock into his mouth until the tip pushed into his throat.

Lips clamped tightly around the velvet-skinned rod, he moved. Up and down, again and again. His mouth sucked and his tongue swirled and teased, painting intricate patterns of lust up and down Zeb's rigid cock. From the time he'd taken that first, sweet drop, Jace's entire focus had been on Zeb's cock. That focus began to expand.

Slowly he awoke to the sounds of Zeb's cries, the movement of his body as he strained upward, thrusting himself into Jace's mouth. There was the sight of Zeb's hips moving forward then back and the tickle of pubic curls against his nose. A wet sound accompanied the sucking of his mouth and the hot tang of male testosterone filled his nostrils. He reached and found the delicate sack that held Zeb's balls and rolled them in his fingers, a treasure newly found and worshiped.

Zeb went rigid for a moment then pushed sharply with his hips. Jace expertly took the slide of his cock deep into his throat and swallowed, compressing the spongy head. There was a hard pulse. Zeb's wail pulled an answered growl from deep in Jace's chest and he pulled back, swallowing again and again. Every drop of cream Zeb released was savored, his waning erection gently licked clean and released.

Rising up, Jace crawled to the top of the bed and studied Zeb's face. His swollen lips were parted, his breath heaving in a hard, steady rhythm that leveled off and slowed. Eyes closed and cheeks flushed, he looked like a debauched angel. Jace smiled and reached into the drawer of his nightstand bringing out a tube of clear lube. He leaned over Zeb and kissed him, purring with pleasure when Zeb's arms encircled him, his hands stroking Jace's back.

"Never felt anything like that before," Zeb confessed against his lips.

Jace eased back. "Gonna take you now, Zeb. Gonna make you mine. Relax. You're gonna like this. It just gets better."

Sliding back to kneel between Zeb's spread thighs, Jace urged his legs up and back. A thrill shot down his spine and a hot surge of blood to his cock had him groaning at the sight. Zeb's tight little ass was exposed, those sweet cheeks parted and his tight, flushed entrance was right there and waiting.

"Oh, now that's gotta be the finest sight I've ever seen," Jace growled.

He coated his fingers with lube. Capturing Zeb's wide-eyed gaze, Jace let his lubed fingers trace the crease between Zeb's cheeks.

Zeb wiggled and moaned, his little hole twitching. Smiling, Jace rubbed his finger over and over the soft, wrinkled skin. With infinite patience and care, he inserted a fingertip and began the first careful movements to prepare Zeb.

His finger slid in and out, deeper with each inward move, easing through the tight tissue, lubricating the tender skin. His actions were accompanied by the tentative undulation of his Zeb's hips. Zeb's mind was thinking, *it's going to hurt*, but his body was telling him a different story. Jace could see and hear the moment Zeb's body took the upper hand. His mouth opened and small breathy moans came flowing out. The rhythm of his hips picked up speed as he attempted to help fuck himself on Jace's probing finger.

With tender care, Jace brought a second finger into play and then a third. By the time that third finger and its two companions were sliding in and out of Zeb's hole, he was pushing into them enthusiastically forcing them deeper and begging for more.

"Jace, please. Need you. Please, please, please! I *hurt*."

"Shh, I'm right here, baby. Gonna take away the hurt. Make you feel fine. Gonna make you fly, lover."

Jace slid his fingers free and replaced them with the lube-slicked head of his cock. A steady, easy pressure took him in, Zeb's sphincter tightening for only a moment before letting go. One sleek glide found him buried to the hilt. Jace closed his eyes and held on against the exquisite, tight heat that held him.

Zeb was whimpering, "So good, so good, so good," over and over again, his hands fisted in the sheets.

Pulling Zeb's legs down, Jace encouraged him to wrap them around his waist. This position brought their bodies tightly together and he started their dance. He pulled his hips back, drawing his cock nearly free before moving forward in a long languid glide. Again and again he repeated the movement. Zeb caught the rhythm and moved with him.

Their lips joined, tongues teasing and tasting as they traded breaths, filling each other's lungs. Together they increased the pace. Slow and easy became a little faster, a little harder, a little deeper. Jace levered himself up a bit, changed the angle and hit gold. Zeb's shocked groan rang out. Jace'd found his prostate. His cock slid across the little gland with each thrust, driving Zeb mad with the pleasure.

They were racing to the finish line and Jace settled in, heading for the final stretch. Hips pumping, breath heaving, he reached for Zeb's cock and pumped. Three strokes was all it took. Zeb's eyes rolled back in his head, a lusty yell piercing through every other sound in the room. His body was bouncing and shuddering, his cock straining to empty every last drop of seed his body had.

The tight vise of Zeb's inner sheath clamped around Jace's cock. Rhythmic pulses squeezed, begged and insisted on his release. Jace wasn't about to try to fight it any longer, even if he could. The wild rush of orgasm pierced his gut and he imploded. His hips jerked with every fierce pulse of his cock, his seed, warm and wet, inundating the sleek passage that held him. He collapsed on top of Zeb, rolling and pulling Zeb with him so they lay face to face.

Zeb was still emitting a soft whimper every now and then and Jace kissed his forehead, softly petting his back, chest and belly. "You all right, baby?" Jace asked softly.

Zeb opened his eyes. They were huge, dark and dazed, but he managed to nod. Jace felt a rush of emotion so deep it took his breath away. "Look at you. Pure sugar, sweet and fine," he managed gruffly around the lump in his throat.

The slow smile Zeb gave him made his heart thump. "You know what I need now?" Jace asked.

Zeb shook his head.

"A shower and some sleep. This bull is plumb tuckered."

A chuckle met his words. "This horn work takes some effort, doesn't it?"

"You bet. Come scrub my back?"

"Anything you want, Jace."

"Anything? I might take you up on that. In the mornin'."

They rolled out of bed and headed for the bathroom. The shower was hot and quick. After drying off they settled back in Jace's bed, cuddled close and went to sleep.

* * *

Late morning sunshine and birdsong brought Jace out of a sound sleep. He lay on his side quietly for a moment, remembering last night and the reason he was still in bed so late. A slow, lazy smile curved his lips as he remembered Zeb's promise to do anything. He reached out for him. His hand found cool sheets and nothing else. Jace rolled. The other side of the bed was empty.

He felt his chest constrict and admonished himself to calm down. Zeb was probably just in the bathroom. Throwing back the covers, Jace went to the bathroom. No Zeb. He turned to face the room across the hall, dread filling his heart. The door to Zeb's room stood open. He crossed the hall and looked in. It was empty. Zeb's things were gone.

On the table that had held his small computer was a piece of paper. Feeling oddly light-headed, Jace crossed the room and picked it up. As he read he backed up, his knees giving way as he sat heavily on the bed.

Dear Jace,

I have to go. Thanks to you I have enough data to give the Casithians. They should be able to take good care of the cattle they will eventually receive from you. But I don't really want to talk about that.

I want to talk about us, but what's the use? You can't leave your home and I can't stay. We both have duties and obligations that prevent us from being together. If that was something you might have wanted. I did, I do. I love you. Thank you for holding me, for touching me, for maybe loving me a little.

Zeb

"Zeb. Oh, God. Please. No. *Zeb.*" Jace's words rang in the empty room. He sat still and quiet as outside, the sun rose high overhead.

* * *

Zeb stared blankly at his computer screen. An error message blinked again and again, silently screaming at him. It was the third time today and his shift had barely started.

He'd been home for almost three weeks. At first he'd buried himself in the project for the Casithians, collating the data and passing it on. New projects came and he tried to immerse himself in them, but each time it got harder and harder.

He wasn't sleeping, he wasn't eating and the pain was growing harder and harder to ignore. A soft whimper passed his lips. He wanted surcease from the hopeless ache inside. An image came to mind. The home he'd shared with Kiel and Rick. Suddenly he knew what he had to do and where he had to go.

Zeb shut down the computer and put in a call for an automated transport vehicle. He was going home.

* * *

Kiel and Rick walked arm in arm down the long pathway that led to their front door. They'd gone for an evening out and chose to walk home, enjoying the balmy, moonlit night. As they approached their front door, a figure huddled on a nearby stone bench rose up.

Feeling a frisson of alarm, Kiel moved forward and put himself between Rick and the stranger. "Who are you? What are you doing here?" he asked, his voice steady and firm.

"It's me. Zebian."

Kiel let out a sigh of relief. Crimes were few and far between but one never knew.

"Zeb!" Rick stepped forward. "Why didn't you tell us you were coming? We'd have stayed home this evening." Zeb stepped forward into the light and was rewarded with stares and a gasp from Rick. "Oh, my God, Zeb are you ill? You look terrible. Come inside."

Kiel opened their door and the two of them got Zeb inside and seated, taking a place on either side of him on the sofa. Kiel reached for Zeb's hand. "Zebian, little one, what's wrong?"

"I… I just… can't." A broken sob escaped Zeb's throat.

Kiel didn't hesitate. He pulled Zeb to him and eased him into his lap. Even though Zeb was full grown, Kiel was a big man, very strong and very determined. This was how he'd comforted Zeb as a child and Zeb needed him now just as he'd needed him then. Rick moved close and the three of them cuddled together, Kiel and Rick offering words of solace and comfort, rocking and petting him as Zeb cried out his hurt.

When his tears abated, he sniffed and took the tissue Rick handed him. Sheepishly he blew his nose. "I'm sorry."

"For what? Coming to us when you felt bad? We love you, Zebian. Where else should you go?" Rick softly admonished.

Kiel gave him a squeeze. "Want to talk about it now?"

"Yes."

Zeb told them about his time on Earth, halting now and then to swallow down emotions that threatened make him cry again. "So you see, I found my mate, but we can't be together. I don't know how I can live like this. I keep wondering if Jace is all right. I'm so afraid I may have hurt him somehow by forming the bond then leaving. I don't know what to do."

"Well, I do," Kiel said confidently.

"You do?" Zeb asked.

"Of course. It's simple, Zebian. You're going back to Earth. Back to your mate."

"But how can I? My duty is here as one of the Maleri'. The Beltholan High Council will never let me just leave."

"Zebian, do you honestly think the Maleri' Council will let them force you to stay? The union between a Maleri' and his mate is as necessary as the air we breathe. No one will insist you put your duty before your life. Besides, with the kind of work you do, you could do it from Earth and just transmit back to Belthola."

"But Councilor Ruran insisted it was time for me to get more involved with field work."

"Councilor Ruran was acting on a recommendation I made to him when you left us to go to work for Division Seven. We felt it was time you got out to meet people. Take an interest in the world around you." Kiel pinched his chin lightly. "Zeb, you built a wall around your heart. We were afraid for you. Afraid that when the time came you'd keep yourself even from your mate. You certainly proved us wrong, but I still feel we were right in our decision to send you to Earth."

Zeb sighed and leaned forward. He pulled Rick and Kiel close so their foreheads were all touching. "I love you both. So, so much. Thank you for being my family."

"Ah, Zebian, you're so very welcome," Kiel answered.

"We love you, Zeb. We'll always be here for you," Rick added.

"Now," Kiel said with a grin. "Let's get you home."

* * *

The sun was setting in a blaze of glory, but Jace watched it with little pleasure. There wasn't much in the past few weeks that had brought him any kind of happiness. Zeb had been gone almost a month, and the hurt was still enough to bring him to his knees if he let it sneak up on him. Even now, sitting here, concentrating on the chores he wanted to see done tomorrow, the pain and sorrow was trying to sneak in.

Jace's breath caught a little and he rapidly blinked his eyes while forcing himself to taking deep, calming breaths. He was no small amount of grateful when a distraction in the form of a strange red pickup truck came up the lane and stopped in front of the house.

At first he thought his eyes were playing tricks on him. Some trick of the light on the windshield made the man inside the truck resemble Zeb. Then the door opened and Zeb stepped out. He was just the same. Dark blond hair, blue eyes and that tight little body that sent Jace's libido over the moon. Jace stood slowly as Zeb climbed the stairs.

Zeb stopped a few feet away. "I'm back. They let me come back."

"To stay?"

Zeb nodded, his eyes bright with unshed tears.

Jace swallowed hard and opened his arms. "Welcome home, Zeb."

Epilogue

"Hey, you! Get your sweet ass in here."

"I'm comin'."

"You better not be," Jace growled.

Zeb, with a smile on his face, walked through the open bedroom door, stark naked. "Hey, I just took a shower."

Jace walked over and nuzzled his neck. "I can see that."

"Mmm," Zeb groaned. "Did you get the tractor parts you went into town for?"

"I sure did. I got somethin' for you too." Jace indicated the box lying on the bed. "Open it."

Zeb gave him a grin and bounced over to the bed, pulling back the lid on the big box. Inside was a cowboy hat and a pair of boots.

Jace crowded close, lips nuzzling the sensitive spot behind Zeb's ear while he ran his hand over the naked flanks of his lover. "Try 'em on," he insisted, his voice low and rough.

Zeb shivered. "Now? Shouldn't I save them for tomorrow when I go riding on Molly?"

Jace started peeling off his clothes. "I got somethin' you can ride."

Naked in no time, he settled on the bed. Hard cock in hand, he slowly stroked himself and watched as interesting parts of Zeb's anatomy jiggled while he stomped into his boots. Zeb settled his hat on his head and crawled up the bed toward Jace's waiting arms.

A huge grin wreathed Jace's lips. "Time to saddle up and ride 'em, cowboy."

Zeb did just that.

Bonds of the Maleri' 5: Redemption

Kate Steele

Chapter One

Another flawless landing. It was a seamlessly smooth transition from space to dock and yet Jorrian Tavaris felt every nuance of vibration and movement the ship made. Pain lanced through his head, his vision momentarily blurring. Grimacing, eyes squeezing tightly shut, one hand went to his temple while the other stretched forth to search for the edge of the bed. Finding it, he flopped down with a groan and lay still, waiting for the pain to recede.

The attacks were coming with more and more regularity. In the darkness behind his closed lids, he let himself admit to a little of the fear he'd been successfully holding at bay. It wouldn't be long now before the darkness claimed him for all time and, depending on popular beliefs, there would be eternal rest, a place paved with streets of gold or a fiery pit of never ending torment.

Jor snorted, a cynical if pained smile curving his lips. If it were up to his fellow gamblers, his reward would be the fiery pit. More than one had claimed he had the devil's own luck, doling out curses along with the valuables they relinquished. At least he had the satisfaction of knowing it wasn't only luck but skill that made him a winner. He never used his Maleri' abilities while playing games of chance. One spectacular misuse of his empathic powers had lost him everything. No one could say he didn't learn from his mistakes.

Suppressing the sharp stab of grief that the memory of Belthola and his lost position amongst the Maleri' brotherhood brought, Jor massaged his temples. *I'll settle for the eternal rest. Peace, quiet, no hunger, no need, no pain. What's not to love about that?* Yet even as he thought it, deep inside a part of him rebelled. To sleep forever, to do and be nothing seemed an awful waste, not to mention boring as hell. *Although I suppose if you're asleep it's a moot point. The universe could explode and you wouldn't know a damn thing.* He sighed. All this afterlife speculation was a melancholy and frustrating thing at best.

Experimentally opening his eyes, Jor blinked. He focused on the ceiling. The pain was receding. He'd been granted a few more hours, days or weeks. There was no way of knowing when his inner mind shield would give way, and no salvation was coming. Only the touch of his true mate could save him and Jor had never searched for him. He refused to burden anyone with his disgrace. He sat up, then stood. Satisfied when his legs remained steady, Jorrian took his already packed black leather duffle and left his cabin in search of the nearest drinking establishment.

Tired of metallic walls and recycled air, Jor bypassed the usual space dock bars and went in search of a little local color. A quick shuttle trip planet-side saw him debarking at the planet's shuttle station on the outskirts of a medium-sized town with a rustic air. Buildings of different designs and heights housed a variety of shops and eating establishments. Quite a few people walked the sidewalks and ranged from browsers to serious, package-laden shoppers. On the street, a steady stream of personal and public transport units cruised.

Three blocks from the port he found what he was looking for. The bar was well appointed, not fancy but definitely not a dive. The clientele looked average, middle class. There was music playing loud enough to be heard but not raucous. The ratio of men to women was approximately three to one, most of the women obviously with a male partner. The servers seemed to be equally divided in number as to male and female, but all were young and good looking. The smell of food mingled with liquor. A small menu was posted behind the bar with simple offerings of sandwiches and finger-foods.

With a practiced eye, Jor quickly found a table with a card game in progress. The men who sat there were focused on their cards and the other players, not in the least interested in what went on in the room around them. This was exactly what he was looking for. Some obviously serious players.

Jor made his way to the bar, took a seat and ordered a shot of whiskey. In all his travels, whiskey was a form of liquor that seemed to be universal. No matter what it was called, every culture he'd come across had discovered a way to ferment whatever kind of grain their planet produced. Taking the small glass the bartender poured for him, he took an experimental sniff. The smell was potent but refined. This brew had an aged scent that caressed the palate as well as a clear and deep reddish-amber color that was visually pleasing.

He took a sip and savored the smooth and smoky bite while it slid down his throat. It settled in his stomach, its warmth easy and persuasive as it encouraged him to relax. Jor let a small curve lift his lips and finished his drink, taking the comfort it offered. He was about to rise from his seat when a tentative hand on his arm caught his attention.

He looked over to find a boy of perhaps fifteen or so giving him an inviting yet nervous smile. "Is there something I can do for you?" Jor asked politely.

The boy's smile widened. "Maybe we can do for each other."

Jor's brow rose. The boy was propositioning him. Not that it hadn't happened before, but this child was much too young to be offering himself in barrooms. "Go home to your mother, boy."

A stricken look came over his face. "She's sick."

Before he could stop himself, Jor reached out with his senses. He'd met his share of flim flam artists but none could ever fool his empathic ability to sniff them out. What he felt from the boy was heartrending. Fear, sadness, shame, determination, they mixed and mingled with a dozen other raw emotions that beat at Jor's shield.

Suppressing the urge to throw his arm up to ward himself from the boy's roiling emotions, Jor reached into his jacket and drew out a small, leather case. Opening it, he took out a card and handed it to the boy. "Do you have a comm unit at home?" The boy shook his head. "Go to the shuttle station and use one of the public comms. Have you heard of the planet Belthola and the Maleri'?"

"Yes, sir," the boy acknowledged with wide eyes.

"Put a call through to the number on that card. You won't be charged for the call. This is going to put you into contact with Chastien Kaldor. He's Maleri' and head of the Taskin City Security Bureau on Belthola. Chase will vouch for me, then he's going to put you in contact with some people who will help you and your mother. All right?"

The boy's emotions soared. Hope warred with distrust. "Not that I don't appreciate it but why... um, why are you helping me and what do you want in return?"

"Let's just call it my way of helping to balance the universe. And as for what I want in return? Make something of yourself. Don't waste this opportunity, boy."

"Val, sir, Val Cammor."

"Pleased to meet you, Val Cammor. Now get your young ass out of here."

Val grinned and dashed out the door.

The bartender, who'd been busy up till then, noticed Val leaving. "I hope he didn't bother you, sir. I've had to chase him out on more than one occasion. Sorry as I feel for him, I can't have underage kids in here trying to sell their, um, assets to the customers."

"Not a problem. I predict you won't be seeing him again. At least not until he's old enough to drink," Jor mused, then shook his head at the puzzled look the bartender gave him.

He rose from his seat and sauntered over to the table of card players. Within minutes he'd caught their attention and, after making his wishes known, was invited to join the game. Jor seated himself and bought markers, unaware of the attention he'd garnered through his exchange with Val.

* * *

Stiff with indignation, Dane Jeffers started to rise from his seat but settled when he saw the stranger hand Val Cammor a card instead of money. He'd lectured Val about coming into places like the Benitenta, but apparently Val was too desperate to take heed. Even after the last incident that left him beaten in an alley with nothing to show for the services he'd performed for his customer but bumps and bruises. He was lucky he hadn't been raped.

Dane's gut twisted. He was treating Val's mother but the supplies he had and the care she needed were far from meeting in the middle. Casithia was a backwater, agriculturally driven planet with very little to recommend it to high powered industry. The medical facilities planet-wide were inadequate and understaffed. Most doctors went where the money was and of those who practiced here, some had shady pasts and reputations.

Dane had trained at the Johns Hopkins School of Medicine in Maryland, in the United States on the planet Earth. His credentials were impeccable, his skill welcomed and appreciated by those near and far, but even that didn't make needed medical supplies appear. The government was poor and the available resources were spread thin.

He kept his eyes on Val and the stranger. Especially the stranger. Dane had noticed the man the minute he'd coolly walked in the door. It would have been hard to overlook someone so distinctive. He was tall and well formed. His black coat fell in an elegant line from his broad shoulders. A crisp, white shirt was tucked into black pants that hugged slim hips and muscular thighs. When he'd sat himself down at the bar, Dane berated himself for letting his gaze wander to the man's ass. It became a half-hearted rant when he found, to his amusement, that the stranger's coat was long enough to hide his backside from view.

What really drew the eye was the man's hair. It was blond, a blond so pale it was nearly white. It was also long. When he'd walked in, Dane could see that it was pulled back. When the man turned and seated himself at the bar a thick and solid rope of shimmering frost pale hair ran down his back and ended just short of being long enough for him to sit on. The man had cocked a booted foot on the rung of the barstool and ordered a drink.

Dane had gone back to his food, ready to dismiss the stranger, when Val had slipped in. He'd watched them, saw the emotions playing over Val's face and his impudent, yet joyous grin as he'd fled the bar. Something the stranger said or did had made Val very happy. Dane was making it his business to find out what... although, for some reason, he had the feeling this man meant Val no harm. There wasn't much he could do for Val and his mother. Keeping Val from being hurt further was one thing he could and would do. No matter what his instincts were telling him, he was determined to talk to Val and find out just what he and the stranger had discussed.

Sighing and shaking his head, Dane returned to his meal and the medical journal he'd been perusing. Peripherally he was aware of the stranger joining the card game. Dane kept his eyes on the journal, he'd had enough of watch dogging the man's actions. Until the commotion brought him once more to Dane's attention.

Dane looked up to find a growing crowd around the card players' table. He could just make out a body lying on the floor. Rising from his seat, he pushed his way through the crowd. "Excuse me, I'm a doctor. Let me through please."

The crowd parted. At the center of the ruckus was the stranger. He was lying on the floor, his pale hair turning red with the blood that was seeping from the back of his scalp. "Sariel, get me a towel or some napkins," Dane ordered the server who stood on the other side of the table. As the girl ran to obey, Dane examined the man. His already pale complexion had gone pasty white. Dane took up his wrist to feel for a pulse. His own heart jumped at detecting nothing.

Wasting no time, Dane quickly opened the man's shirt. He placed his head against the stranger's chest but detected no heart sounds or movement of his chest. "He's not breathing," Dane said aloud.

There was a disconcerted rumble from the crowd but Dane paid them little heed. He tilted the man's head back to check his airway, pinched his nose closed and leaned forward. Covering the man's mouth with his own, he breathed out and into the man's mouth twice. There was no response. Undaunted, he began chest compressions. Silently he counted thirty compressions then returned to again breathe twice into his mouth. Back and forth he worked, thirty chest compressions, two breaths.

The fifth time he placed his mouth over the stranger's an odd feeling took hold of him. At first he thought he was getting dizzy. The feeling of lightheadedness increased and he tried to pull away and sit up only to find himself caught in an invisible web. Dane gasped. A silent scream his only recourse as the unthinkable happened.

Noooo!

Thoughts, images, touches, scents and sounds inundated his mind. The stranger's life was paraded before him, indelibly ingrained into his conscious and subconscious until he knew this man as he'd known only one other before. Once more the mate gift of the Maleri' was bestowed upon Dane, and he wailed his despair into the darkness of this unwelcome joining.

As suddenly as the power took him, he was released and Dane scrambled away, his being filled with horror at what had overtaken him. Jorrian -- Dane knew the stranger's name now -- stirred and moaned. Pale lashes fluttered against his cheeks and frosty brows drew together in a frown as his eyes opened. Stormy green orbs pinned Dane in their sights, comprehension replacing confusion in their depths.

"You bastard," Jor managed before his head lolled and hit the floor with a small yet solid thump.

There was a shocked silence until the serving girl waved a towel in front of Dane's face. "Doc? Are you okay? You're gonna take care of this guy, right?"

Dane blinked and sought for control of his agitated emotions. He took the towel from Sariel and forced himself back to Jorrian's side. The wound in his scalp was still bleeding profusely. Letting his training brace him, Dane put all other considerations on hold and got to work.

"Can someone tell me what happened?" Dane questioned the crowd. "How did he end up on the floor?"

"I can answer that, Dr. Jeffers."

Dane looked over in time to see one of the card players, Mont Bartel, squat down across from Jorrian. Dane nodded. "Mont."

Mont acknowledged the greeting. "We hadn't been playing very long, just a couple of hands when I noticed him frowning. Unusual behavior for a card player, especially one as polished as he seems to be. We'd just started the hand when he threw in his cards. He said there was something important he'd forgotten to take care of. He stood up, grabbed his head and keeled over."

"That's it?"

"That's it, Doc."

"Thanks, Mont. Do you think you and couple of these other men could help me get him to the clinic?"

"Sure thing. You got your TU here?"

"Yeah, it's parked out front."

"Noan, give me a hand with this guy," Mont said, directing his fellow card players. "Crayl, how about you follow us to the clinic, then Doc won't have to drive us back."

The arrangements made, Dane secured a makeshift bandage to Jorrian's head and followed the men out, watching as Jor was settled in Dane's transport unit. The trip was quickly made -- his clinic was a few miles out of town, just beyond the shuttle station. Jorrian was brought into the clinic and settled on a narrow bed.

"Anything else we can do for you, Doc?" Mont asked.

Dane shook his head. "You've gone above and beyond. Thanks, Mont, Noan. And thank Crayl for me, would you?"

"You bet."

The two men shuffled out and Dane went to his patient. He stared silently at him for a moment, then went to work.

Chapter Two

Jor woke with the headache from hell. A pounding reverberation had taken up residence in his skull and he frowned, both hands coming up to rub at his temples. It was then he discovered the bandage that encircled his head. Frowning, he puzzled at its presence until memory came rushing in to fill the gaps. Dr. Dane Jeffers. He sat up and swung his legs over the side of the bed.

A picture filled his mind of dark curly hair, falling forward to frame a tanned and perfect visage. A chiseled jaw, straight nose, full lips and a pair of wide blue eyes the color of Beltholan skies that stared at him in horror.

Jor dropped his head forward and pinched the bridge of his nose. It was nothing more than what he'd come to expect if by some monumentally abysmal twist of fate he should find himself with a mate. Dane Jeffers' horror was perfectly understandable. His own feelings were hardly less harsh. He was appalled. The man had once been mated to another Maleri'.

Jor tore the bandage from his head and flung it away.

"Hey! I put that there for a reason."

Turning his head, Jor watched Dane enter the room. He turned his gaze away. "You wasted your time."

"I'm a doctor. It's my duty to waste my time fixing things that are broken. That includes your head."

"What's wrong with it?" Jor asked and without waiting for an answer, he sent one hand searching over his head. He hissed when his fingers came in contact with a large lump and a row of bristles. "What the hell is this?" he demanded. "What have you done?"

"I stitched the split in your scalp. I don't know if you remember, but you fell and hit your head."

Jor glared. "I remember perfectly. Why did you stitch the wound? That's barbaric. Why didn't you use lacerseal?"

"Because I don't have any," Dane explained with gentle sarcasm. "The health facilities are government funded and the government has no funds. Therefore, I make do with what I can come up with. Laceration sealant is a luxury we can't afford."

"It really wouldn't have mattered if you'd left me alone," Jor spit resentfully. "Who asked you to interfere? Why couldn't you have just left me there? I was ready to…" *Die*, he finished silently, as though saying the word aloud would really make his acceptance a fact and not just let it be something he truly didn't want to believe.

"After what happened, I wish the hell I had," Dane replied with equal vehemence. "This, this thing that's happened between us. Don't even think for one minute that I intend to honor this bond. I was mated to a Maleri' once. He was a good and decent man. I loved…" Jor looked up to see Dane swallowing hard, his eyes glittering with unshed tears. "It doesn't matter. That's done and over, and this will never be. As soon as you're able, I want you gone."

"I'm able and more than ready now," Jor answered, hiding the wince of pain, shame and anger that Dane's words brought.

Dane walked back to the doorway and halted before stepping through, "I'll drive you back to town. Where are you staying?"

"The shuttle station hotel. I'll walk."

"It's three miles. I'll drive you," Dane insisted and left the room.

Jor wanted to argue but when he stood, his head vigorously protested the movement. He was very much afraid that even a walk as short as three miles was beyond him at the moment. Sighing in resignation, he followed in Dane's footsteps.

***

The drive was accomplished in silence. Each man caught up in his own thoughts. Thoughts they struggled to keep from slipping through the bond that formed and strengthened between them. The Maleri' bond was inescapable, breakable only by the death of one partner. In most cases the death of one heralded the death of both.

That Dane had escaped his departed mate's fate was a fact that brought him an anguish so deep he wished it was possible to die of sorrow. When Teleran had come to Earth, Dane was a practicing physician, so lost in medicine and his patients there was little time for anything else in his life. In reality, his involvement in his work was a cover for the fact that there was nothing else in his life.

He had no family, few friends and his last relationship had ended with a whimper. Tel had changed all that. While it had been a shock to discover that other sentient beings existed, when the Maleri' bond formed between them, Dane had reveled in it. To know without a doubt that this person was *the* one he'd thought never to find? To know that he wouldn't spend his life alone? To give of himself, heart, body and soul and find it returned in equal measure? It had been a gift, a treasure of incalculable worth. And it had been his for all of four weeks.

Dane had readily agreed to go with Teleran, but his responsibilities were such that he couldn't just pick up and leave. With his lover's blessings he'd set about placing his patients with other doctors and closing his office. He was near the end of his preparations when Tel had been called back to Belthola. Trade agreements he'd helped negotiate on the planet Gefrin were breaking down and his presence was urgently needed.

Promising to return in a few days, Tel had gone and never come back. An overzealous and unbalanced mine worker had decided to give the manufacturing heads a demonstration of the miners' power. The explosion had injured a dozen people and killed three, Tel among them. Dane felt the wrench of Tel's leaving to the bottom of his soul and Tel's whispered, *I'm so sorry, love*, that had traveled the distance between them, haunted Dane's dreams.

Tightening his grip on the transport's steering wheel, Dane clenched his teeth and fought to blank his mind. The treacherous Maleri' bond was calling, enticing him to share his pain with the man at his side, and Dane silently fought it tooth and nail. His mate was dead. This man, Jorrian Tavaris, was an interloper, a betrayer of everything Tel had stood for. What did it matter that he'd spent years atoning for his mistake? Why should the fact that he helped countless people like Val Cammor influence Dane's view of him?

Dane steeled himself, mutinously pushing away the feel of Jor's shame and remorse and his own traitorous need to offer comfort. The port came into view and Dane parked at the nearest entrance. He waited silently as Jor carefully levered himself out. He watched for a moment until Jor disappeared inside then drove away, trying to ignore Jor's softly whispered *sorry* as it echoed Tel's sentiment from long ago.

* * *

Jor made his way to the hotel and from there to his room. Once inside he dropped heavily into a chair. His entire being hurt. Physically, mentally and emotionally, no matter what part of himself was explored there was pain. Every moment spent in Dane's company had been agony. Though he'd struggled to hide it, Dane's hurt had beaten Jor until he was wired tight with guilt and self-hatred.

And what was worse? He'd known Teleran Bokra. Tel's death had come just months before Jor's disgrace. Dane had been on Belthola, taken in by the Maleri' Council in an effort to heal the damage Tel's death had inflicted on him. He'd been on Belthola when Jor had been forced to leave. Jor was struck by the irony of the situation. His future mate had been mere miles away when Jor had all but destroyed his own life. The laugh he uttered held little in the way of humor.

He rose from the chair and went to the stand that held his bag. Riffling through the right side pocket, he found the bottle of pills he sought. He opened the bottle and shook two into his hand, closed it then opened the small fridge unit by the low mirrored dresser. Several sealed bottles of water were there. Taking one, he removed the cap before tossing back the pills and chasing them down with the icy, cold water.

A staggering flicker of despair crashed over him and he grabbed for the dresser's edge, holding on. As suddenly as it came it disappeared. He stared at himself in the mirror, moisture gathering in his eyes. "Dane," he whispered, watching dispassionately as a single tear slid down his own cheek. "And the angels wept," he murmured, his mind filled with the vision of Dane's tearful blue eyes and the sound of his harsh sobs.

Jor staggered to the bed, crawled in and eased himself down. His mind and body had reached the end of their endurance, refusing to acknowledge any further outside influences. With the help of the pills Jor had taken, his body shut down while his mind sent him deeply into slumber.

* * *

Jor stirred restlessly, a memory forming in his sleeping mind. Gentle fingers touched him. A gruff voice spoke, the words soft and reluctant. "So beautiful. I've never seen hair this color. And so soft. What a mess. This blood has got to go."

He felt someone pull him toward the head of the small bed. The bulk of his hair was freed from confinement beneath his body and something soft was placed under the back of his neck. There was silence as the person with him moved away. Jor felt them return and a scent tickled his nose. A subtle musk, masculine and arousing, surrounded him and suddenly he knew who those gentle hands belonged to. Dane.

The sound of water caught his attention a few seconds before wet warmth cascaded over his hair and scalp. He nearly moaned at the sensuous feel of it and the tender touches of Dane's hands washing the blood from him. Jor drifted in the sensations, all care and worry gone. The water was taken away and his hair wrapped in a towel. Moments later the towel was replaced by warm air flowing over him. Dane dried his hair and a brush made an appearance. The ends of his hair were seen to first. The soft bristles moving higher, closer to his scalp as any tangles were smoothed away. The brushing ended and he was resettled on the bed.

Still asleep, Jor rolled to his side, silently protesting the loss of such tender care. There'd been precious little meaningful contact in his life since leaving Belthola. His eyelids fluttered. The rapid eye movement beneath them signaled the beginning of a dream that replaced the memory.

A hand took hold of his, strong, masculine fingers, entwining with his own. Jor raised their joined hands to his lips and placed a kiss on the back of the hand holding his.

"Such a romantic," Dane accused softly.

"Only with you," he admitted.

He opened his eyes and squinted. Above him, Dane's dark curls were silhouetted by clear blue skies, his face a shadow in the bright sunshine. Below them a blanket was spread across a cushion of green grass, the remains of a picnic relegated to its edge. Jor slid his free hand behind Dane's neck and pulled him down into a slow, tender kiss. Dane moaned softly, his pleasure evident, his mouth opening for the strokes of Jor's tongue.

Encouraged, Jor wrapped his arm around Dane and drew their bodies together, then rolled bringing Dane beneath him. He eased back, staring at his lover. Dane's eyes were closed, his lips parted, and Jor's breath caught in his throat. Dane was his angel. He'd rescued Jor not only from death but from a life filled with loneliness and self-loathing. His blue eyes opened and Jor lost himself in their depths. He waded deep into the love reflected there and felt his spirits soar. All the shackles that had chained him disappeared.

Dane's smile went from angelic to mischievous. "I had an ulterior motive for bringing you out here, you know."

Jor returned his smile. "You did?"

"Mmmhmm. And it wasn't just to feed you."

"Hmm. I wonder what that motive could be."

"Come here and I'll show you."

Dane reached up and Jor went willingly into his arms. Their lips came together, opening, welcoming the sweet invasion of each other's tongues. Their coming together was natural and easy, their passion for each other intoxicating and ever present. Practiced *fingers loosened buttons and fasteners while the heat grew between them. Dane groaned when Jor's fingers slid into his open pants and wrapped around the thick stalk of his already erect cock.*

Jor's stomach clenched at the sound of Dane's pleasure. The feel of the rod in his hand, iron hard with skin like silk, sent a rush of pure lust down his spine. His mouth sought the hollow of Dane's throat, tasting the salt and musky sweetness. Licking and sucking his way downward, Jor groaned as the flesh of their chests, exposed by their opened shirts, slid together. He stopped at a muscled pec, the tight brown nipple surrounded by a lighter copper-brown areola drawing his gaze.

He slid his tongue over the taut bead, taking it carefully between his teeth. Dane arched beneath him when Jor lashed his tongue repeatedly over the tiny nub before sucking it. Dane's moans went straight through Jor, making his pulse pound harder and his blood rush faster. His hips jerked reflexively at the further influx of blood that filled his cock to bruising hardness.

Pushed by the urgency of his growing need, Jor moved down the length of Dane's body, hands and mouth caressing Dane's ridged abs and flat stomach. The muscles under his hands rippled under his touch and Jor smiled, pleased at Dane's response to his touch. As much as he wanted to worship every inch of his lover, Jor's hunger drove him to the hard cock he still held trapped in his fist.

A growl inched from his throat. He pushed his face into the dark nest of pubic hair, inhaling the tart, masculine scent while soft yet wiry wisps of hair caressed his cheek. Opening his hand, he kept it cupped around Dane's cock but free enough to let his tongue play over the thick length. To the music of Dane's moans, he traced a wet path over the raised, pulsing veins, letting his tongue skim over the velvet heat. Reaching the head, he deftly explored the curve of flesh where the straight shaft blossomed into a plump, reddish cap.

Jor followed a wet trail of pre-cum to the tiny slit that topped Dane's cock and delicately probed with his tongue. Dane's cry was all the encouragement he needed. His mouth descended, taking the thick length to the root. He closed his eyes, lost in utter bliss. This act, to fill his mouth with Dane's cock, to feel the wet silk of Dane's skin against his tongue, to breathe his unique scent and taste the sweet pearls of Dane's pre-cum was magic. The world fell away. Dane was everything and all. Jor's beginning and end. He tightened his lips around the shaft and sucked.

With an expertise born partly of experience and partly of sheer joy in the doing, Jor worked Dane's cock. His tongue danced and teased while his lips slid up and down the hard length. His cheeks hollowed and released with the force of suction he applied. Dane was babbling incoherently, words and moans interspersing while his hips strained upward, following the movement of Jor's mouth.

Jor threw his leg over Dane's and ground himself against his thigh. His own desire was growing unbearable, his cock pulsing with the need for release. Jor gently cupped Dane's balls and rolled them, rhythmically squeezing, pushing him over the edge. Dane's body stiffened and arched, the first rush of his semen bathing the back of Jor's throat as he came. He pulled back, wanting the taste, fresh, mild, salty and sweet.

Unconsciously he ground himself against Dane and shuddered, groaning out his own climax around Dane's cock while swallowing each spurt of seed his lover released. Using his lips and tongue, Jor massaged Dane's cock, encouraging the aftershocks, the quivers that tightened Dane's body and brought more of his flavor to Jor's seeking mouth.

Dane's cock lost its rigid hardness and Jor, assured he had every drop, let it slip from his mouth. Dane's hands landed on Jor's shoulders and fisted in his shirt, pulling him up. He obeyed his lover's summoning, and found himself rolled to his back with Dane's tongue lazily exploring his mouth.

"Mmm," Dane rumbled before pulling away. "We taste good together. I wanted to suck you too, you know. That was my dessert."

Jor smiled. "Sorry. You're just too sexy. I couldn't help myself."

"It's all right. I'll get my chance in the shower when we go in."

"You're pretty sure of yourself. Am I that easy?"

"Only with me," Dane replied, echoing Jor's earlier confession about being romantic.

They shared a quiet laugh, a few more kisses, then helped each other to their feet. Dane packed the picnic things while Jor folded the blanket. Joining hands, they walked from the back yard and into the house.

Jor woke slowly and stretched. A smile curved his lips while the dream replayed in his head. He stroked his hands slowly down the length of his body, stopping at the wet spot that covered his groin. At least that much of the dream had been true. He'd come in his pants. He rolled out of bed and began shedding his clothes while walking to the bathroom. *Too bad the rest wasn't real*, he mused sadly before stepping into the shower.

* * *

Dane took a deep breath and yawned, his eyes fluttering open. Totally relaxed, he let his thoughts drift. A picture formed in his mind, a sunny day, a shared picnic, the sweet rush of love and the aching arousal that found fulfillment in his lover's mouth.

Jor's mouth.

Dane frowned, dismayed at where his dreams had led him. His first thought was to blame Jor, but common sense won out. How could Jor be held responsible for Dane's dreams? As much as Dane wanted to blame him, Jor couldn't even be held accountable for the bond that now locked them together. He certainly hadn't been in a position to warn Dane away. It was Dane's own fears that had made him reject Jor so vehemently. And it was Dane's fears that made him see Jor as a threat, instead of a second chance. A chance to experience the love he'd been denied. Dane rapidly blinked his eyes against the tears that threatened.

When Tel had been killed and their bond broken, Dane had nearly broken as well. If the Maleri' Council had not come for him, Dane had no doubt he'd be living the rest of his life in some mental institution. It was only the Maleri' healers with their empathic abilities that had brought him back from the near catatonic state in which they'd found him. What would happen if he accepted Jor only to lose him as well? Stranger things had happened. Hadn't they?

When did I become such a pessimist?

Dane sighed. *When Tel died.*

He shook his head, partly in protest of the thought and partly in disgust at his own cowardice. Deliberately Dane brought the memory of the dream forward and let it fill his mind. Through the Maleri' bond that formed between them Dane had learned more about Jorrian Tavares than any one person had a right to know about another. He squirmed, knowing that Jorrian had received an equal portion of him. Jor knew about Tel. He knew about Dane's breakdown and his recovery on Belthola. He knew about his time spent with Tel's mentors and how they had grieved together then shared their love of Tel in memories of him.

But Dane wasn't the only one with problems and scars. Jor's need was also evident. Not just the desires of his body but the requirements of his soul. His pain was endless and blackened his spirit. Even his efforts to atone did little to lift the stain that blighted every aspect of his life. Jor had given up. He was going through the motions, waiting for the end.

No wonder his anger had turned on Dane when Dane had inadvertently saved him.

He shook his head. Together he and Jorrian were a complete mess. Both hurting, both angry, both trying to fight the Maleri' bond, a force that took no prisoners. If it weren't so tragic, it would be laughable. *Oh, Tel, what am I going to do?*

You're a healer, Dane. Do what you do best.

Dane froze. Had Tel spoken to him or was that his own subconscious providing answers? How could he know? The one thing he was sure of was that he was tired and scared. Tired of the hurt but too scared to let anyone in to assuage it.

Dane rolled to his side and ended up in a wet spot. He frowned for a second then realized that when he'd come in the dream, he'd come in reality. He couldn't remember the last time he'd had a wet dream. After Tel's death, Dane's libido had taken a lengthy sabbatical. Even after its return, Dane's enthusiasm for sex was lukewarm at best. He bit his bottom lip and worried it for a moment. If nothing else, his body was telling him what to do. The question was, should he let it?

Chapter Three

Jor left his room and walked into town. He found a nice little restaurant and ordered a meal. While eating he watched the people coming and going, inside the restaurant and outside through the big glass windows at the front. The world was moving on apace, yet Jor felt like he was floundering in quicksand. The forming of the mate bond should be the most joyous thing two people could experience, and yet both he and Dane repudiated it.

There were too many obstacles to overcome, too many black marks against him and too many hurts that neither of them could live with nor let go of. The weight of his life was pressing in on him and the only solution was to go. Dane had clearly stated his position. He wouldn't honor the bond. And why should he? He'd had the best. Why settle for someone so far beneath him? With that bitter realization souring his stomach, Jor paid his bill and left, determined to catch the first ship out no matter where it was headed.

Arriving back at the shuttle station, he started for his room and stopped as a disconcerted murmur ran through the crowd of customers and service personnel. Jor frowned in consternation. Blinking red lights came up on every visible monitor drawing attention to the quarantine warnings being posted. The station was shutting down. People began rushing from place to place some with what looked like purpose, others in a fashion that screamed pure panic.

Jor continued to the hotel and once there he grabbed the nearest porter. "What's going on?" he questioned the man.

"Oh, sir, haven't you heard? We're under quarantine. A shuttle arrived with several passengers who were ill. Dr. Jeffers was called and he's diagnosed them with Runcalis Fever."

"But that's not possible. There's vaccine for that. It's standard practice to vaccinate against that. How the devil could someone come down with Runcalis? He's got to be mistaken."

"I don't know, sir, but that's what we've been told."

"Where's Dr. Jeffers now?"

"I don't know, sir."

"Does the station have a med center?"

"Yes, sir, level two, section B."

"Thanks."

Jor headed in the direction supplied and found the place deserted except for a very young and flustered med tech. "Can you tell me where Dr. Jeffers is?"

"He just left with the ill passengers. He was taking them to his clinic." The man ran a hand over his hair in agitation. "Frankly, I'm glad he stepped in. We're only here to dispense bandages and mild analgesics, not handle epidemics. He said isolation was imperative and he could care for them better at his place since this facility isn't set up for any long term care."

With a muttered thanks, Jor went back to ground level and noticed the security men in place at the nearest outside entrance. Checking several others, he was unsurprised to find them all guarded. Jor returned to his room and took up the small tote in which he kept his toiletries. He placed his own bottle of medication in it then returned to the station med center. Once there, he persuaded the med tech, with the help of a little cash, to give him a supply of analgesics, antacids, laxatives and any other pills that rattled nicely in their bottles when he shook the bag.

As prepared as possible, Jor headed for the nearest outside exit. He was stopped at the doors by security. "I'm sorry, sir. No one enters or leaves the station. Haven't you seen the quarantine notices?"

"Of course I have, but I'm Dr. Jeffers' assistant. I have the medicine he needs. It's imperative I get these drugs to him."

Jor took his own prescription bottle from the bag and showed it to the guard while subtly shaking the bag. The guard read the bottle, his brow furrowing with incomprehension. Just as Jor hoped. The guard had no idea what was in the bottle but it looked official.

"Mmm, well, in that case, you can go but don't expect to return until the quarantine is lifted. I'll need your thumb print for identification. And I'll warn you now, your picture is going to be circulated to the security staff here and in the surrounding towns. If you're spotted anywhere you're not supposed to be until the quarantine is lifted, you don't want to even think about how much trouble you'll be in."

"Of course, I understand completely. I just want to get to my boss."

"Get going," the guard invited, opening the door for him.

Jor stepped out, took a deep breath and started the three mile walk to Dane. It was only when he was on the road and almost there that the thought came to mind. *Why the hell am I doing this?*

* * *

Dane was settling the last of his three patients in the infirmary when a steady knocking brought his attention to the clinic's main entrance. He rushed out, yelling as he went. "Don't you see the quarantine notices? Go away!"

"Yes, I see the fucking quarantine notices! Why does everyone keep asking me that? Do I look like I'm blind or so stupid that I can't read?"

Dane's stomach flipped. Jor. He was the last person Dane had expected to see. He threw open the door on the last of Jor's rant. "What are *you* doing here?"

Jor rummaged in the tote bag for his pills then shoved the rest into Dane's hands. "Here, I brought your much needed medicine." He pushed past Dane and stood waiting while Dane looked at the contents of the bag.

"Not that a person could ever have too much laxative, but is this supposed to be a joke?" Dane asked with a raised brow and an edge of sarcasm to his voice. "The station and town are under quarantine. How did you get out and once again, *what* are you doing here?"

"I told them I was your assistant and that you desperately needed this stuff," Jor answered, indicating the bag. Before going on he shuffled his feet as though unsure, then suddenly brought his gaze to Dane's while raising a hand to his head. "These stitches. They itch. They need to come out."

Much to his surprise, Dane felt a frisson of amusement. Jor's transparent reason for being there was laughable. He found himself struggling to hide a smile. "Of course they itch. It's a sign the wound is healing and it's much too early to remove them. They have to stay for at least another five days."

"Five days! Well how was I supposed to know that? I've never had anyone tie bits of my anatomy together with string."

Dane turned away to hide the smile tugging at his lips. *What the hell's wrong with you? You don't like this man, remember?* Something gave him a sharp, mental pinch. "Ow! Don't do that!" He turned back to glare at Jor.

"Do what?" Jor looked totally confused.

"You really don't know, do you?"

Jor shook his head.

"God, I hate this metaphysical Maleri' crap!" Dane cursed then saw and felt the quick flare of hurt his words caused him before Jor shut down. His green eyes lost their luster and went dull. He dropped his gaze from Dane's and headed for the door. "I'll get out of your hair."

Dane's hands fisted at his sides in frustration and anger directed at himself. *Fuck!* "And just where do you think you're going to go?"

Jor shrugged.

"You can't go back to the shuttle station and you sure can't go back to town. You've come in contact with a contagious disease."

"I've been vaccinated against Runcalis Fever," Jor replied, his voice cold and even.

"Doesn't matter. You could still spread it. Besides, what are you going to do? Wander the wilds for the next couple of weeks?"

"What do you care?"

Dane cleared his throat. "Look, I'm sorry about that Maleri' crack, okay? I'm a little stressed here. Runcalis isn't normally serious, but in a place like this it could become so. The majority of the people on this planet haven't been vaccinated against the simplest of contagious diseases. Like I said before, medical funds are stretched tight. We've been lucky that most travelers are fully immunized against a plethora of diseases and are unlikely to bring them planet side. Most adults would make it through a bout of Runcalis with little problem. It's about as severe as measles on Earth. It's the children I worry about. If Runcalis makes a run through the population, we could lose thousands of children to secondary infections like pneumonia."

"Are you sure it's Runcalis and not just some simple cold virus?"

"I'm sure. They have all the symptoms, including the distinctive yellow striations on their arms and legs."

"How is it that these people ended up not being vaccinated against something so common?"

"For the very reason that it is so common. Once a vaccine was discovered for it, Runcalis pretty much disappeared. You've heard the saying 'out of sight, out of mind'? Everyone starts thinking, oh, this disease doesn't exist anymore. Why get vaccinated against it? And just when everyone's guard is down, bang, it sneaks in again."

Jor nodded. "So, I can't go back to town or to the station. What do I do?"

The sound of retching in the next room was loud and clear. Dane met Jor's gaze, a smirk on his lips. "Since you told security at the station that you're my assistant, I suggest you get to work. There's a bucket and mop in the closet in the infirmary along with disinfectant and gloves. You can draw hot water from the sink. Welcome to the medical profession."

"Don't you mean the janitorial profession?" Jor asked with a moue of distaste.

"That too," Dane agreed and left to check on the patients while Jor got the bucket and mop.

* * *

A few hours later the patients were settled, medicated as well as possible to lower their fevers and relieve their other symptoms. They'd each been given a bucket to avoid further accidents on the floor, something Jor was inordinately glad of. While emptying those buckets wouldn't prove to be a treat, cleaning up the noxious mess on the floor had been far worse.

Fortunately Dane had something that settled queasy stomachs as well. "As long as we keep them medicated, they should rest comfortably. No one seems to be showing any particularly virulent symptoms, thank God. I just hope no one at the shuttle station contracts it."

Jor looked up from the sink where he stood scrubbing his hands and arms up to the elbow. "From what the porter at the hotel said it sounds like they were isolated fairly quickly."

"They were," Dane nodded. "The pilot of the ship they were on herded them straight to the station med center."

"He should have kept them isolated on his ship."

"That would have been the best solution but unfortunately theirs was a short pleasure cruise. The ship wasn't a large one and there was no sickbay or doctor on board. They were closer to us than to anyone."

"What about where they came from originally? Do you suppose anyone's thought to backtrack the beginning of the infection?"

"I put in a call to station security and told them to do just that. That's the best I can do. It's up to them to report the incident and make the necessary authorities aware."

Jor finished washing up and dried his hands under the heated air unit, he sighed, suddenly tired. "So what do we do now?"

"Now we relax. Are you hungry?"

"Um, maybe."

Dane furrowed his brow. "Maybe?"

"Well I am hungry and I think I could eat. As long as what we have doesn't resemble any of that stuff I cleaned up off the floor."

Dane chuckled. In the past few hours, working side by side with Jorrian had eased some of the strain between them. "Let's see. As I recall there was some nasty brown stuff in that puddle you cleaned up. Oh, and something sort of yellow-green."

Jor groaned as he followed Dane out of the infirmary. "Now that's just cruel."

"Hey, I'm a doctor. We're gentle, humanitarian creatures."

"Yeah, right." Jor mumbled.

Dane just smiled and led the way to his personal quarters which were across the yard from the infirmary. It struck him as he walked, that the yard they were walking through was the very one that had been in his dream. The thought of that dream had his cheeks heating and his groin tingling. Dane glanced back at Jor. His face was a study in neutrality but his eyes were hooded, his face flushed.

Dane opened the back door which brought them into the kitchen. "Do you like Italian food?" he asked Jor.

"As a matter of fact, I do. I spent a year on Earth. It's a very interesting place. I especially liked Las Vegas."

"Las Vegas! Oh that's right, you're a gambler."

"Mostly. There aren't too many jobs you can have when you wander from place to place."

"Umm, I can see that. I've got leftover lasagna. Will that suit you?"

"Sounds good."

"Good. Do me a favor and get that loaf of Italian bread out of the fresh-keeper. We can have garlic bread with it and I have salad. I assume you like garlic?"

"If one likes Italian, one must like garlic."

"Smart man." He handed Jor a flat metal sheet. "Slice off two pieces for me and however many you'd like. Use this to put them on. There's butter in the fridge and garlic powder in the cabinet above the keeper. Oh, and knives and other utensils are in that top drawer by the sink."

The two of them worked quickly and efficiently. Dane slid the lasagna in the oven along with the tray of bread that Jor prepared. He directed Jor to plates and glasses while filling salad bowls with a premixed concoction of greens. He offered Jor a choice of dressings while Jor filled their glasses with water.

"Would you like something else to drink? I could fix some iced tea," Dane offered before joining Jor at the table. "I don't keep much in the way of liquor in the house or I'd offer you wine."

"The water's fine. I drink but not excessively. I like keeping my wits about me."

"I suppose, being a gambler, you'd have to."

Jor nodded while chewing his first bite of salad. "This is good. And yes, it would be hard to learn the other player's 'tells' through a fog of alcohol."

"Tells?"

"Little habits or gestures they have that give away the state of the hand they're holding. They're usually subtle little things like pursing the lips, a certain way of flexing the fingers, lack of or increase of eye contact."

"In other words, you read their body language."

"Yes, precisely."

"Like outside when we crossed the yard. Your face was flushed and you kept your eyes down. Did you, perchance, have a dream that took place out in my backyard?" Dane had to hand it to Jor. His experience as a gambler paid off.

Except for a slight pause of the fork that was bringing another bite of salad to his mouth, Jor gave nothing away. He took the bite, chewed and swallowed before answering. "And what would happen if I said I did? Will you blame me for invading your dreams?"

Dane waited a moment then shook his head, filling the tense silence between them. "I wanted to, at first," he replied honestly. "But I know I can't. Despite what you may think, I'm not a cruel or unfair person. I realize that what's happened between us is the fault of neither one of us."

"I never thought you were cruel or unfair. You're more than justified in your feelings about this." Jor gestured vaguely. "About me."

The oven timer chose that moment to go off, and Dane rose from his seat to retrieve the rest of their meal. He dished out the lasagna and garlic bread and did his best to alleviate this new tension but the former feeling of ease between them was strained. They finished their meal, limiting their conversation to inconsequential and impersonal matters.

After the cleanup, Dane gave Jor a quick run through of the house. It was a small yet cozy place, consisting of one bedroom, one bathroom, the living room and the kitchen. "There's only one bedroom. I'm afraid you'll have to sleep on the sofa," Dane apologized while pulling a couple of light blankets and an extra pillow from the closet in the short hallway that separated the bathroom from the bedroom.

"Are you sure you want me to stay here? I could sleep in the infirmary."

"With the sickies? Hell, no."

Jor met Dane's gaze, a startled look in his eyes. "Sickies?"

Dane shrugged. "In my profession, if you don't keep your sense of humor you crash. And okay, maybe calling the patients 'sickies' isn't the most politically correct thing to do, but it's not hurting anyone and it certainly doesn't change the quality of care they receive."

"Don't get defensive. I was just wondering if it was some ultra modern medical term I'd never heard."

Dane snorted and smiled. "So you do have a sense of humor. I was beginning to wonder."

It was Jor's turn to shrug. "There's not too much about my life I find amusing." He turned and walked back into the living room, bending to place the blankets and pillow on the sofa.

Dane followed and let his gaze wander the length of Jor's back. His lips quirked in a small smile at the sight of Jor as he bent. This time he got a good look at the man's ass and it had been well worth waiting for. Round, firm cheeks stretched the fabric of his pants. Instead of just a tingle in his groin, this time Dane felt a distinct thickening of his cock.

When Jor turned back, the somber look in his eyes made Dane's amusement fade. Without thinking, he stepped closer. Laying a hand on Jor's shoulder, he gave it a light shake. "You're too hard on yourself."

Frowning, Jor met Dane's gaze, his eyes searching. Satisfied with what he saw, he nodded curtly. "I don't know why you would say that but thank you."

"Maybe it's something you should spend some time thinking about. And you're welcome. Goodnight."

"Goodnight."

Dane retreated to his bedroom and undressed, contemplating the puzzled look on Jor's face. Dane's remark had been a subtle hint for Jor to rethink his perpetual guilt trip. Maybe Jor would get it, maybe not. At the moment Dane was too tired to worry about it.

Sliding into bed he turned his thoughts to his patients and set his alarm to go off in three hours so he could get up and check on them. Lying down, he let his mind play over the events of the day and of all the things that had filled it. It was thoughts of Jorrian that took center stage as he drifted to sleep.

Chapter Four

Dane slapped a hand at the alarm, silencing its strident call. Blinking to clear the sleep from his eyes, he rose and dressed then walked out into the living room. Eyelids at half mast rose fully and beyond at the sight of Jor on the sofa. Jor had undressed and sometime in the past couple of hours had thrown his blanket off. He lay on his back, one arm thrown over his head, the other resting on his torso. He was fully and gloriously naked.

His pale hair was free and pushed to the side. It rippled down the length of Jor's body, resembling a frozen waterfall. His fair skin glowed in the soft light that filtered in through the window from the outside light. Dane admired the sleek, muscled length of his body but what caught and held his fascinated gaze was Jor's fully erect cock.

Slightly darker than the rest of him, it rose from a neat bush of light blond pubic hair. It lay tight against his belly. Dane could almost swear he could see the pulse of blood in the prominent veins that ran just under the surface of skin that cried out to be touched. Knowing that it was natural for men to have several nocturnal erections during the course of a night did nothing to alleviate his instant arousal at the sight.

"Fuck," he breathed. His mouth started to water. What would it be like to simply walk over there, go to his knees and worship at that towering pillar of masculinity?

Dane shook himself and tore his gaze from Jor's body. *Get a grip, Dane.* A second thought immediately answered, *wouldn't I love to.* It was like having his inner devil on one shoulder and his inner angel on the other. Dismissing them both, Dane walked through the kitchen and out the back door.

The cool night air was bracing and cleared his head. In the glow of the outside light mounted on the outer wall of the clinic, Dane made the short, familiar walk and let himself in. Once in the infirmary he went from patient to patient, checking each one. They were all resting comfortably. The medication he'd given them earlier was still doing its job. All the buckets were empty and he breathed a sigh of relief. Vomit patrol was not one of his favorite things, especially at this time of the morning.

Satisfied that everything was as it should be, he returned to the house. Dane opened the backdoor and stepped inside the kitchen, moving quietly so as not to disturb Jor. Once in the living room it was clear to see he might as well have saved his efforts. Jor was awake and sitting up on the sofa, the blanket draped over his lower body.

Even partially covered, Jor was temptation incarnate. Thick ripples of Jor's beautiful fall of heavy hair covered his back and slid over his shoulders. Dane was utterly fascinated.

He swallowed hard and clamped down on the reoccurring surge of need that washed over him. His mind might be having a hard time accepting the Maleri' bond to Jor but his body was having no such problem. In fact, his body was setting up an ever increasing clamor and demand for what it viscerally knew as its mate. His body was demanding Jorrian. Dane raised a hand to his forehead, blotting the sweat that was forming. He shivered at the trickle that ran down his spine.

"Is everything all right?" Jor asked, turning to him, his voice husky with sleep.

"It's fine. I just went to check on the patients."

"Are you feeling all right? You look a little flushed."

"Um, no, I'm fine," Dane moved, turning his back to the outside light that filtered in through the window while effectively putting himself in shadow. Jor's vision was a bit too acute for his liking.

"Will you be checking on the patients at this time every night?"

"For the next couple of days, yes. Every three hours through the night until the worst of the symptoms ease. I can't just call it a day and leave them on their own for ten hours. Plus there's the fact that they'll need to have their medicine again in another three hours."

"All right. I'll switch off with you."

"What do you mean?"

"We'll take turns. You know, switch back and forth. You'll go after the first three hours, I'll go next. That way you'll at least be able to get six uninterrupted hours of sleep."

Dane found himself touched by Jor's offer. "You don't have to do that. I'm used to interrupted sleep."

"I know I don't have to. I'm your assistant. Remember?" Jor sent him a tentative smile. "Seriously, let me do this. If there's a problem with anyone, I'll wake you. You said yourself they weren't displaying any particularly virulent symptoms."

"All right," Dane agreed. "But I have to take the next shift so I can administer their medication."

"Agreed. You'll get any shifts that involve dispensing medicine."

"It's a deal. What are you doing up, anyway? Did I wake you?" Talking to Jor while being enveloped in this near darkness made Dane relax. There was something about communicating with voices only while everything else was shielded by the dark that made it easier to be more open.

"I rarely sleep more than a few hours at a time."

"Unless you take something, right?" Dane watched as Jor dropped his gaze to the bottle of pills resting by his clothes on the low table in front of the sofa.

"Yes."

"So why didn't you take one of your pills? The ones you brought with you? I assume that's what they're for,"

Jor nodded. "I took two last night. I don't like to take them every night. I don't want to become addicted to them."

"That's an admirable sentiment but it must not be very comforting when you're sitting up in the wee hours of the morning because you can't sleep." The thought of Jor's lonely night vigils pulled at Dane's heart.

The more time Dane spent with the man, the more Jor's vulnerabilities emerged. Dane thought his own loss was difficult to deal with but he certainly didn't hold an exclusive on heartbreak. It amazed him that Jor held up under the load of guilt he heaped upon himself let alone the permeating sense of sadness and loss that filled him.

While they tried to keep their emotions from slipping through the bond, it was impossible to catch everything. Bits and pieces broke through. They were each given small glimpses of each other in the form of emotions or budding thoughts. Dane knew himself well enough to know that while he still grieved for Teleran, he'd at least managed to find some pleasure in his life. Jor's all pervading inner doom and gloom led Dane to believe Jor's earlier admission. It seemed he did find very little in his life to be amusing or pleasurable.

He fought the urge to go to Jor and offer comfort. Whether it was the bond between them or his own innate urge to heal what was broken, he knew Jor wouldn't welcome him. His pride would make him reject anything less than a full capitulation to the bond. Without the intimacy the bond would afford them, anything less would make Jor self-conscious, defensive and perhaps even angry.

Dane knew that most men had difficulty dealing with and exposing their emotions. Even with someone with whom they were intimately involved. *Purposely make yourself look weak in front of another man?* Dane silently scoffed. *Not bloody likely.*

He blinked. Pulling his mind from those silent thoughts, he found Jor staring at him.

"You should put away whatever thoughts are making you frown so and go to bed. You'll have to be getting up again, sooner than you'll like."

"You're right," Dane agreed. "You should try and get a little more sleep yourself."

"Umm," Jor grunted with a noncommittal nod.

Dane shook his head. "Stubborn." Without waiting for a reply, he returned to his room.

* * *

The next few days passed without incident. Jor and Dane harmoniously worked together to care for the patients. They took shifts checking the patients at night, fixed meals together and in the early evenings before bed, watched news or other broadcasts that were distributed planet-wide from an independent vendor of off-world programming. Everything was running smoothly but for one slowly growing glitch. The increasing sexual tension.

If Jor had found it difficult to sleep before, it was quickly becoming impossible. Lascivious dreams starring himself and Dane kept yanking him from sleep. He was afraid they might be broadcast through their link as the first had. He didn't want Dane to know how much and how quickly this need for him was growing and so he kept himself awake as much as possible. The pain was also returning. During their initial joining, Dane must have siphoned some of the energy that was straining against his shields but with no further outlet, it was rebuilding.

Jor admitted to himself he'd rather die than let Dane know. He wouldn't take Dane's charity, and knowing him as Jor did now, he was sure Dane would cross his own self-imposed boundaries against the Maleri' bond to help him. It was a cruel twist of fate that draining the energy required him to engage in sex with his mate. Jor had never had sex with a reluctant partner and he wasn't about to begin now. There was no way he would ask for Dane's help. But that didn't stop his growing desire for the man.

As though thinking of him caused him to appear, Dane walked in through the infirmary doorway, scattering Jor's thoughts. Just the sight of him caused Jor's belly to tighten in anticipation. Dane's arms were filled with a neat stack of clean linen.

"Come help me change the sheets?" he asked Jor with a charming smile and a hopeful gleam in his eyes.

Jor felt his lips twitch with unaccustomed amusement. Dane was irresistibly cute and Jor had the feeling that once upon a time he knew it. For some reason, which Jor couldn't understand, Dane had taken to subtly flirting with him. Whether Dane was aware of what he was doing, Jor wasn't sure. All he knew for sure was the pleasure he took in it. It was worth wrestling later with the unfulfilled lust Dane's flirtation raised.

He joined Dane by the first bed to be changed. Standing one on either side of it, they lifted their groggy patient into a sitting position and stripped the old sheet down. Jor held the man upright while Dane got the clean sheet tucked under his side of the bed then held the patient while Jor finished his side. They laid him back down, eased the old sheet from under his hips and stripped it off the bed. The clean sheet was maneuvered under his hips as well and his legs elevated slightly so that it could be smoothed the rest of the way down and tucked under at the foot of the bed.

The bed was narrow and each movement seemed to bring them nearly face to face. Dane's scent, clean and masculine, teased Jor's senses. His heart began to beat faster at their close proximity to each other while his cock inevitably stiffened. As much as he kept telling himself to relax, it was useless. His body was screaming for Dane. By the time they got to the last patient, Jor was fighting to keep his trembling hands from reaching for Dane. He made the mistake of making eye contact with him.

Their gazes locked and the world stood still. For one blazing moment the Maleri' bond took control. It flared wide open between them and left them utterly naked to each other's desire. Jor's stomach clenched. His semi-erect cock went rock hard. He fought to breathe. His pulse pounded in his ears, a roaring beat to accompany the hot demand of his body. Dane's easy manner had fled. He stared back at Jor. Jor could hear Dane's breath, audible pants slipping between his parted lips. Jor shook with the tension between them, dying to break the spell yet wanting it to last forever.

It was Dane who recovered first. "I, um, forgot something at the house. I'll be back in a few minutes."

Jor watched as Dane pivoted on his heel and strode from the room as though the hounds of hell were after him. Jor was trapped in the web of lust that had spun between them. He stumbled to the infirmary bathroom and locked the door. Any thoughts of propriety or control were gone. He tore open his pants and grasped his demanding cock.

"Demons and deities," he groaned, his clenched fist pumping his swollen flesh. He slid to his knees.

The ache was unbearable, the pleasure quickly growing. Jor pulled at himself, his strokes long, hard and fast. Images of the intensity of Dane's eyes bored into him and he groaned. It felt as though Dane was actually watching him. This was no gentle build of sensation. It was a harsh, abrupt need that screamed for fulfillment. The feelings were big, huge, overwhelming.

Heat radiated from his body, centering in his balls it slid up his spine. Orgasm was coming. He was teetering on the brink when his essence and another's merged. Dane. Dane was at the house, in his bedroom jacking off. Jor could feel Dane's lust and pleasure. He could almost taste the tart musk of his sweat. A phantom hand joined Jor's on his cock and he knew that Dane felt him as well. It was a touch of divinity. It was exquisite. It was too much. His cock spewed.

He managed to cup his hand over his pulsing cock head. Thick ribbons of pure creamy seed jetted forth, splashing into his palm. Jor retained enough sanity to swallow his scream, settling instead for a harsh guttural groan. His body shuddered and he curled inward, rocking with the aftershocks that grabbed his gut and twisted with slowly decreasing tugs of pleasure.

Jor rested for a few moments allowing his quivering muscles to regain their strength. When he thought his legs would hold him, he rose and went to the sink. Turning on the water, he washed away the semen that had pooled in his hand and looked back to check the floor. A few drops had escaped. Taking a disinfectant wipe from the wall dispenser, he cleaned them up.

Returning to the sink, Jor splashed his face with water and dried it. He looked at his reflection in the mirror. His familiar stoic expression was back, his mask firmly in place. The ethereal joining with Dane had been the most joyous and lust fulfilling experience of his life. And knowing how it felt, knowing there would be no joining for real made him wish more than ever that his life was over. Determined to avoid Dane for the rest of the day, he sighed and left the bathroom.

* * *

Dane sighed as he made his way back to the house. He'd gotten up to the sound of his alarm to check the patients. As he'd passed through the living room he could see Jor lying on the sofa wrapped in his blanket, asleep. If he wasn't pretending. Dane wouldn't put it past him. Ever since their bond-shared masturbation Jor had been unusually quiet and withdrawn. His depression was near palpable. Dane, on the other hand, was experiencing a quiet joy. A fact he struggled just as hard to hide while he wrestled with the implications of the feeling.

Forced as he was to finally take a good look at himself, Jor and the situation between them, Dane came to the only logical conclusion. They belonged together. It was a conclusion that caused him initial dismay in the face of his love for, and loyalty to, Teleran. And yet, if he was honest with himself, he knew that Tel would want him to be happy and he himself wanted that happiness. Dane wanted to love and be loved. He craved the touch of another. Who didn't? At this point, the actual love was in question but the need was certainly in place.

He and Jor needed each other, and Dane knew that Jor's need was even greater than his own. Jor needed Dane for his very existence. While he wasn't saying anything, Dane hadn't missed Jor's surreptitious rubbing of his temples or the slight frowns and almost imperceptible winces. Jor was in pain. Dane had taken a look at the pill bottle Jor had left on the table in front of the sofa. It was a combination sleep aid and pain medication. Dane also noted the bottle had gotten lighter in the past few days. Despite his aversion to it, Jor was leaning on his medication more and more.

Dane decided it was time to act. The patients in the infirmary were very close to full recovery and would be released from his care in two days. Dane knew that Jor would leave as well. He was already withdrawing. His decision made, Dane was determined that Jor would be going nowhere, except hopefully to his bed. The thought brought a smile to his lips even as his cock jumped. He chuckled and softly groaned. *God I can't wait to touch him and get my hands on all that long, silky hair. Fuck.*

Reaching the kitchen door, Dane let himself in but paused when he heard voices.

"So do you think they might help? This planet's medical programs could use a serious boost."

"I'm sure they will. I'll run it by them. But, Jor, why don't you come and talk to them yourself? Your banishment's been lifted for five years now. Santorel and Thomas have told me how much they wish you would come home."

Dane moved closer to the doorway but stayed in the shadows. Jor was speaking to someone on the comm unit.

"I can't. We're under quarantine."

"That's temporary and you know it. Stop avoiding my question."

"Chase, we've been through this. I can't come back to Belthola just because I've managed to buy my way in."

"No one has voiced a sentiment like that. The things you've done since you've been gone, the people you've helped. Did you do that to buy your way back?"

"No, of course not, but no one would have to say that that's what I've been doing. Not when I know it's what they really think."

"You are so damned stubborn and you're so sure you're right. Your reinstatement was unanimous but you're determined to never let the guilt go, aren't you?"

"You didn't cost a man his life!"

"Neither did you!"

Breathing hard, his expression mutinous, Jor looked away from the screen and spotted Dane standing in the shadows of the kitchen. Their gazes locked for a moment before Jor turned back to the comm unit. "I have to go. Just... please check on what I've asked you about."

"All right but this conversation is not over Jorrian."

Jor gave him a humorless smile. "It seems I'm not the only stubborn one. Thanks, Chase."

Jor ended the call and looked down to his blanket covered lap. "I hope you don't mind my using the comm. The call won't cost you."

Dane stepped into the room and crossed to the sofa. He seated himself beside Jor. "I don't mind. Tell me about it," he demanded softly.

Jor looked up, surprise in his eyes. "Um, I called my friend Chase. He…"

"No, not that. Tell me about what happened. Why you were banished from Belthola."

Jor's body went rigid, his eyes cold as he shut down, leaving Dane to face a blank wall. He looked away. "You already know what happened. You saw it when the bond formed."

"I saw something of it, yes. But I want to hear it from you. Please?"

Dane's gentle request loosened Jor's unyielding stance. He relaxed slightly and took a deep breath but remained silent. Dane thought for a moment that he would refuse but he gave in, again looking down at his lap before speaking. "I was twenty-four. It was the most important assignment I'd ever been given to handle on my own. Two major factions on the planet Mefthru were nearing an internal conflict that could throw their country into civil war. I won't go into the details of the conflict but suffice it to say I lost my objectivity. Instead of being impartial, I took sides. A man, one of high rank, was taken hostage and killed. It was my fault. If I'd done my job, the hostilities would have ended before things went so far. The Maleri' Council sent another of my brothers to help when negotiations broke down but it was too late. I don't know if you're aware of it, but all Maleri' are bonded to each other."

"They are?" Dane asked, appalled that his relationship with Teleran had been shared among all the Maleri'.

"Not in the way that mates are bonded. We don't live inside each other's heads. It's a subtler, gentler bonding but it's also enough to keep us from lying to each other. Not that an honorable man would lie. When Geral arrived, I immediately confessed what I'd done."

"And what was it you'd done? Something besides losing your impartiality?"

Jor nodded, his fists clenching. Dane reached out and took one of Jor's hands in his own, soothing his fingers over the tight skin of Jor's hand. Jor let his gaze rest on their hands and again relaxed. "I knew they were going to do something. I didn't know that taking a hostage was their plan but I knew something was going to happen. I didn't warn the other side. I let it happen."

"How much time passed between when you knew something was going to happen and when it actually did? Days?"

Jor shook his head. "When negotiations broke down I retreated to the quarters I'd been assigned at a neutral embassy. An hour later the man was dead."

Dane frowned. "So you had an inkling of an idea that something bad was going to happen and an hour later it did. How could you possibly hold yourself responsible for that?"

"If I'd done my job the way I should have to begin with, it wouldn't have happened!" Jor insisted vehemently.

"You don't know that," Dane shot back. "You may have these wonderful empathic powers but you can't predict the future. Did you work directly with the person or people who killed the man?"

"No."

"Did you work directly with the man who was killed?"

"No."

"For all you know, the people who did the killing could have been a rogue faction within that particular organization. The man who was killed could have done something to provoke things. Was he considered to be a good man?"

"There was talk. Rumors of torture and other atrocities the man had ordered done and even participated in."

"Oh, my God, Jor! It sounds like his demise at the hands of the other faction was inevitable. Even if you'd gotten both sides of the conflict to come to a peaceful agreement. How many times have fanatics or people who have suffered and want revenge restarted the whole mess all over again by killing someone they think deserves to die? Jor, it wasn't your fault."

"I'm tired of arguing it. Fault or no, I was banished from Belthola and the Maleri' brotherhood."

"For taking sides, but not for causing that man's death."

"Yes."

"And how long ago was that?"

"Fourteen years. I haven't been home since then."

"And yet your banishment was lifted five years ago. And yes, I was eavesdropping."

Jor nodded.

"And so you travel the universe, gambling, drinking a little and helping boys like Val Cammor while wallowing in your pain and waiting to die." Dane held on tight as Jor tried to jerk his hand away. "Stop that," he ordered and smiled when Jor subsided. "So you're thirty-eight." Dane stated quickly calculating in his head. He continued to pet Jor's hand. "I'm thirty-five. I'm a doctor. I've lived here since leaving Belthola after Tel died, not wanting to go home for fear of the memories. And I've been wallowing in my pain and waiting to die." Dane's voice shook.

Jor shook his head, the loose fall of his hair shimmering with the movement. "What are you doing? Why are you doing this?"

"Because I don't want to end this way, bitter and alone. I want joy in my life and I've decided I want you."

"No. Don't think you can fool me this way. You know what's going to happen to me unless I'm fully bonded with my mate and you don't want that on your conscience. This has nothing to do with you. My coming here, this bond between us, was an accident of fate. *I don't want or need your pity,*" Jor growled.

"Then take pity on me," Dane pleaded softly. "If you don't touch me, I'm going to explode."

Jor met his eyes and Dane opened himself not only to Jor's physical perusal, but his mental one as well. Dane dropped his shield, leaving himself wide open. The bond flared but met resistance from Jor.

"Don't leave me out here alone," Dane whispered.

Jor resisted, again shaking his head. Dane could see the fear and longing in Jor's eyes. He had to make Jor see, had to make him let go. The words formed and Dane spoke them with all the sincerity in his soul.

"Listen to me. The past is over and done. All that's left are memories. If they're good, you treasure them. If they're bad, you do your best to forget them. And if there's a lesson to be learned, you learn it and move on. I wasn't ready to admit that Tel was in the past. I didn't have the strength to let him be just a cherished memory until you came. I don't want you to go. I don't want to live in the past anymore. Neither should you."

"Dane," Jor whispered, his body shaking, "you deserve so much more than me."

"Oh, no." Dane's voice was sure and steady, his conviction unshakeable. "I deserve you. Just because you've spent years beating yourself up for making a mistake and telling yourself that you're worthless doesn't make it so. I see your worth and what's more I feel it," Dane put a hand to his chest, "here in my heart. You're kind and generous to a fault, sensitive and caring. And let's face it, you're sexy as hell. Are you going tell me I don't deserve to have a man like that?"

Jor's face crumpled, a few slow tears sliding down his cheeks. His shield dissolved and the bond opened between them, wrapping them in silken tendrils of budding need and acceptance. Wordlessly, he reached for Dane.

Dane opened his arms wide and took him in. "Will you come to bed with me, Jorrian?" The head on his shoulder nodded and Dane smiled, stroking his hands down the length of Jor's back. "I love your hair," he confessed, his fingers slipping through the heavy strands.

"You washed the blood out of my hair when I hit my head."

"I thought you were still out," Dane accused, his tone teasing.

"I was mostly. It felt like I was dreaming. A really good dream."

"We'll have to make it a reality again very soon." Dane stood and pulled Jor up with him. His blanket slipped and fell to the floor. Dane hummed at the sight. "Oh, I was right. You are beautiful."

"Not me. You," Jor whispered. He raised his hand and tentatively combed his fingers through Dane's hair. "You're an angel. My angel."

Dane smiled, his eyes dancing, the skin crinkling at their corners. "Me? An angel? Sweetheart, you're delusional."

Jor laughed softly. "Maybe just a little addled. I haven't felt in my right mind since I met you."

Dane's laugh rang out, low and sweet. He took Jor's hand and tugged him down the hall to his bedroom. "I think we're in the same boat."

He pulled Jor into the bedroom and closed the door behind them. Doing so made everything feel intimate, so cozy, real and right. Dane's breathing began to speed up, his eyes on Jor while he unbuttoned his shirt.

Jor moved to stand before him and brushed his hands away. "Let me."

"Yes," Dane murmured, the sound of Jor's voice brushing over him, the feel of Jor's hands making him quiver. His shirt was opened and spread wide. "Want to kiss you," Dane confessed. "So much. Please."

Jor's hands came up to cup his cheeks. He tilted Dane's head slightly then took his mouth. Two moans joined and mingled when Jor's tongue slipped into his mouth. Dane shivered, accepting Jor's tongue, his hunger rising fast and hard. His head whirled. Jor's taste was wild, intoxicating. The kiss grew deeper, hotter. Jor devoured him. Dane was no longer leading the way. He'd silently given his permission and Jor was taking charge.

Jor was hot and hard against him. Hands on Jor's forearms, Dane pushed into him, rubbing against him, Jor's groan setting him on fire. Jor's hands released Dane's head to wander over his shoulders and down his back. They slid under Dane's shirt to caress his skin and the sleek line of his spine before returning to his shoulders, pushing the shirt back and off. Dane straightened his arms, letting it slide free then wrapped them around Jor, bringing their bared chests together.

The touch was electric. Dane's nipples tightened. He groaned at the sweet pinch. "God, yes. Touch me. Need to feel you," Dane panted.

"Shh, I know. I feel it every bit as much as you. Need it every bit as much."

"I know you do. We're a pair, aren't we? So pathetic."

"Hush," Jor ordered softly. "Not pathetic. Just lost. Until now."

He brought their mouths together again, the kisses deep and drugging. Dane went willingly into the fog Jor's kisses spread over him. Jor's presence was strong and steady, holding him close and he knew it to be true. He was no longer lost. Dane let himself go, melting into the heat, the need, the sweet flavor of Jorrian.

Jor's hands slid over his back one moving down, sliding under the waistband of his pants. A large, warm hand cupped the cheek of his ass and squeezed. Dane pushed into the touch and moaned when Jor's other hand worked his pants open. Dane's cock was solid and full, standing tall and begging to be touched. His head rolled back and he pushed into the hand that wrapped around him. His pants slid to the floor.

"Bed," Jor insisted, his voice a husky rasp. He released Dane and stepped back.

Dane's stomach quivered at the look in those stormy, green eyes. He walked past Jor to the bed and bent to pull the covers back. When Jor's hands smoothed down his back and over his ass, Dane moaned and arched into the touch.

"I knew you were a sensualist," Jor chuckled. "The way you move. You're like some glorious feline, all sleek muscles and grace."

"Can't help it, it feels good."

"Let's see if we can make it feel better."

Dane crawled into the bed and rolled on his back. Jor followed him in and slid between Dane's thighs, laying himself over Dane's body. He held himself up on his elbows, his hips undulating. Their cocks pressed together, sliding and rubbing. Their gazes locked, Dane could clearly see the growing pleasure in Jor's eyes. His own need rising fast, Dane pushed up, grinding their bodies together while increasing the friction between them.

Dane lifted his head, seeking a kiss, and Jor hummed his approval. Their mouths came together, tongues meeting, exploring arousing. Dane knew he was whimpering, moaning, small constant little noises that broadcast his pleasure but he couldn't stop. It all felt so good. The growing heat had sweat rising. In turn their scents, musky and pure male became more intense, mingling together. But most of all it was the sensation of skin on skin, the weight of Jor pressing against him that had every nerve in his body shooting invisible sparks. Jor released his mouth and moved to his throat, licking and gently biting. Dane tensed, small shudders shaking him.

"Oh, God, Jor! So gooood," Dane groaned, his balls pulling up tight.

"I know, love. So hot. Come for me, Dane, come with me."

A whip of white-hot pleasure zipped straight up Dane's spine. He cried out, his body going rigid when the first hard shot of semen spread wet heat between them. Jor's mouth slammed down on his and he swallowed Jor's groan, holding him close. A second spray of heat joined Dane's. The kiss was almost suffocating in its intensity as they rocked together, slowly coming down from the heights of orgasm.

Jor broke the kiss and lay his head on Dane's shoulder. Dane panted, his mouth open, a half grin stretching his lips. He uttered a short breathless laugh.

Jor echoed it before rising up. "I hope we're laughing because that felt so good and not because either one of us did something really amusing. If it's me, I'm not sure I want to know. It's been a while since I've had sex so I may have forgotten some things. My ego may not withstand the blow."

Dane chuckled and reached up to brush Jor's hair back. "You did just fine and it felt amazing. How's that for your ego?"

"Oh, very nice. You keep that up and this having a mate thing won't be hard at all."

"Umm, having a mate won't be hard but something else is. You never got soft."

Jor's expression was shyly pleased, belying the flush that suffused his cheeks. He reached down and wrapped his fingers around both their cocks. Holding Dane's gaze he lightly stroked his hand up and down. "I'm not the only one."

"No, you're not," Dane agreed, his eyes half closing while the need returned. "Jor, uh, baby, please. Fuck me?"

"With pleasure, love."

Dane expected Jor to get straight to it, but instead he leaned in, taking a kiss. It was soft and slow, an exploration of lips and tongue, a sharing of taste. The kisses went on and on, accompanying the gentle, barely there glide of Jor's hand. Dane floated. The pace was unhurried, undemanding. The pleasure stirred to life, the fire starting as a soft glow that warmed from the inside out.

Jor fed him kiss after kiss. Unconsciously, Dane started playing with Jor's hair. He ran his fingers through it, wrapped strands around his fingers and shivered when it sifted down against his chest. One hand cupped the side of Jor's head and Dane traced the whorls of Jor's ear with his fingertips. He was unsure when the movement started, the rocking motion of his body pulling him from his Jor-induced trance. The fire had grown from a glow into a flickering flame. The heat was rising.

He whispered against Jor's lips. "Soon? Need you."

"I know. I just want to love on you for awhile."

"I'm not going anywhere," Dane assured him, wiggling his hips a little more urgently.

"Is this your subtle way of hurrying me up?"

"Exactly," Dane admitted with a smile.

Jor returned his smile and upped the ante with a wink. "All right. If you insist."

Dane closed his eyes for a moment, savoring the gentle wash of joy that tightened his chest. Jor's happiness was palpable. He was inordinately pleased to know that he was responsible for it. Of course it was a two way street. Who'd have believed this guilt-ridden, lonely man could in turn bring such happiness to him? Jor had called him his angel. Dane knew he was no such thing but he was almost sure an angel or two came into the equation somewhere.

All such thoughts fled when Jor gave their cocks a final stroke, released them and sat up on his knees between Dane's thighs. Dane watched Jorrian's eyes and caught the flicker of mischief that lit them. Jor reached out, his fingers sliding through the semen that pooled on Dane's belly. Dane's muscles rippled at the touch.

"Will this serve as a proper lubricant?" he asked, rubbing the viscous fluid between his fingers. "It's still warm."

Dane's stomach tightened. He cleared his suddenly dry throat. "It should work."

"I'm glad you approve. Pull your legs back for me, love."

Dane bent his legs and lifted them exposing the rounded cheeks of his ass and the tempting valley that lay between. He shivered at Jor's growl. Jor leaned forward, sliding his tongue the length of Dane's cock from base to tip. Dane gasped then moaned when a gentle finger circled his puckered opening and lightly teased a few times before sliding in. He moaned again, a thrill of sensation gliding up his spine.

Jor looked up at him. "Mmm, so hot, Dane. How does it feel?"

"Good. So good," Dane breathed, pushing himself down on Jor's buried finger.

Jor went back to Dane's cock taking the plump head inside his mouth. His hum of pleasure sent vibrations straight to Dane's balls, distracting him as a second finger slid inside with the first. Dane pushed into it, loving the slight stretch and increasing fullness. When Jor's fingertips brushed his prostate the touch was electric. Dane arched, his hole clamping tight on the teasing fingers.

Jor lifted up slightly. "I'll bet you know what that is, don't you, doctor?"

"Umm, yeesss. More."

"Demanding, aren't you?"

"*Jor*, need it."

"I know, love. There's more, I promise."

Jor found Dane's gland and slid his fingers over it again. Without preamble he deep-throated Dane's cock and sent a third finger thrusting deep into his hole. Dane retained enough sense to limit his movement to a modified thrash, but the sensations Jor was building in his body were almost overwhelming. He wasn't sure whether to be grateful or sorry when Jor lifted off his cock with a sucking pop.

"Ready?" Jor asked, withdrawing his fingers.

Dane nodded, loving the harsh husk of his voice and the flame of desire he could see burning in Jor's eyes. Jor took more of their combined semen from Dane's abdomen and slicked himself up. Taking his own raging erection in hand, he nestled the tip against Dane's waiting hole and pushed. Dane bore down, trying to relax his opening and cried out triumphantly when Jor's cock pushed through and past the tight ring of muscle.

"Easy, easy," Jor groaned. "So tight. Are you all right, Dane? *Please* say you're all right. It feels incredible."

Dane managed a short laugh which tightened his muscles around Jor, pulling a groan from both of them. "*Oh fuck!* I'm fine, baby, please. *Move.*"

Jor rocked forward, his cock sliding deep. Dane's head reeled with the feel of Jor's thick heat stretching him. He rocked his hips, pushing into the pressure, needing it, needing Jor. Jor's withdrawal had him ready to cry out in protest until his return tore a moan of appreciation from Dane instead. Jor moved slowly at first, long, teasing glides of his cock in and out that had Dane panting, moaning, reaching for more.

Jor lowered himself over Dane and kissed him, taking his breath and giving it back. "You feel so good, taste so sweet. And those sexy little whimpers are turning me inside out."

Dane moaned again, reaching down to grasp Jor's ass. "I don't whimper. *Jor, please.* Faster."

"Like this?"

"Ahh, yes!" Dane yelled, his head thrashing on the pillow.

Jor had pushed up on his arms, changing the angle and speed of his thrust. Dane matched his movement, pushing up to meet each inward stroke. His gaze was locked with Jor's, the pleasure rising fast, drawing moan after moan from his throat. Once more he was enveloped in his lover's heat, scent and touch, all of it combining into a drugging aphrodisiac that blanked the mind and sent the body spinning out of control.

Again Jor moved. Resting back on his knees, he grasped Dane's legs then pushed forward, slamming their bodies together. Dane cried out at the hard, pounding rush of Jor's cock. Nothing existed but the rhythmic slap of flesh and the thick rod that reamed his hole and drove him to the edge of sanity. The flame that started as a small flicker, blazed out of control. Dane felt the fire, reveled in the heat and jumped straight into that white-hot center. Pleasure ignited a powder keg in his gut and exploded, wrenching another wild cry from him. His cock pulsed with the shudders of his body, stream after stream of liquid heat rushing out to anoint his chest and belly.

Jor's cry echoed his. From far away, Dane could feel the echoing pulses of Jor's cock and the rushing pressure of seed that filled his grasping passage. His body shook beneath the slow pleasure until tense muscles eased allowing him to collapse against the bed in a sated heap. Jor withdrew and managed to move a bit before becoming part of the heap.

They rested quietly for a time, both drifting, neither speaking until Dane opened his eyes and turned his head. Jor's head was resting on the pillow beside Dane's and he opened his eyes.

"Hey," Dane offered with a lazy smile.

"Hey, yourself. Are you all right?"

Dane stretched. "Mmm, excellent. You?"

"I'm... so good I can't describe it. And hungry."

Dane grinned and sat up, Jor following his example. "I think we should celebrate. I want to do something in honor of your courage in coming here that first day."

Jor blushed. "That wasn't courage. It was stitches. You know you still have to take these things out."

"Oh, I know and if you think I believe that transparent excuse you have a lot to learn about me. Anyway, as I was saying, I'm going to celebrate by fixing you a special meal. In honor of your first act as my assistant, I think I can come up with something brown." Dane edged his way off the bed. "Oh, and we mustn't forget something yellowish-green."

"I think I just lost my appetite," Jor growled, crawling across the bed. "And you are in big trouble."

"How much trouble? About eight, nine inches worth?" Dane asked, eyeing Jor's filling cock. "I think I can handle that." Instead of running he pounced, leaping on Jor.

The two of them wrestled on the bed, tickling each other and laughing. Laughter gave way to moans, tickling to kisses and teasing to touching. They made love again, finding redemption in each other's arms.

Kate Steele

What is it they say? Watch out for the quiet ones? Kate Steele has found that writing is the ideal way to release all those wild inner urges and she's just getting started. "I'm aging in reverse. With the help of lots of plastic surgery and vitamins I fully expect to have my own male harem by the time I hit 90." For now she's settling for the quiet life in rural Indiana with family and pets. Guilty pleasure: Singing in the car. "With the volume loud enough I sound just like Celine Dion!" You can contact Kate and sing-a-long at katesteele27@yahoo.com or visit her website at www.katesteele.com

Changeling Press E-Books
Quality Erotic Adventures Designed For Today's Media

More Sci-Fi, Fantasy, Paranormal, and BDSM adventures available in E-Book format for immediate download at www.ChangelingPress.com -- Werewolves, Vampires, Dragons, Shapeshifters and more -- Erotic Tales from the edge of your imagination.

What are E-Books?

E-Books, or Electronic Books, are books designed to be read in digital format -- on your computer or PDA device.

What do I need to read an E-Book?

If you've got a computer and Internet access, you've got it already!

Your web browser, such as Internet Explorer or Netscape, will read any HTML E-Book. You can also read E-Books in Adobe Acrobat format and Microsoft Reader, cither on your computer or on most PDAs. Visit our Web site to learn about other options.

What reviewers are saying about Changeling Press E-Books

Ciarra Sims -- Possession Obsession

"Ms. Sims is a talented author with a knack for creating characters that evoke an emotional response in the reader. The sex scenes are hotter than a fireworks finale on the fourth of July."
-- *Susan White, Coffeetime Romance Reviews*

Lacey Savage -- In His Dreams

"I was in suspense as to where the ending might go and was very happy to get what I wanted (nope, not going to give it away!). Definitely a must for all paranormal fans."
-- *Glenda K. Bauerle, The Romance Studio*

Shelby Morgen -- C.H.A.S.E. 1: All I Want for Christmas

"Sensual and extremely erotic, All I Want for Christmas is also achingly sweet and heart-rending."
-- *Sharyn McGinty, In the Library Reviews*

Aubrey Ross -- Lilith's Legacy

"The characters in Ms. Ross' Lilith's Legacy are magnificent and addictive... The story is, well; it is just magical."
-- *Keely Skillman, eCataRomance Reviews*

Lexxie Couper -- Shifting Lust 2: The Warlord's Vengeance

"5 Cups! This fast paced, action packed, and erotically charged story has it all... It is like the greatest of all chase scenes, leaving you breathlessly holding on to your seat. So, buckle your safety belts and get ready for another wild read from Ms Couper."
-- *Jenn, Coffeetime Romance Reviews*

www.ChangelingPress.com

Printed in the United States
117100LV00002B/100/P